ARCADIA MON AMOUR

Nathaniel Webb

PRESS

Published by Vulpine Press in the United Kingdom in 2021

Cover by Claire Wood

ISBN: 978-1-83919-081-0

www.vulpine-press.com

King and queen of Cantelon,
How many miles to Babylon?
Eight and eight, and other eight.
Will I get there by candlelight?
If your horse be good and your spurs be bright.
How many men have ye?
Mae nor ye daur come and see.

– Scotch, early 19th century

Rupert's Land

Madawaska

Cascadia

The Secret
Commonwealth

Pembina

The Divide

The Great Plains Confederacy

Free
California

Deseret

The Grand
Kingdom

Alondra

Sabine
Free State

The Gifted Nations of
AMERICA

Mikael Asikainen 2021

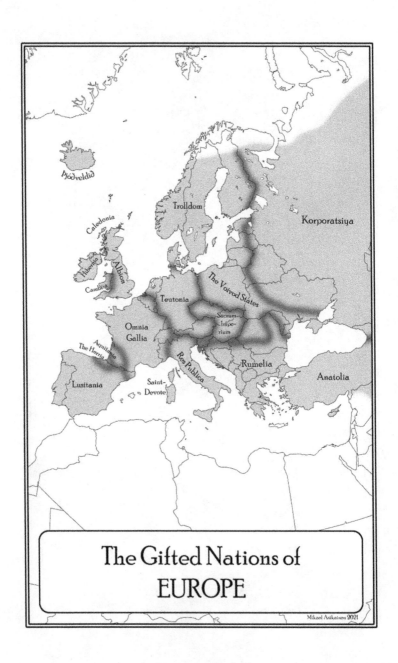

Þjóðveldið

Trolldom

Korporatsiya

Caledonia

Hibernia

Albion

Cambria

The Voivod States

Teutonia

Sacrum-
Impe-
rium

Omnia
Gallia

Aquitania

The Horia

Res Publica

Rumelia

Anatolia

Lusitania

Saint-
Devote

The Gifted Nations of
EUROPE

Mikael Aukanen 2021

CHAPTER 1

Compared to the dragon she'd slain, this little wyvern didn't scare Emily.

The Gray of Finalhaven had been the size of a house, with foot-long fangs that could shred armor, wings that beat like a hurricane, and four feet capable of grabbing and crushing boulders. The wyvern was more like a giant purple bat, hardly bigger than Emily, with a snub-nosed lizard face and leathery, blue-veined wings that stretched between its body and its front claws. The green flames it belched defiantly in her direction petered out a yard from its mouth. All it could really offer in terms of threat were the gleaming talons at the ends of its two feet, but even those were only an inch long at best.

If it weren't trying to kill her, it would have been cute.

Emily leaned her hammer against the base of the red striped cliff where she'd cornered the wyvern—or thought she'd cornered it, until the thing flapped its wings and made a single huge hop backwards up to a jutting stone shelf some thirty feet overhead. Now it sat there watching her, wings still spread, head cocked, occasionally spitting out a warning lance of flame.

Emily checked that her long knife was secure at her hip, spat in her hands, and began to climb. She had a plan, sort of. Unlike true dragons, wyverns couldn't really fly, nor were they much good on the ground. They flew like chickens, flapping around energetically without ever really taking off. They could flap a whole lot higher than chickens, though, which was annoying, but eventually she would catch the wyvern somewhere it couldn't get down from and then she could kill it.

Halfway up the cliffside, the view made Emily admit that it really was beautiful in the southwest. She'd never been to Deseret before, but the broad orange sands, low scrub plants, and towering white-tipped rock piles were as attractive in their own way as the chilly Secret Commonwealth where she'd grown up.

Arizona—that was what they called this area outside the Gifted world. To Emily, it was the Gifted Nation of Deseret, a scattered community of practitioners of magic and mad science. More than that, it was the home of Jack Twelve-Fingers, whom she'd fought alongside and spent one wonderful night with on a forgotten island thousands of miles from here.

She paused, letting herself relax into the rock of the cliff face, which felt cool against her overheated cheek. A few rogue memories of those extra fingers of Jack's flitted through her mind, but she pushed them away. So what if she'd taken this job with thoughts of him in the back of her mind? He didn't even live here anymore. He was on an island off the north Atlantic coast, as far away as possible from Deseret and its ruler, the Baron Wasteland, his father. There was no chance, Emily reminded herself, that she would just randomly run into Jack here among the rocks.

Besides, the wyvern population really *was* getting out of control; they had attacked a number of Gifted living in the desert, and Baron Wasteland had shown no inclination toward dealing with the problem. So Emily had been sent by her employer, the Sabre & Torch Society, to see what she could do before the mundanes started to notice.

With her mind back on the job she began to climb again; she was five feet below the wyvern when it jumped. It hopped clear of its little ledge, out and away, pumping its wings so hard as it tried not to fall that Emily could feel the air around her swirling. Soon its unsteady descent brought the wyvern level with Emily, but some ten feet out from the face of the cliff where she hung by her fingertips.

She jumped too, shoving off from the rocks and stretching out toward the taloned feet that hung tantalizingly close. The wyvern shrieked and spat flame, but the stream of fire died away before it could touch her, then her reaching fingers found a scaly leg and she closed her grip, leaving her swinging one-handed from the thing's foot. Woman and wyvern lurched a yard toward the ground together before the monster beat its wings again and steadied their fall.

Emily pulled her knife loose with her free hand and slashed upward, hoping to catch the thing's wing, but mistimed the attack and cut only air. If she could tear that thick membrane it would be forced to descend and then they'd see who could handle a thirty-foot fall better—but the wyvern obviously knew that too, because it screeched and tried to kick her off with its free foot, lashing out with talons that looked much longer up close.

Emily jammed her knife between her teeth and waited for her moment; when the claws came in reach of her empty hand she grabbed those too. Now she had both its legs; trapped, the wyvern could only thrash her awkwardly up and down, which was jarring but not immediately threatening.

They sank slowly as Emily's weight dragged the monster toward the earth, but she was in range now and the creature ducked its head down to cough fire directly into her face. The jet sprayed her for a searing second then flickered out almost instantly, leaving her scorched and blinking but otherwise whole.

She had to get at those wings. Squinting as the sun flashed over the wyvern's shoulder, she let go with her left hand and yanked with her right, dragging the creature a few inches down, then grabbed hold again a little higher up its leg. The red ground wheeled beneath her as she repeated the trick in reverse, climbing her way up the wyvern's body. It was beating its wings wildly now, trying to simultaneously maintain altitude and shake her off. Hand by hand she struggled upwards until her hands were on the thrashing monster's narrow shoulders and she was nearly face-to-face with it. But a wing struck her in the temple, its little terminal claw raking her burned cheek painfully. The sun hit her eyes again as she jerked away from the blow.

Emily checked her left-hand grip, took a breath, and let go with her right. As the wyvern lurched she snatched the knife from her teeth and slashed at the wing that had just hit her; this time she connected, tearing a huge gap in the leathery membrane. The wyvern gave a roar unlike anything she'd heard from it so far and wind whistled through the rip as it beat its wings in a sudden thrash that levered her hand free from its shoulder. Emily scraped down the monster's twisting body, freefalling, until her numb hand closed reflexively around its leg and she hung, gasping, far above the swinging landscape.

The wyvern began to turn as it fell, corkscrewing toward the ground, the torn wing unable to keep up with its opposite. The earth was coming up quickly now and Emily braced for a rough landing. A moment later the two combatants hit red dirt together, tumbling in a beating, shoving mass to come to rest near the foot of the cliff.

Emily lay dazed, her chest heaving, her limbs weak. The fall had hit her harder than she'd expected—her breath refused to come in anything more than short, fluttery pants. At least the wyvern didn't seem to be moving as Emily stared up into the flat blue sky over the desert.

No, there was no chance she'd run into Jack here. They always seemed to miss each other. A day after the dragon's attack she'd left the island of Finalhaven to join the Sabre & Torch Society while Jack stayed behind, helping clean up and get things in order. There was no cell phone reception that far out in the sea, no internet. So they'd exchanged a few handwritten letters, but even those were hindered by the fact that Emily had no home address.

That was how it was in the S&T. Rootless, restless, homeless. Traveling the world, solving supernatural problems, fighting monsters that came through the Veil. It had always been her dream to join and when she'd earned her spot by killing the world's last dragon, she hadn't hesitated. She'd jumped into the Society life feetfirst and with stars in her eyes.

Now she was just seeing weird blotchy shapes waver against the blue of the sky. Emily forced a full breath painfully into her lungs and staggered to her feet. Her knife had been lost in the scuffle—maybe it was under the wyvern—but as she glanced shakily around she found her hammer right where she'd left it, leaning against the rocky base of the cliff.

Something scratched in the dust behind her. She jumped for the hammer as the wyvern righted itself and spat fire at her back. Heat kissed her neck as she grabbed her weapon and spun blindly, swinging it in a wide arc.

It connected with the wyvern's head as the thing rushed at her with its clawed wings leading. A fat smack echoed off the rocks and the shock rang up her arm; the wyvern stumbled one way and Emily went the other, shaking her head to try to clear the last of the haze from her mind.

A high-pitched screech, different from the wyvern's cries, sounded somewhere far above. Emily glanced up wildly and was blinded by an eyeful of sun. Hissing, she ducked her face into her elbow to help her vision clear, but before she could recover, hot pain lanced down her arms as something pierced deep into her shoulders.

The hammer fell from her nerveless hands as she was lifted bodily into the air. She could hear, could feel, the sweeping beat of huge wings just above her. They had to be much bigger than the wyvern's.

Dragon? The word rode on a sting of panic.

Finally her vision cleared, thanks in part to the great shadow blocking the sun above her. Emily was thirty feet or more from the ground and climbing. Gulping, she looked up: she was in the clutches of a wyvern twice the size of the one she'd been fighting, its talons digging into her shoulders and gripping tight. A second huge wyvern above them carried her injured foe in a gentle grasp.

Even these great creatures couldn't truly fly and soon they set down on a ledge not far from the one Emily's prey had first fled to. There was a wide gap in the rocks here, invisible from below thanks to the ledge and, as she was dragged toward it, Emily guessed that it led to a cave where the wyverns made their nest.

If the Irregulars could only see me now, Emily thought. Ernest would have something clever and cutting to say, probably a play on words. The young poet was still on Finalhaven as far as Emily knew. He'd taken over running the Irregulars for Captain Queen, who had lost her memory. Nobody knew where she was.

Michael and Elizabeth might have been a bit less snarky than Ernest, but they were missing, too. They'd gone on the run almost the moment the dragon's severed head hit the ground. Elizabeth Pendragon was the rightful ruler of Albion, firstborn child of the old king Arthur XXIX, but apparently queens weren't welcome in the royal line that had spawned only boys for the thousand years leading up to Elizabeth. She'd spent her entire life in hiding. Michael Fletcher, the soft-voiced healer, had happily joined her in a life as quarry for Albian knights.

What a mess. It had almost been easier when they were all cooped up in the Castle Forlorn, waiting for the dragon and its mercenaries to come kill them. The whole thing seemed like a dream now, fading in the light of morning until the details were a faraway haze and only a few raw emotions remained. The Irregulars were scattered to who knew where and Emily was injured, trapped, and alone.

She couldn't fight as the great wyvern half flew toward the cave mouth. Struggling just seemed to dig its claws deeper into her muscles. It rose a few feet in the air on a single wingbeat, then tossed Emily into the opening almost lazily. She tumbled through and fell to the floor of the cavern beyond.

In the slanting sunlight, Emily could make out the shapes of bones of all sorts and sizes covering more than half the cave floor. Most were tiny, probably from birds and rodents. A tall set of broad ribs stood out from the pile—a cow, maybe? Emily stood shakily, trying to work some of the pain from her shoulders. Her foot kicked something that rolled into a shaft of dusty sun: a human skull.

"Shit," Emily said. She had no time to reflect, though, as the wyverns pushed through the cave mouth to join her. The one she'd been fighting had to be an adolescent at best, if the other two were its parents. She couldn't see any indication of sex—both the adults were absolutely massive, at least twice her size.

6

There was no way she could take all three on, that much was obvious. The wyverns advanced on her as a group. All three had their wings out in a threat display that Emily had to admit was working excellently. The massed creatures blocked the cave mouth, cutting Emily off from both escape and sunlight. At this point her best bet was to flee back to civilization, where she could reach out to the Sabre & Torch for backup, but flight was looking more impossible by the second.

Even as she backed away from the wyverns, Emily couldn't take her eyes off them. Their heads were lowered, weaving slowly back and forth as they tracked their prey. At any second, one of those heads might lash out for the killing strike, ragged teeth snapping at her throat. Another might leap on her, its claws cutting open her stomach and pulling out her guts. She could fight off one for sure, but two or three would overwhelm her by sheer mass.

"Hey!" barked a voice from the mouth of the cave. The three wyverns turned as one and, through the gaps as they lowered their wings, Emily could see a tall, muscular shape silhouetted against the sunlight.

"God dammit," she said. She was saved, but at the cost of her pride.

Durgan dun Raven, Emily's mentor in the Sabre & Torch Society, leaped into the cave, laughing. Sensing a threat, the wyverns wasted no time playing with him. The adolescent jumped clear as the two adults darted at dun Raven from either side, spitting flames. The warrior's huge sword flashed up, turning one gout of fire aside as he rolled his broad shoulders under the other. He turned the roll into a downward slash of his blade that made a red arc as it cut a wyvern from shoulder to wing. The beast fell back, screeching.

The other adult darted its head towards dun Raven, snapping at his exposed back. Quicker than seemed possible for such a huge man, he spun on one heel. His sword flashed again and the wyvern's head separated from its neck and tumbled over his shoulder, mouth still open and ready to bite.

The surviving adult, though bleeding heavily, renewed its attack. Dun Raven fell back against a vicious onslaught of snapping teeth and slashing claws. None of them seemed likely to connect, but it was all the warrior could do to intercept them all.

Protecting its child, Emily thought suddenly, but the younger wyvern had no intent of staying back. It approached dun Raven slowly, rearing its head back in a motion that Emily recognized. The thing was about to spit fire in the fighter's face, which under the vicious attack of the parent might be enough to distract him.

"Look out!" Emily shouted as she scrabbled through the bones around her, trying to find something that could serve as a weapon. Her hand closed on a long, heavy bone that might have been a femur and she leaped toward the adolescent, planning to bring the makeshift weapon down on its head.

At the last second she changed her mind and as the thing began to cough up its fire she jammed the bone into its mouth. It choked as the femur went down and the fledgling flame came up. They met somewhere in its long neck, which burst open with a wet pop as the fireball exploded against the obstruction. Hot blood sprayed Emily's face as the wyvern fell away and landed with a clatter amongst the detritus of the cave floor. A second later, the last of the wyverns fell too, both wings sheared off by Durgan dun Raven's flickering sword.

"Thanks," grunted the big warrior. He was far bloodier than Emily, but he wore it like war paint while she just felt sticky. Emily never failed to feel awe when she looked at dun Raven. He was easily over seven feet tall, fully filled out with muscle from his hunched shoulders to his tree-trunk legs. The left side of his face drooped under a long, jagged scar. His shaggy blonde hair looked like he had cut it himself with a dagger. He had been born to fight, perhaps the most appropriate man ever to receive the Gift of Combat. Emily was theoretically his equal, but she felt puny next to him.

"Don't even," she said, wiping blood from her eyes. "How long have you been following me?"

Dun Raven's shrug was like a mountain shifting. "Whole time. It's your first solo job, so."

8

"Apparently not," said Emily.

"Come on," said dun Raven. He turned to leave the cave, which was starting to smell from all the gore. "I'm hungry."

"Wait," Emily said, following him. "How bad is this? In the eyes of the S&T, I mean."

"Bad?" asked dun Raven.

"My first time on my own and I screwed it up," Emily said, blinking in the Deseret sun as they left the cave. "I let myself get snatched—I think those things dove out of the sun, by the way, in case you were wondering—and almost eaten."

Out on the ledge, dun Raven knelt and prepared to climb back down the cliff. "You're sad because I saved you?"

"I'm upset because you had to!" said Emily.

Dun Raven looked up at her from the cliff's edge. "That's good."

"Good?" Emily gaped at him. "How is it good?"

"Because." Dun Raven had an even more serious look on his face than usual. He'd been mentoring her for four months and it had mostly been fighting and eating, but every once in a while he actually imparted some authentic wisdom. When he did it was always with that face. "You should be upset. S&T agents work alone. Too much to do, not enough fighters. Learn to rely on yourself or die."

"I thought I could." Emily shook her head. "I really thought I was ready to go solo."

#

Dun Raven bought them lunch, at a tiny roadside diner where he and Emily were the target of many suspicious stares as they plowed their way through two steak-and-fries combos, five hamburgers, three Reubens, an additional plate of fries with gravy, and a vanilla milkshake that Emily ordered with fond thoughts of the ice-cream loving Captain Queen of Finalhaven.

9

They were both quiet through the meal. Dun Raven—scrubbed free of blood and changed into a tight T-shirt and jeans, but still every inch the warrior—sat with a sandwich in each hand and his mouth constantly full, and did the lion's share of the eating. Emily had similarly cleaned up—the trunk of their rental car was crammed with bloody towels—but unlike dun Raven, she had to force herself to put food in her mouth despite her ravenous hunger. Halfway through chewing each bite she would see the lowered, weaving heads of the wyverns coming for her. Then they would morph into images of the dragon of Finalhaven that were burned into her memory like photographs: its wings huge against the midnight moon, its smile as it told her to run after biting the old Marcher Lord in half, its jaws closing down on Sir Maximilian.

It's dead, Emily reminded herself. *You killed it yourself. You're just tired.*

As Dun Raven paid the bill, Emily took the car across the street to a gas station.

Food and fuel, she thought. *All I need to keep moving.* In fact, those were the only options; the diner and gas station had been dropped seemingly at random on either side of a black line of tarmac that ran in both directions to an empty horizon. Dun Raven joined her as she stood filling the tank.

"Where to next?" she asked. Before he could reply, her mentor's cell phone rang.

It was ridiculous to watch that huge man answer a phone that looked tiny in his hands, but the common methods of magical communication—telepathy, automatic writing, voicecasting—were taxing on the caster and less reliable than a decent satellite connection. Emily watched dun Raven's scowl deepen as he listened, then grunted an acknowledgment and hung up.

"Get your stuff out of the car," he said. "I need it."

"What is it?" Emily asked. "Can I come?"

Dun Raven shook his head. "No. I'll be gone for a few months." He opened the back door of the car and tossed Emily her duffel bag. "Don't take any jobs."

Emily finished gassing up the car and gave dun Raven the keys. He got in the driver's seat, adjusted it as far back as it would go, and slammed the door.

"See you, Sledge. Think about what I said." The car came to life with a roar and dun Raven peeled out into the street, cutting across two lanes of active traffic.

"Wait," Emily said after him. "Where am I supposed to go?"

#

A few hours later, bedsprings squealed in complaint as Emily sat exhausted on paper-stiff motel sheets. The ten-mile walk from the gas station had been more boring than challenging. She could have run the whole way in a sliver of the time, but she was supposed to keep a tight lid on her Gift around regular people and she'd been under close watch from squint-eyed locals as she strolled into town.

"Town" was a generous term; aside from a run-down grocery store, a little local bank, a bus station, and the motel, the only sign of civilization was a series of chain-link fences dividing weedy undeveloped lots into unwelcoming rectangles. There was no more reason for this town than there was for the diner up the road. Still, a triangular tower of steel behind the bank promised cell service and that was all Emily really needed.

She opened her duffel bag, feeling a pang of longing for a laundromat as she surveyed the dirty, balled-up clothes within. Buried under the clothing was a laptop and Emily's weapons. She'd lost her best long knife but found her hammer where she'd left it at the base of the wyverns' cliff, and she still had a small pile of other knives, a pair of throwing axes, and a set of brass knuckles.

She pulled out the laptop and a small clasp knife, which she flicked open one-handed as she set the laptop on her bed. It hummed to life when she opened it and a small camera set above the monitor promptly scanned her retina. The computer unlocked. Emily tapped through a touchscreen

11

menu and opened an app that connected her to the central hub of Sabre & Torch Society information. The S&T logo, a crossed sword and burning torch, appeared on the screen.

Emily pricked her thumb with the knife, drawing a single bead of bright red blood. Whispering a few words in Latin, she let the droplet fall on a flat silver square embedded below the keyboard.

Kayo Jackson, one of Emily's best friends from her school days and a talented magician, had once explained how the system worked, but that knowledge had long since been replaced with more crucial information. By pricking her thumb and speaking the Latin, Emily wasn't casting a spell herself, just activating the spell woven into the silver plate. The magical energy created by her blood meeting the plate then somehow got transferred to the computer—Emily's imagination failed around this point—and granted her access to the S&T's extremely private site.

The sword-and-torch logo faded away, replaced by a rather mundane list of content. The S&T's data team aggregated worldwide news, rumors, police reports, social media chatter, and a hundred other sources, all in a search for the supernatural. The raw data was all available, but most members went right to the job board, where verified reports and requests for help from other field agents mingled with the occasional emergency notification.

Emily scrolled through the jobs, looking for anything that would get her out of Deseret. She had no intention of following orders and sitting in her dad's tiny apartment in Boston while dun Raven was off adventuring. Her failure in what was supposed to be her first solo mission stung, but her mentor's sudden absence was an opportunity for another shot— ideally as far from here as possible.

She paused on a report of lindworm sightings in Trolldom, the Gifted Nation that encompassed most of the area known as Scandinavia, then scrolled on. She'd fought lindworms during her school days and the cold in Trolldom had worn her down despite her superhuman toughness. There were always lindworms out in the snows there; their public defenders could handle it.

12

She flipped past a few North American listings before the name "Albion" caught her eye. She had no love for that Nation, given how they'd treated Elizabeth, who should have been their queen. Still, Albion included England and England was far from here, not too cold, and somewhere she'd never been.

The post was a request for backup from an S&T member named De Soto Rigmaiden. She didn't recognize the name—she was pretty sure she'd remember if she'd heard it before—but then again, she'd hardly met anyone yet beside Durgan dun Raven. Rigmaiden was American, from a tiny Nation in the south called the Sabine Free State, but he'd gone to Albion chasing reports of antlered men in the rural southwest of England. He'd spent a month or so following rumors and had finally come face-to-face with a creature that left him hanging half-dead from a tree before disappearing into the forest.

Rigmaiden wanted revenge and for that, he needed help. His post was light on details, but Emily could easily imagine the fear and frustration hidden beneath the sparse words of the report. He'd made a request to the Albian government under King Arthur XXX, Elizabeth Pendragon's younger brother, and been rebuffed, told that the Albian knighthood had better things to do than chase phantoms. Emily shook her head, thinking that those same knights were being wasted hunting Elizabeth across North America when they could be used at home. Her opinion of Arthur XXX fell even more.

As her adrenaline got pumping and her exhaustion sloughed away, Emily forgot entirely that she'd meant to pick up a solo gig. She tapped a button to send a message directly to Rigmaiden. It only took a moment for her to write it up, sticking to the details: "I'm currently in Deseret but on my way. I'll take the earliest flight to London and get a car from there. Don't go hunting without me."

She hit send and hopped off the motel bed before the message had even left her outbox. There was no question of loitering around the motel, or even getting a few hours' sleep before setting out for the airport. It would be hours before she could set foot on a plane and there was no telling how many connections she'd have to suffer through before she landed in London. She'd forgotten all about the embarrassment of that morning. Somewhere out there action and danger were waiting for her and she had no intention of wasting time getting to them.

CHAPTER 2

Less than forty-eight hours later, Emily stood at the edge of a dark Albian forest with De Soto Rigmaiden at her side. Night was falling, bringing an autumn chill that got its fingers under Emily's hoodie and raised goosebumps on her skin. She shifted her grip on her hammer nervously as she watched the still, dark eaves of the forest.

Rigmaiden sniffed and wiped his nose with the back of his hand. He was an older man, tall, lean, and wiry, with lank gray hair to his shoulders. His skin was sallow except where it was red and peeling over his sharp cheekbones and sunken cheeks. He had bags beneath both gray eyes and a fading purple circle under the left. He wore a John Deere cap and a long, striped serape over dirty blue jeans and carried a machete in his left hand and a battered, splintering wooden shield in his right.

"You ready?" he asked. It was the third thing he'd said since meeting Emily in a little rural town called Kennetsbridge, about three hours' drive from London. The first two had been, "You Emily?" when they met and "We're here" upon reaching the forest a few miles from Kennetsbridge.

"Ready," said Emily. She'd slept on the plane and eaten in London, so there was really nothing left standing between her and the upcoming monster hunt. It had all happened so quickly, between the decision in the Deseret hotel room and now, but Emily told herself she preferred Rigmaiden's no-nonsense approach to endless debates and discussions. That was the strength of the Sabre & Torch Society, after all. It empowered its agents to make snap decisions when lives were on the line. If this monster, whatever it was, was lurking in a forest so near to Kennetsbridge and its outlying farms, people were definitely in danger. Then there was the prospect of a publicity mess if some innocent mundane should stumble upon the thing, or worse, get killed by it. It was the duty and mission of every citizen of the Gifted Nations to drive back things that came through the Veil between worlds, but the real constant work was keeping those same things under wraps.

Rigmaiden set out for the tree line and Emily followed close behind. She had to hustle to match the old fighter's long stride. Soon they passed beneath the first boughs of the forest. The trees were still thick with leaves despite the chill, and the darkness beneath them was nearly absolute.

Rigmaiden pulled a flashlight from his pocket and flicked it on. It made a pale circle that flickered over the trees and ground as they walked, but did nothing to illuminate the black space around them. With only the faint beam to guide them, they headed toward the heart of the wood.

"So what have you got on this thing?" asked Emily after a few quiet minutes. She had whispered, but in the hush of the forest her voice was like a shout. "Anything I should know before we meet it?"

"Tall," said Rigmaiden, looking up from his examination of a patch of moss hidden by rotting leaves. He managed to speak with a full voice yet keep his tone soft. "Strong. Shaped like a man, but with antlers like a buck. Eyes like a cat in the dark."

"You nearly died, didn't you?" It was a rude question, but Emily wanted all the information she could get.

"Been closer," grunted Rigmaiden. He played his flashlight over a gnarled growth of roots that blocked their way, then traced up a massive oak tree whose branches stretched far beyond the little beam.

"Wasn't there anybody local who could handle this?" Emily whispered. "You'd think the Albian government would be a little more concerned with a monster running around."

"Shush." Rigmaiden held up a hand. In the faint glow of the flashlight Emily saw the fighter's brow furrow as he examined the oak tree. She tried

16

to keep her breathing silent, but as her heart beat harder and her pulse quickened it was tough not to gulp down air.

The flashlight played across the lower branches of the oak, then abruptly stopped. Emily squinted—what had Rigmaiden seen? The branches creaked and shifted. But there was no breeze this far into the thick wood...

"Come out, you bastard!" Rigmaiden shouted, making Emily jump. A clump of branches shifted away from the tree and suddenly they weren't branches at all, they were antlers, wavering nearly ten feet off the ground. The circle of light flashed down the length of the thing as Rigmaiden dropped his light and Emily caught a glimpse of a human-like shape peeling away from the trunk of the oak. Its skin was like bark, cracked and rough, but patches of fur sprouted here and there along the thick torso and arms.

The flashlight clattered to the ground and stuck there, pointing up at a skewed angle to catch the eyes of the creature far above Emily's head. Rigmaiden was right; it had eyes like a cat's, flashing in the darkness like headlights. They floated in the night, shifting as the thing turned its head to stare at her.

Emily cut to the right and Rigmaiden went left, instinctively splitting up so each could attack from the best possible angle as they darted in at the creature. Its antlers creaked and its eyes disappeared as it turned on Rigmaiden. There was a crack like a splinty sword hitting a ball flat on; Emily guessed that Rigmaiden had caught the monster's attack on his shield.

Emily braced herself and swung, guessing at where her target should be. Her hammer whistled through the night air and collided with a bang that dwarfed the noise of the shield. She stumbled under the impact, her arms shaking. It was like hitting an iron wall.

Something rustled in the darkness and then Emily was staggering breathless as a limb like a tree branch slammed into her chest. Antlers moved through the flashlight beam and eyes gleamed as they turned on her. She ducked purely by instinct and something rushed over her head, missing her by an inch. Seizing the opening, she darted in with her hammer leading, coming up under the limb that had slashed at her, and shoved her weapon forward with both hands.

The hammer connected and the thing made a sound for the first time. It was loud, a cross between a screech and a whine, high-pitched and piercing. A fluttering rose all around them as spooked birds took off in panicked flight. Emily fumbled to steady herself after the blow she'd landed unbalanced her as much as her foe. The flapping of startled wings masked the rush of the creature's next attack.

Clawed hands shoved Emily backwards, driving her away and leaving her staggering in the darkness as the world reeled around her. She shook her head and tried to orient toward the sound of scuffling nearby. She turned her head in just the right direction as something lashed out, catching her full in the face and driving her to the ground.

Emily felt blood pouring from her nose, which had shattered like a dropped wineglass under the blow. She spat as much as she could from her mouth and hastily wiped the rest away. Sounds of Rigmaiden and the creature scuffling came from the darkness to her left and she could make out their dim shapes. She grabbed her hammer and headed in that direction, stumbling over the reaching roots of the oak.

A crunch and a pained grunt sounded, then Rigmaiden shouted, "Damn you!" in a slurred voice. Emily homed in on his yell and leaped forward with a hammerblow ready, but checked herself suddenly, uncertain whether she was chasing the monster or her partner. The creature's eyes flashed to life only a foot above her head. Something jagged and hot sank into her shoulder and she felt a flare of wet breath on her face. Under the copper smell of her busted nose, the thing stank of rotten undergrowth.

Pain burned down Emily's chest as the creature bit deep in the same spot where the wyvern had grabbed her not two days earlier. Hissing, she dropped her hammer and twisted to grab the monster's jaws, but it let go before she could get a grip. She shoved it bodily away from her, succeeding more in pushing herself backwards but at least making space.

Emily felt around with her foot, but her hammer was lost. She pulled a knife from her belt and flicked it open. There was no reason to think a knife would succeed where her hammer and all her strength had failed, but she had no intention of giving up.

The creature screeched again as it moved through the flashlight's hazy beam toward her. It had its head low and Emily caught a glimpse of an elongated skull-like face beneath the spreading antlers, soft with mossy growths and missing a few teeth. Its mouth clacked and its breath came in a soft rush. Emily stood completely still, her empty left hand open in front of her and the knife in her right ready to strike.

The crash of a gun filled Emily's ears as sparks flared in the black. Emily blinked, trying to clear her vision, but all she could see was a bright orange blaze.

"Come on, old boy!" someone shouted off to the left. A man's voice, with an Albian accent. Not Rigmaiden... but who?

Creaking and rustling sounded as the creature turned toward this new arrival. The gun roared again and behind the sparks Emily could vaguely see a human shape. A clattering noise followed—the sound of someone breaking a shotgun open to replace its cartridges.

Her vision was filled with orange light, but Emily had been blind anyway in the wooded night. Whoever the newcomer was, he was on her side and he was in trouble. She crept toward the clattering noise, one questing hand out. A moment later she touched heaving, mossy bark. She jumped straight up and threw her arms around the creature's neck; it was like trying to get a tree trunk in a submission hold. The creature shrieked and bucked beneath her as Emily held on tight, riding the thing like a bull. Her knife was still in her right hand and with shaking fingers she twisted it into a reverse grip and plunged it into what she hoped was the creature's throat.

The thing's scream became a strangled gargle. Its back arched in a sudden convulsion and Emily was thrown clear. Her head hit a rock-hard root as she landed among wet leaves. She jumped to her feet as quickly as she'd fallen, shook her head, stumbled, and righted herself.

"Emily, that you?" It was Rigmaiden, somewhere in the dark in front of her. The flashlight had gone out at some point and the forest was fully black. Off to her left the monster was still roaring wetly and thrashing among the leaves.

"Stay back!" barked the Albian voice again. There was a sharp snap and a click and then a gout of blue flame and orange sparks exploded into the night with a boom. A clack, then the gun roared again. Burned into Emily's vision was a silhouette, a tall antlered shape bent halfway backwards as it caught the blast only a foot or two from its origin.

The boom of the gun echoed away and then there was silence. By some silent agreement, all three stood stock-still, waiting and listening for the faintest sound of motion from the creature crumpled on the forest floor between them.

"He's dead," said the Albian. "It's all right now. Come on, it's all right."

Emily moved toward the voice as Rigmaiden shuffled slowly through the leaves. A moment later his flashlight came faintly to life, blinked out, then shone again after a series of sharp taps. Emily blinked as the beam hit her square on.

"You okay?" asked Rigmaiden. "You look like shit."

"Fine," said Emily. "I can't tell you how many times I've broken my nose. How about you?"

"Leg's busted," said Rigmaiden. "Can't hardly walk. Be okay, though." The beam flashed over to illuminate the third man. "Who are you?"

In the flat white light, Emily saw an exhausted-looking young man. He was probably in his mid-twenties, but the weak light on his drawn features made him look twice that. He had thinning, windblown brown hair and brown stubble on his jaw, thin lips, and a broad nose. His skin looked naturally pasty, but like Rigmaiden he had the chapped red of sunburn on his cheeks. Looking in his eyes was like seeing an old man peering from a young man's face.

20

He was dressed in old-fashioned hunting clothes, a heavy tweed jacket with leather-patched shoulders over a V-neck sweater and thick corduroy pants tucked into tall Wellington boots. Tucked under his arm was a shotgun, broken open, with smoke still weaving up from both barrels.

"Marlow Bright," he said warily, eyes sliding back and forth between Emily and Rigmaiden. "I take it you're Americans?"

"That's right," said Rigmaiden.

"This isn't really tourist country. You've wandered far off the beaten path here," said Bright. He snorted decisively. "But! You are in luck. My house isn't far. Fair good chance that I happened to be walking tonight. You must let me help you. You can get cleaned up before we find your car and get you on your way."

#

The walk to Bright's house was hampered by Rigmaiden's leg, which they saw was crushed badly as soon as they escaped the forest. The old Free Stater refused to admit to any trouble, but as Emily and Bright half carried him slowly along the tree line, every breath of his was a hiss of pain.

"You must let me call you an ambulance," said Bright as they hobbled across a broad field. "They'll be at the house in no time. We do have roads, even if you've chosen to ignore them."

"No need," said Rigmaiden. At the sight of Emily and Bright's skeptical looks he continued, "I'll see a doc once I'm back home in… America. Looks worse than it is."

Bright said nothing and Emily wondered what he must think had happened. Obviously they couldn't tell him the truth, that they were agents of a secret group of globetrotting monster slayers. It was lucky that it had been so dark in the forest. Come to think of it…

"That was a hell of a stag," Emily said. "Do you think it was rabid, maybe?"

"Must have been," said Bright.

21

"We have moose that size where I come from," Emily went on. It would be good to make a friend of Bright and better to put plenty of ideas other than monsters in his head, but if she was honest, her adrenaline was draining away and she just needed to talk to someone as the horror of the fight started to creep up on her. "Do you have moose in England?"

"No, no, not in the slightest," said Bright.

"Must have been a deer, then," said Emily.

"Must have been."

They struggled on under the thin moon, Rigmaiden grunting and wheezing between them. Eventually the forest fell away as they climbed a gentle rise covered in clover. They paused at the top and Emily saw the lights of a small stone farmhouse in the dell below.

"Ah, there we are," said Bright. "Barley Bright. Not far now. Aminah will have a kettle on. Come along!"

It was only a few minutes to the door of the farmhouse. It stood a few hundred yards back from a modern road and was ringed by a low wall of crumbling stone with a white picket gate standing open. Ivy climbed from the ground up the house's two stories; the upper was dark, but lamplight glowed cheerily from all the windows of the ground floor. All the fear had drained from Emily, leaving her empty and worn out, making the house look very inviting.

Bright left Emily to sit with Rigmaiden on the stone wall as the old fighter gathered his strength. The farmer strode up a neat gravel path and opened the door of his house, which was unlocked. They heard the low tones of a conversation within, then Bright waved to them from the doorway.

The front door opened directly into a kitchen. A broad oak table stood to one side, with six chairs around it and four steaming cups of tea sitting on top. A wide brick hearth took up the entire back wall, with an old-fashioned oven and stove inside it. The whole place was so quaint, so charming, that Emily expected to see oil lamps hanging from the ceiling, but the lights were simple glass balls with normal lightbulbs in them.

"It's lovely," she said.

"Thank you," said a female voice. Emily turned to see a young woman, about Bright's age, come through an open doorway across from the big oak table. She had golden olive skin, deep brown eyes, and a square jaw. The thick black hair that hung straight down to her elbows suggested someone who never worked, but that impression was instantly dispelled by her battered duck boots, patched jeans, and a cable-knit wool sweater as quaint as the house itself. She approached with a smile, an honest, toothy grin, but her face fell as she took in Emily and Rigmaiden. "My Lord, your face!"

"Oh—right," Emily said. "Do you have, like…"

"Don't move!"

The woman dashed out of the kitchen and returned a moment later with a damp washcloth, which she used to dab at Emily's bloody face. The bruising felt pretty minor, but her nose stung. Even with the blood cleared away, her nostrils felt clogged, and now there was a faint whistling when she breathed. Definitely broken.

"There now, that's a touch better. Gonna be purple tomorrow, though. Not much we can do about that." Long hair swinging, the woman went to the kitchen sink to wring out the washcloth, still talking over her shoulder. "Tourists, is that it? Don't see many tourists around here." Her voice had a humor to it, as though she knew a secret joke she wasn't telling. She spoke with a northern Albian, maybe a Caledonian accent—Scottish, that's what the mundanes called it, Emily reminded herself firmly. Mainland Scotland was under the rule of Albion, but the outer isles had stayed independent since before Roman times. Emily sniffed and tried to return the young woman's smile. Mundane politics always added a layer of confusion to Gifted history.

"Yeah," Emily said. "Are you Mrs. Bright, or…?" She trailed off as a wave of emotion passed over the young woman's face; she didn't even seem to be trying to hide it. Obviously she wasn't Mrs. Bright but wanted to be.

"Aminah Mirza," she said, brightening again. "That's just Aminah to you, and 'Mister Bright' is just Marlow, thanks. He may be the master of this house but he's not so old yet."

"Nice to meet you, Aminah," Emily said. "I'm Emily and this is Rigmaiden."

"De Soto," grunted Rigmaiden. Clearly the young woman had softened his heart as well.

"Aminah, where's that tea?" Bright—Marlow—came in from the same doorway as Aminah. He had cleaned up and shaved and looked twenty years younger than he had in the forest. His brown eyes were bright as he rubbed his hands together. "And perhaps some biscuits, don't you think?"

Aminah stayed in the kitchen as the others decamped through the back doorway, which led to a warm sitting room where a fire burned in a stone fireplace. The stairs to the second floor were here, along the back wall of the house, with overflowing bookshelves built into the triangular space underneath. The books all looked old, with wide, ribbed bindings in faded greens and grays.

Emily crossed the room and dropped into a squashed leather chair that promptly fitted itself to her body. Turning toward the fireplace, she saw a large painting of a romantic countryside hanging on the wall above it. Beneath, on the mantel, sat a relief sculpture carved from white stone. It showed a heroic figure with curly hair and a billowing cloak grabbing a bull by the mouth and plunging a knife into its neck.

"Roman," said Marlow, following Emily's eyes. "Been in the family for generations. My father once said we've had it since Trajan's day, but I like to think some ancestral cad nicked it from the British Museum."

"The painting is nice, too," Emily said politely. She'd never had much interest in art, but she had to admit that the landscape had a certain peaceful appeal. Lush green hills rolled toward a low forest, from which a pale blue river ran in broad curves. It almost looked like the Albian landscape they'd tramped through that night, except for the white marble ruins that dotted the hills and a low, gray castle that sat in the far background.

24

Drawn in despite herself, Emily stood to get a better look. Up close, the detail was amazing. Every ripple of the river was rendered in fine brushstrokes. A few tiny people in togas lounged at the foot of one of the ruins. Under the shelter of the forest, a bear stood looking out at the sunshine.

She stepped back again to take in the whole picture. There was a label on the gold frame, hand-painted in neat letters: ARCADIA.

"Arcadia?" Emily said. "Where's that?"

"Nowhere," said Marlow. He sat in a low couch across from the painting and sipped his tea gingerly. "It's not somewhere you can go. It's… an ideal. An idea."

"I see," Emily lied. Rigmaiden limped to the leather chair Emily had vacated, pulled a flask from his back pocket, and added something to his tea before tasting it.

"We must do something about that leg," said Marlow.

"Looks worse than it is," Rigmaiden said. "Got my medicine right here."

Aminah came in from the kitchen, a tray of cookies in one hand and a fresh damp washcloth in the other. She set the cookies down next to Marlow and sat on the far end of the couch.

"Well, aren't we quite the group?" she said. "A broken nose, a broken leg, and Marlow all cut up. I almost feel left out."

"Don't," said Marlow.

"It's a tough bunch, that's all I mean." Aminah shrugged and helped herself to a cookie. "Stoic."

"Well," said Marlow, standing. "It's been quite a night, we're all tired, and you'll be off to hospital in the morning. Let me show you the guest room."

Emily was debating asking if she could take the plate of cookies to bed with her when a motion in the corner of her eye caught her attention. She looked back at the painting and blinked in surprise. Maybe her exhaustion was playing tricks on her, but it sure looked like the painting was moving. Two tiny human figures, one painted all in shades of white and the other with dark skin, were walking along the river. They'd come from the forest and were headed for one of the little marble ruins.

"Marlow?" Emily said.

"Mm?" The young man glanced over at her, then jumped like a scared cat, confirming Emily's suspicions.

"You're an Arcane, aren't you?" Emily said. Marlow went white, but Aminah started to laugh. Emily hurriedly went on, "It's all right! We're Gifted too. Rigmaiden and I are fighters."

"Tourists!" Aminah said through gales of laughter. "I knew it!"

"I suppose you were in the forest looking for the same thing I was," Marlow said, scratching his chin. "Lucky we found each other."

"Yeah, thanks again for the save," Emily said. "I was blind as a bat in there, but I'm guessing you weren't."

Marlow smiled. "Just a little spell. Most useful for finding lost sheep at night." He looked at something over Emily's shoulder and snorted. "There you are. Perfect timing, as usual."

Emily turned, confused, to see Elizabeth Pendragon and Michael Fletcher standing between her and the fireplace. The figures in the painting had disappeared.

Chapter 3

"Emily!" A shocked grin split Michael's face.

"Michael! Elizabeth! Elizabeth?" Emily shook her head, unable to choose which of her friends to look at and trying for both at the same time.

"Emily," said Elizabeth and she put out her hands. Emily grasped them, felt for a dizzy moment that she should kneel, then threw the exiled queen into a hug. Michael joined them a moment later and when they finally broke apart, his eyes were bright.

"I don't even know where to start," Emily said. Her friends looked just as she remembered them from their fearful days on Finalhaven. Elizabeth was like a ghost, all pale skin, bone-white hair straight down to her back, and a plain white dress of lace and cotton. Michael's grin was just as white against his brown skin and he had his long black dreds tied back from his forehead with a strip of red cloth. In sneakers, jeans, and a T-shirt, he could have gone unnoticed anywhere in the mundane world. They both looked whole, healthy, and happy to see Emily.

Emily squeezed Michael's shoulder as she tried to order her thoughts. One jumped to the top of the heap and she laughed as it registered. "Were you just in the painting?"

"Yes," said Elizabeth. She smiled gently. "Are you all right? Your nose—"

"Wait, stop!" Emily said. "I have so many more questions. Okay, first—first, Elizabeth, are you safe?"

27

"We're with friends," said the queen and her glance turned to Aminah and Marlow. "I'm afraid we don't have much to report."

"Quite all right," said Marlow. "We clearly have our hands full getting caught up. Aminah, why don't you put the kettle back on?"

"I'd rather not miss this," said Aminah. Marlow raised an eyebrow; she met his look with one of her own, but hurried back into the kitchen.

They made themselves comfortable, filling the little sitting room. Elizabeth and Michael snuggled together on the couch, leaving enough room for Emily as well. Rigmaiden stayed where he had dropped into the leather chair, his hurt leg sticking straight out. Marlow pulled up a wooden chair from along the wall, then hesitated.

"Michael, would you give me a hand?" He chewed his lower lip. "I'll take a look at Emily's nose if you can help Mr. Rigmaiden with his leg."

"That's me," said Rigmaiden, holding up a hand in a lazy wave.

"Of course, sorry!" Michael hopped up from the couch and went to kneel at Rigmaiden's feet as Marlow took over the spot next to Emily. If Rigmaiden was offended at being forgotten about, he didn't show it.

"I guess you found it, huh?" said Michael as he prodded gently at Rigmaiden's busted leg. The only sign the old fighter gave of his pain was a narrowing of his eyes as Michael felt the break.

"Your friends found it," said Marlow. "I just followed the sounds of trouble. It's dead now, though, thank Mithras."

"Thank your shotgun, I bet," said Michael. "Now, Mr. Rigmaiden, this is going to feel strange."

"You think I never been healed before?" said Rigmaiden sourly. "Just get it done."

"My, you're a barrel of laughs," Marlow said. "You may be my guest, but so is Michael and I'll thank you to treat him civilly."

Rigmaiden wrinkled his nose. "Appreciate it."

"Don't worry about it," said Michael. "I'll bet this hurts a lot more than you're letting on."

"So what was that thing?" Emily asked, watching Aminah come back in with two more cups of tea on blue saucers.

Marlow put his spread fingers on Emily's nose and cheeks, turned her head gently to face him, and frowned as he examined the damage. "Well, we're not rightly sure," he said. "But we suspect it came from Arcadia."

"So it *is* a place!" Emily laughed, then winced as Marlow pressed on the crooked bridge of her nose. Despite the pain she couldn't help but snort, which made her sinuses whistle. "*Oh, it's just an ideal...* you're not much of a liar, Marlow."

"Thank you," said Marlow. He twisted his hand sharply and Emily's nose cracked as it snapped back into place. Emily leaped up from the couch, gasping with the sudden pain.

"The hell was that!" she yelped.

Marlow smoothed the front of his sweater. "Well, I could have said 'it won't hurt a bit,' but I'm not much of a liar." He made a little more room for her on the couch. "Come now, I just needed to set it. Now that's done I can heal it up."

"We're done over here," said Michael. Rigmaiden was standing gingerly up from the chair, testing his weight on his broken leg. He pressed his lips together, then relaxed as whatever he felt satisfied him.

"Not bad, kid," he said. "You got talent."

"So this thing came out of your painting, like Michael and Elizabeth?" Emily asked, forcing the conversation away from broken bones and back to the topic that most interested her. "Must have been tough to fit its antlers in here."

"It is more complex than that," said Elizabeth from the couch.

"Of course it is," Emily muttered. She had no problem with magicians, but magic itself was... frustrating.

"The painting is like a window into Arcadia," Michael said. "For a long time, it was the only one. But now, other windows seem to be opening. Nearby, but not right in this room—mostly in the forest, we think."

Emily flashed back to the moment in Elizabeth's rooms in the Castle Forlorn when Michael had sat and explained the memory spell that trapped the castle. It was all about entrances and exits back then, too. Even his tone was the same.

"Put another way, every entrance to another world is a rip in the Veil," said Elizabeth. "The painting cut the first hole to Arcadia, but the hole is growing."

That was remarkably clear for Elizabeth. Michael must be rubbing off on her.

"Okay, so can we close the hole? What if we destroy the painting?" Before she'd even finished the sentence, the looks on Michael's and Marlow's faces told Emily it was a bad idea. More than that—they seemed almost scared at the suggestion.

"We can't do that," said Michael.

"Out of the question," Marlow agreed.

"Why?" Emily asked.

"Aside from its obvious value," Marlow said, "destroying it just wouldn't help. The damage to the Veil has been done."

"So instead," Michael said, "we've been making sorties in. Trying to figure out why monsters are coming out."

"Well, mostly Michael and Elizabeth have," said Marlow. "Whilst Aminah and I keep an eye on the home front, and a good thing, too."

"Are you an Arcane as well, Aminah?" Emily asked.

Aminah laughed, a single sarcastic bark. "Me? Lord, no. Just regular folk, me." She pushed her thick hair behind an ear. "My only Gift is making the tea."

"But you—"

"Know about Marlow and that?" Aminah smiled. "I do. Figured it out all on my own, too. Like you said, he's not much of a liar. Had to admit the truth when I confronted him with everything."

"She's sworn to secrecy," Marlow said tightly.

"Oh, sure, no need to worry about old Aminah." She laughed. "I'm just happy to be here."

"Happy to have you here," Emily said. Aminah nodded. "So have you found anything? About what's going on, I mean?"

"Not yet," Michael said, and Marlow shook his head.

"Well," said Rigmaiden, standing up noisily. "I need to sleep. Sounds like we're going in that painting tomorrow."

"Sleep is a good idea," Marlow agreed. "Come along, I've got guest rooms upstairs. They're cozy."

"He means small," Michael put in. Elizabeth laughed.

"Oh, Emily, let me heal your nose," Marlow said. Emily had forgotten all about it in her curiosity about the painting, but she let Marlow lay his hands on her face again. A cool tingle flowed across her skin and sank deep into her bones as the throbbing sting of her nose faded, along with a headache she hadn't even realized she had.

"Thanks," she said. "Now point me at that guest room."

Three sharp raps sounded at the front door. Everybody froze except for Aminah, who stood up.

"You expecting anyone?" asked Rigmaiden.

"Not at this hour," said Marlow. "I think our chivalric friends are back for another round."

"Chivalric?" Emily repeated.

"Best hide," Aminah said. She pointed to the stairs, where Elizabeth was swinging aside a column of books to reveal a low stone tunnel, Michael hovering anxiously behind her. "Priest's hole. Go on, they'll show you. You too, De Soto."

Emily hustled after Michael into the little tunnel. Rigmaiden followed, surprisingly quick now that his leg was healed. He swung the bookcase shut behind him, leaving them in darkness until a little globe of light flickered to life between Elizabeth's fingers.

Michael put a finger to his lips and pointed down the tunnel. They were on a small landing; Elizabeth was already hurrying down stone steps that led to a further tunnel underground. The other three followed after her as quickly as they could without making noise. It was even lower down here than on the landing, probably no higher than five feet, and Emily had to hunch awkwardly to get through. After a minute of cautious scurrying, Elizabeth held up her hand. They stopped as the young queen turned. Her face was as white as paper in the light from her hand.

31

"We should be safe here," she whispered. "I believe I owe you two an explanation."

"What is it?" Emily asked. "Who's here?"

"Our old friend Arthur Chesterfield," said Michael. "And a squad of knights."

"Arthur... was he the tall one or the fat one?" Emily asked. Back on Finalhaven, a contingent of Albian knights had searched in vain for Elizabeth's hiding place until the day the dragon attacked, when she'd burst from her secret room in a blaze of flame to come to Michael's rescue. Alongside Sir Richard and Sir Maximilian—both now dead, Emily remembered with a twist in her stomach—there had been two knights named Arthur, a popular name for Albian boys thanks to a thousand years of kingship.

"The tall one," Michael said. "They were both promoted, I think. Fat Arthur is still in America, leading the hunt there."

"And Tall Arthur is here harassing you?" Emily asked.

"Not us exactly," said Michael. "We don't think he actually knows we're here. His team seems to be sweeping the southwest. They come knocking every once in a while."

"And you hide out while Marlow sends them away."

"Pretty much," Michael agreed. "He's gotten pretty good at it, but he's had a lot of practice. Sometimes Aminah does it instead, to change things up, I think. It's almost gotten boring... until I remember they want to kill her."

Elizabeth squeezed his arm. "No need to worry."

"I could stop worrying if you would just agree to defend yourself," Michael said.

"We've discussed this, Michael," said Elizabeth. "They're my subjects. I'm their queen. I won't use magic against them."

"They want to kill you, Lizzie," Michael said, but Elizabeth shut him up with a kiss on the lips.

Emily shook her head, glad the Sabre & Torch stayed neutral in Gifted politics. Another ten minutes passed as they hunched under the low ceiling of the priest's hole, straining to hear any noise from above. The tunnel, built from old stone and buried in the dense earth, was as solid and silent as a mausoleum, and Emily reminded herself again and again that if she couldn't hear the knights, they couldn't hear her. But it was small comfort as she began to cramp up. She was about to ask Michael if he could do anything about her back with his healing magic when a knocking echoed down from the head of the tunnel. Two raps sounded, then one, then another two.

"That's our sign," Michael said, and they began the slow, awkward trip back to the house.

#

Full of biscuits and wrapped up in a cozy old quilt, Emily dropped into a weary sleep as soon as she shut her eyes. She dreamed of the dragon again. She was back on the gatestation, facing the thing in its glass globe. She thought she was safe—it couldn't break free, couldn't attack from behind the glass—but then the glass was gone and the dragon stood over her, wings wide against the moon. She ran and the dragon chased her down an endless blood-crimson staircase. The dragon ate Captain Queen. It ate Jack. It sprayed her with flames and she could smell her own flesh burning…

Emily woke to the scent of bacon and bright sunlight glowing through the white curtains of the guest room. She pulled on yesterday's clothes and slumped downstairs, wondering if it counted as exercise if you spent the whole night running from nightmares. The sitting room was empty, but the bacon smell led her to the kitchen where Michael, Elizabeth, and Rigmaiden were in various stages of a meal provided by Aminah. Elizabeth had finished—if she'd eaten at all; Emily was still a bit doubtful that the elfin queen operated like a normal person—Michael was sipping coffee and Rigmaiden was digging into a second heaping plate of bacon and eggs.

"There we are," said Aminah cheerily. "I've got more bacon on if you wait a tick."

"Did you sleep?" Michael asked as Emily pulled out a chair at the long kitchen table. "You look... yeah."

"I'm fine," Emily said. "It's good to see you guys."

"We've missed you," said Elizabeth.

"How's the Sabre & Torch treating you?" Michael asked.

"It's good," said Emily. She put her hands on the table then moved them back to her lap. "It's fine. It's... oh, there's that bacon." She looked up gratefully as Aminah set a hot plate down, then immediately filled her mouth with food. Michael shared a raised eyebrow look with Elizabeth.

"So when are you leaving?" Emily asked around a mouthful of breakfast.

"Leaving?" Michael said.

"Running." Emily swallowed heartily. "Away. From Arthur."

Michael glanced at the pale young woman at his side. "We're not running."

"Are you nuts?" Emily set her fork down. "The king can field a thousand knights like Tall Arthur. I'm not fighting all those guys."

Michael blinked and opened his mouth to respond, but the front door cut off his reply with a bang.

"That damned fox!" Marlow fumed as he stormed into the kitchen, muddy nearly to his knees. He unslung his shotgun from his shoulder and leaned it against the table as he picked up his rant. "That's the third time this month! The chicken coop was a bloody wreck. Total loss."

"Eat something," said Aminah. She pushed a plate of eggs into his right hand and a fork in the left. He began to eat without so much as a look at the food.

"I'll have to run him down," Marlow went on, his mouth full. "This can't keep on, it simply can't. We needed those eggs." He looked around

34

as though noticing his audience for the first time. "Everybody up? Good. Time for a fox hunt."

Rigmaiden opted out and Aminah just rolled her eyes at the expedition, but Emily, Elizabeth, and Michael bundled up for the cool autumn day. Emily wore one of Aminah's sweaters, which was a bit snug on her muscular frame but pleasantly warm. Soon they gathered in the front yard under watery morning sunshine.

"Is it safe for you two to be going out?" Emily asked as they waited for Marlow to finish his breakfast and wash the mud from his boots.

"Lucky for us, the Albians are pretty predictable," Michael said. "We think they're basically doing a circuit of the southwest, knocking on all the Gifted doors. They come by about every two weeks, talk to Marlow or Aminah, and move on."

"Still, what if they change up their schedule?" Emily persisted. "Should you be out in the open like this?"

"Emily," Elizabeth said gently. "I was raised behind castle walls. A captive of kindness, perhaps, but a captive all the same. This…" She indicated the broad blue sky, the yellowing grass of the yard. "To feel the wind, the sun. To smell the old leaves. To be cold. To be *too* cold. This is freedom."

Emily looked around. It really was beautiful. The autumn air was crisp and a few fat, twisted trees in the corners of the yard were half-turned to flaming reds and oranges. Beyond the stone wall, a clover-laden hill rose to a rounded summit and Emily knew that beyond it lay the old oak forest. The farmhouse behind her, a pile of stone and ivy with smoke rising lazily from the chimney stack, looked like a part of the landscape rather than a work of human hands.

"I'm just worried," she said.

Michael put a hand on her shoulder. "Don't be."

"Here we are!" called Marlow from the doorway. He was fully dressed again in his old-fashioned country clothes and he carried his shotgun, broken open, under one arm.

"Tally ho," Michael said.

They set out up the clover hill and toward the forest. Marlow was certain that was where the fox made its den and Emily was happy to defer to his obvious expertise. As she reached the top of the hill, Emily looked back to find she'd outpaced her companions. She smiled at the thought of being the lone Combat Gifted among a bunch of Arcanes—usually the reverse was true, as it had been at the Castle Forlorn, with only Michael to support a whole gang of knights, squires, and other fighters.

"Somewhere in there," said Marlow, puffing as he crested the rise, "lurks my nemesis." He scanned the tree line as though he could see the fox if he just squinted hard enough.

"This feels personal," Emily said.

"You have no idea," Michael agreed. He reached out a hand to Elizabeth, helping her up the last few steep steps of the hill. "Marlow has been after this fox for as long as we've been here."

After a moment they set out down the gentler back slope toward the forest, Emily checking her naturally long stride so she didn't outpace her friends again.

"How long *have* you been here?" she asked as they walked.

"Four months? Pretty much since we left Finalhaven," said Michael. "We were in Boston by the time the Arthurs got moving and London not long after that. Marlow has been very patient with us."

A little ways down the hill, Marlow gave them a lazy wave at the sound of his name, but didn't look back. He was stalking toward the forest with fierce concentration in the set of his back.

"How do you know him, anyway?" Emily asked. She wasn't sure there was anybody she could crash with for so much as a week, let alone four months. Her friends from Harkness would have happily put her up, but they were all busy with their own fledgling careers, living out of suitcases in little one-room rentals.

"We met when we were in school, at Starling." Marlow waited at the bottom of the hill, only a hundred yards from the woods.

"Starling?" Emily asked. "Michael, I thought you went to Killoke with Bronwyn."

"I knew her my freshman year," Michael agreed. "But she's three years older. Junior year I did a sort of exchange program with Starling and that's where I met Marlow."

"And yes, I'm an Albian citizen," added Marlow. He put two cartridges into his shotgun and snapped it closed. "Who went to a North American school. Bit of a story there, but it's not relevant."

"I can't imagine either of you at Starling," Emily said.

"We didn't exactly fit in." Marlow shook his head. The Starling School for Gifted Youth, in the Grand Kingdom that comprised most of the southern United States, was the most conservative and traditional of the North American Shadow Academies. As far as Emily had heard, their dress code still included powdered wigs for both students and professors. Despite that, it had a reputation for strict academic standards. Unlike Harkness or Killoke, it had a difficult entrance exam and only accepted a tiny portion of applicants each year.

"Worst year of my life," Michael said. "And I'm counting the time I spent thinking I was going to die on Finalhaven."

"We'd have been done for, both of us, if we hadn't met each other." Marlow set out for the tree line, the determined look back on his face, and the others followed.

"We had a little clique," Michael explained. "Outcasts, basically. Arcanes who were interested in something other than blowing people up. Mentals who didn't want to build fighting machines. A fighter who— Marlow, do you remember Teddy Chase?"

"That poor fellow." Marlow laughed. "He wanted to be a Mental so terribly much. One semester he actually convinced the school to let him take a theoretical physics class. I've never seen a man fail so badly at anything in my life. Would have been a laugh if it hadn't been so sad."

"He was a good guy, though," Michael said.

37

"The best," Marlow agreed softly. They'd reached the tree line and spread out as they moved in among the underbrush and sprawling oak roots.

"Could you stay with him, maybe?" Emily asked. "In North America, I mean. Was he from the Grand Kingdom?"

"He was," said Michael. "We're not going back to America, though."

"Why not?" Emily said. "I know you think you're safe here, but come on. The knights are coming through every couple weeks. It's only a matter of time—"

"It's much worse in America," Elizabeth said. She took Michael's hand as they walked. "Every Gifted Nation has heard about my appearance at the Castle Forlorn. In addition to Arthur and his knights, most of the American Nations have search teams out as well."

"I'm sure the Commonwealth—"

"Even the Secret Commonwealth," Michael said. "Apparently protecting their relationship with Albion is more important than doing the right thing."

Emily thought of the people she knew who worked in the government of the Secret Commonwealth and found she couldn't honestly disagree.

"Shh," hissed Marlow, holding up a hand. The others immediately fell silent. Marlow knelt, touched the soft ground gently, then held two fingers up to his nose and sniffed. He pointed to a place where the body and branches of a fallen tree screened a small hole in the earth.

Marlow laid his shotgun gently on the ground. Emily pursed her lips, about to ask why he would put the gun aside when he was possibly about need it, but kept the thought to herself. Marlow reached into an inner pocket of his tweed jacket and drew out a small charm of white stone. It was a tiny man with a lion's head and four wings. A snake wrapped up his legs and chest. He held a key in each hand.

Marlow began to murmur something in a language Emily didn't know. Latin, maybe? The Harkness Combat education didn't include much in the way of linguistics.

Emily looked up at the sound of shuffling in the leaves. A twitching nose poked out from under the fallen tree and the fox it belonged to slowly appeared from its hole. Marlow kept speaking under his breath until the fox had come all the way out, then he gently set the charm down and spread his hands.

"Hello there," he said. "I'd like to speak with you, if you please."

The fox blinked, its whiskers quivering.

"Good," said Marlow. "Now, I know you've been hungry. But my chickens aren't for you. I've got kits of my own to feed." He glanced back at Elizabeth and Michael and the fox looked up at them too. Its black eyes glittered and for a second Emily expected it to reply in English.

"Do you understand?" Marlow went on. "I needed those chickens for my kits. I'll be happy to bring you some food, but please stay away from my den."

The fox barked, making Emily jump.

"That's fair," said Marlow. "I'll see you next week." The fox scampered back into its hole, white-tufted tail flashing as it disappeared underground. Marlow picked up the charm and put it away, tucked his shotgun back under his arm, and stood, wiping dirt from his hands.

"There we go," he said with a nod. "Been meaning to get that done. Thanks for coming with."

"That's it?" asked Emily. "You just had to ask him nicely?"

"Her," said Marlow, "and yes. Why, what would you have done?"

"I don't know," Emily said. "I just thought…" She gestured to the shotgun.

"For a fox?" Marlow looked like he didn't know whether to laugh or yell. Instead he broke open the shotgun and pulled out the cartridges. "Heavens, no! I've never hurt an animal and Mithras willing I'll never have to. This old thing was just for insurance. Never know when you'll find a gang of knights lurking about."

CHAPTER 4

The farmhouse door stood open, swinging in the wind that had picked up when they left the forest. They saw it as soon as they crested the hill. Marlow fumbled to reload his shotgun as Emily, sensing his immediate panic, began to run. She made it to the door and pushed into the house before the magicians had even reached the stone wall.

"Hello?" Emily called. The kitchen was empty. She bolted past the table and through the door to the sitting room, then came skidding to a halt as she took in the scene in front of her. A knight stood with his hand on Aminah's shoulder as another leaned halfway into the priest's hole behind the bookshelf. All three faces were turned toward her; Aminah's was streaked with tears, but the knights' were hidden behind the smoked-plastic faceplates of ballistic helmets that stood at odds with their medieval-looking tabards.

The knight guarding Aminah flipped his faceplate open. Emily blinked in surprise—it was Daniel, squire to the taller Sir Arthur. He must have grown an inch since she'd last seen him on Finalhaven only a few months ago. His jaw was better defined and showed the first hints of pale stubble. His eyes were wide.

"Emily?" he said.

The knight at the secret door opened his own helmet as he straightened to his full height. It was Sir Arthur Chesterfield.

"Miss Sledge, I hereby place you under arrest by the power devolved upon me from the Crown of Albion. The charge is aiding a wanted criminal, the pretender Elizabeth Pendragon, daughter of Anne of Avon. Please stay where you are."

"What's going on?" Marlow tumbled into the room, shotgun in hand. "Oh, you bastards!"

"Drop the weapon, sir," ordered Sir Arthur. "Marlow Bright, I hereby—"

"Certainly not!" barked Marlow. "Out of my house, both of you!"

"Oliver, Rowan, to me!" Sir Arthur shouted down the tunnel. The clattering of two more knights echoed up from the secret door.

"I've no interest in fighting you," Marlow said, his voice tight but calm. "I've been nothing but polite as you call at my door at all hours of the night, week after week. But this is simply too much. The governor shall hear of this."

"The governor sent us," Sir Arthur replied. He flipped his faceplate down and put a hand on the pommel of the longsword that hung at his hip. "Now, if you're quite finished with your outrage, I'm placing you under arrest. Put the gun down."

Sir Arthur stepped forward as the other two knights emerged from the priest's hole. One of them grabbed Aminah by her upper arms. Rigmaiden appeared behind them a moment later, moving slowly.

"I've committed no crime," Marlow said. He shifted his grip slightly on the shotgun.

"Put the weapon down," Sir Arthur said. "I won't ask again."

"Arthur, Daniel, come on," said Emily. "We fought together so recently. We drank together. We're not enemies here either."

"Where is Elizabeth Pendragon?" asked Sir Arthur.

"Arthur, we *killed a dragon together*," Emily said.

"No." Sir Arthur's voice was icy. "You killed the dragon and you killed my best friend into the bargain."

"He wouldn't have died if he'd stayed out of my way."

41

"How bloody dare you!" Arthur barked. "You killed Max! *Now get on your goddamn knees and tell me where the pretender is!*"

"I'm right here," said Elizabeth from the doorway. Michael hovered behind her, anxiety creasing his face. "Marlow, put the gun down. It's all right."

Sir Arthur flipped his faceplate open again, revealing a stony expression that betrayed no hint of shock or intimidation.

He must be hell to play cards with, Emily thought dumbly.

"Miss Pendragon, I hereby place you under arrest by the power devolved upon me from the *rightful* Crown of Albion. The charge is conspiracy to usurp the throne. Please stay where you are."

"I have no intention of usurping the throne," said Elizabeth. "I wish only to be left alone."

"That's for a magistrate to decide," Sir Arthur said. He stepped into the center of the room, moving toward Elizabeth, one hand still on his sword.

Emily picked up the couch and brought it down on his head.

The room exploded into action as the couch drove the knight to his knees and split in two with a sharp crack. Marlow racked his shotgun and shouted at the other knights to stay where they were. Aminah broke away from them as they drew their swords and ran to Marlow's side. Michael began chanting in a booming voice that echoed over the chaos. Daniel ran to Sir Arthur and began trying to pull him from under the shattered couch.

Elizabeth yelled, "Stop!" but nobody was listening.

One of the knights, either Sir Rowan or Sir Oliver, came at Emily, his longsword gleaming. He had to go around the wreckage to get to her and as he turned to face her full on, she kicked him in the chest. The impact sent a shiver up her leg—there was clearly proper ballistic armor under that tabard—but the knight staggered back and fell over a leg of the couch.

Emily grabbed his sword almost before it hit the ground. She leaped for the door, where Elizabeth was still shouting for them to stop fighting.

A glance over her shoulder showed Sir Arthur shaking free of the couch, so Emily grabbed a little wooden chair with her left hand and threw it at him. Sir Arthur slashed it in half with his longsword and one of the pieces bounced harmlessly off him as the other clattered against the far wall.

"My grandfather made that chair!" Marlow exclaimed.

"Elizabeth, you can't go with them," Emily said, ignoring Marlow's outburst.

"I won't harm them," she said. She put a hand on Michael's arm and he stopped chanting. "Nor will you. They are my subjects."

"They're going to harm you," Michael said. His voice was quiet but his eyes were burning.

"Perhaps I should take my chance with the magistrate," Elizabeth said.

"There's no way he'll find you innocent," Emily said. "Come on, we need to—"

"Look out!" Michael grabbed Elizabeth around the waist and pulled her backwards into the kitchen as Sir Arthur's sword arced down toward her. Emily stepped into the empty space and threw her own blade up into a hasty high guard. Sparks flew where the swords met. She bulled forward into Arthur and they went down together in a crash and tangle.

Emily was up first. She put her foot on Arthur's chest and her sword point on his throat. A glance back showed Elizabeth and Michael arguing in the kitchen. In the sitting room, the other three knights were advancing warily, but a meaningful look from Emily stopped them as they realized she had their captain's life in her hands. A wary stillness settled over the room.

Elizabeth and Michael turned in surprise as the front door crashed open.

"Ah, there are my reinforcements," Sir Arthur said from the floor.

"Elizabeth, come here!" Emily shouted. She didn't wait for the young queen to obey, but darted into the kitchen and heaved her up in a fireman's carry. Dashing back through the door she kicked Sir Arthur, who was halfway risen, then darted for the fireplace.

Daniel, the squire-turned-knight, leaped for them and drew his sword. Emily skidded to a stop as Daniel got between her and the hearth. His eyes were wide, his breathing heavy. The sword wavered in his hands.

"Daniel, come on," Emily said gently. He hesitated and looked past her to Sir Arthur. That was all the invitation Emily needed. She settled Elizabeth on her shoulder and jumped into the painting.

#

They tumbled to the mossy floor of a glade where light slanted green through rich, broad leaves. Unlike the wood near Kennetsbridge, which was chilly and dark, the forest where Emily and Elizabeth found themselves glowed under a summer sun. The emerald greens around her were richer than any color Emily had seen before. The same was true for the azure sky. Even the white bark of a nearby stand of birch trees seemed somehow deeper and fuller than usual.

Emily shook her head. There was no time to admire the scenery. She pulled Elizabeth up by both hands.

"Those knights are coming after us, guaranteed," Emily said. "You've been here—where do we hide?"

Elizabeth looked around in obvious uncertainty. "I don't recognize this place."

"Fair enough," Emily said. She grabbed Elizabeth's hand and ran for the tree line, half-dragging the queen behind her. Elizabeth stumbled to keep up and Emily forced herself to slow to a more human pace. They reached the birch stand a few seconds later and plunged between the slender white trunks.

Soon the birches fell away, revealing a landscape of rolling grassland that reminded Emily sharply of the painting they'd just come through. White marble ruins dotted the hills. To their left, maybe two hundred yards away, was a lazy, winding river.

Emily aimed them at a row of columns, all of them broken off at different heights. Their feet sank into soft, trim grass as they climbed a long slope toward the ruin; by the time they reached the first marble pillar, Elizabeth was gasping for air. Emily pushed her behind it and dashed along the row to the next column tall enough to hide her. Her feet clicked on flat paving stones that lay scattered and half-hidden among the grass. She reached the pillar, put her back to it, and slid down to the grass.

From this point of relative safety, Emily dared a glance back at the forest. Half a dozen knights were emerging from the trees, about halfway to the river and at least a hundred feet from the birch stand where she and Elizabeth had come out. She watched them form up and move toward the river, then huddled back behind her column.

A look at Elizabeth showed the young queen staring at Emily, awaiting their next move. If only Emily had any idea what that would be... they had a moment while the Albians went the wrong direction, but they needed somewhere to go. On either side of them, here and there among the curves of the land, were other ruins. They were lovely, but they didn't offer much more protection than their current hiding spot.

Could they make it to that low square of stones? It looked like an old foundation wall—maybe there was a basement beneath it. If not, though, they'd be exposed. A short stretch of aqueduct caught her eye, standing out above the hills. They could climb it—at least she could, and she could carry Elizabeth—but then they'd be stuck there.

She looked up the slope they were on. A low, flat shape at the crest caught her eye. It was a small rectangular structure that resembled a mausoleum and it looked in better repair than the other ruins nearby. Emily blew out a breath. She wasn't crazy about how prominent it was, there at the top of the rise. Still, it had proper walls to hide behind and at least one window to reconnoiter from.

Emily glanced back at Elizabeth. She sat with her back against the column, looking up at a few clouds with her hands in her lap, but she looked like she'd gotten her wind back. It was time to move. Emily waved to get her attention, then pointed up at the building at the top of the hill.

"On three," she mouthed. She held up one finger, then two, then three.

Elizabeth and Emily jumped to their feet and ran up the hill. Their paths met halfway to their goal and Emily grabbed the queen's hand. She pulled Elizabeth off her feet as they flew up the slope, going full tilt for the last dozen yards.

There was a door on the far side, made from beaten bronze, with a big bronze ring for a handle. Emily tore it open and shoved Elizabeth through, then ducked in after her. The interior of the building was a single small room, maybe ten feet by fifteen. There were windows on the left- and right-hand walls, but otherwise the only feature was a marble fountain depicting a young man in a toga and crown. The fountain was still and silent, its shallow pool empty.

Emily dropped down next to Elizabeth where she sat panting against a wall. They sat in silence for a minute as the queen caught her breath.

"Have they followed?"

Emily nodded. "Yup. I saw them coming out of the forest. I don't think they saw me, but we should get moving soon."

"To where?" Elizabeth asked. "The land is mostly open."

"I'm not sure yet," Emily said. "But this is the most obvious hiding spot around. We just have to keep running and we should be okay. How much have you guys explored?"

"Very little, mainly in the forest. We hoped to discover the origin of the monsters that have come through the Veil, so the wood seemed the best place to start."

"Did you find anything?" Emily rose to a crouch and sidled toward the nearer window.

"No," said Elizabeth.

Emily stood cautiously, rising just high enough to see through the window. A corner of the forest and a curve of blue river was visible, but no sign of the knights. She crept to the other window, but saw only green hills.

"Time to go," she said, reaching out a hand to help Elizabeth up. She looked paler than usual and her dress was torn along the hem and stained at the knees. It was strange to see her like this—so human. The Elizabeth who rose from the wreckage of the Castle Forlorn with wings of smoke and fire, who tore a dragon from the sky, was like an alien compared to the panting girl who stood looking to Emily for direction.

Emily led her out into the sunshine. They seemed to be alone. But where could they go? Back to the forest, maybe—the knights might not expect them to double back and if Elizabeth knew her way around at all it would give them an advantage.

They ran down the back side of the hill. At the bottom of the slope, in a crease where their hill met another, was a faint dirt track that Emily hadn't noticed before. It wound between the hills and disappeared around a far curve. Thinking they might circle around and come at the forest from a new angle, Emily set out along the track, Elizabeth close behind.

She heard them before she saw them—the clatter of armor and weapons, the murmur of furtive conversation. It was the Albians, no doubt, coming around the curve. Emily grabbed Elizabeth's hand and bolted in the opposite direction.

Elizabeth could barely keep up and soon she was panting again, with a wheeze that hadn't been there before. It occurred to Emily in a flash of head-slapping insight that a life spent in two small rooms probably wasn't too good for your cardiovascular health. She glanced back at Elizabeth and saw the young queen's face was drawn and gleaming with sweat.

The track dipped as the hill on their left fell away. Emily glanced at the small field that opened up on that side, then stumbled to a stop. A circular hut, low and gray, stood in the middle of the grass. She looked up over her shoulder and spotted the ruin where they'd hid, right where she expected it atop the hill behind her—how had she missed this obvious shelter?

"Have you been here?" She turned to Elizabeth, who shook her head as she gulped down huge breaths, her hands on her knees. Emily looked at the hut, looked back down the track, and nodded. "Good enough. Let's go."

#

Emily shut the door of the hut behind them just as the first Albian knight came out between the hills. It closed with a final *click* and plunged them into darkness. The hut had a musty, earthy smell and Emily felt a dirt floor beneath her sneakers. From what she'd seen before she shut the door, the hut was like something from a fairy tale: a single room, cluttered with all sorts of sinister junk stacked along the walls and hanging from the thatch roof. She'd half expected a big, bubbling cauldron in the center of the room, but it was just empty space.

"Can you see?" Emily whispered.

"Give me a moment," said Elizabeth.

Light sprang up from a candle on the floor near their feet. Then another candle stuck in the door a few inches further in. Then another and another and another, tracing the curve of the wall as they flickered to life one by one. Soon they made a full circle, illuminating the hut with a wavering yellow glow.

"Was that you?" Emily asked.

"It was me," said a hunched shape within the circle of light. The shape unfolded into a woman in a heavy gray cloak with the hood up. Long hair, black streaked with white, fell from the hood. Her face was in shadow, but she seemed to be middle aged, with light brown skin and fine lines around her eyes and mouth. She stood as tall as Emily, her back straight, her shoulders squared.

"Who are you?" Emily asked.

"I can help you," the woman said.

"Who are you?" Emily repeated, putting herself between the woman and Elizabeth.

48

"Mm." The woman moved to one wall of the hut, stepping over the ring of candles. She moved a curtain aside, revealing a small, dusty mirror. With the sleeve of her robe, she wiped the glass clean, then lifted her chin and held that pose for a moment.

Apparently satisfied, she murmured a few words and nodded to the mirror. Something moved in it—Emily couldn't make it out from where she stood, but the woman watched the image for a moment, then said a few words Emily didn't understand, made a small gesture with her left hand, and nodded again.

She turned back to Emily and Elizabeth. "That's better. One needs space to think, time to talk. Best not to be interrupted." She stepped back into the circle of candles. "Now then. Let us make our introductions. I invite you to begin, as you have come into my home uninvited and will not be guests until I know your names and your purpose."

"Emily Sledge," said Emily, trying to make it sound important. "Of the Sabre & Torch Society. And Harkness Academy. And the Secret Commonwealth."

"Certainly," said the woman politely. Her gaze passed over Emily's shoulder to Elizabeth. "And you?"

Elizabeth stepped out from behind Emily, smoothing her rumpled dress. "I am Elizabeth Pendragon, daughter of Arthur XXIX Pendragon, formerly of the Castle Forlorn, rightful Queen of Albion."

"Mm." The woman turned back to the mirror. "That explains the boys hunting you."

"You know who we are," Emily said, "so how about you?"

"I am Valeria Tall and Gray, a witch." She plucked a mote of dust from her sleeve. "And as I said, I can help you."

"How?" Emily asked.

"With what?" Elizabeth said at the same time.

Valeria Tall and Gray gestured toward the mirror. "There they stand, poor confused things. With a word I might clear their thoughts, let them see truly again. No doubt at that point they will realize where you've run to and come a-calling at my door. It would be a shame, it seems to me. Royalty is so rare in Arcadia."

"Are you threatening us?" Emily asked.

"Not at all," said Valeria Tall and Gray. "To repeat myself, I am offering to help."

"Why?" Elizabeth said.

"My reasons are my own," said the witch. A faint smile played over her face. "I see something of myself in you, let us say."

"Let's say you do help us," Emily said. "How? What would you do?"

"The men out there are my subjects," Elizabeth said. "I will not see them harmed."

"Making requests, making restrictions already, I see." The witch frowned. "Impolite, I think. But let us say we make a deal. How do we define harm? They might easily be made pigs, or frogs. I might put them to sleep for a thousand days. I might steal their breath for an hour, though I suspect a minute would do the job."

"No," Elizabeth said. "None of that. That is all harm."

"What, then?" Valeria Tall and Gray made a lazy circle with her hand. "What would your rules be, if we made a deal?"

"Send them away," Elizabeth said. "Whole, awake, and unhurt. All we need is enough time to escape."

"I see," said Valeria Tall and Gray. "I can do this, but it is not easy. To change a man from one thing to another is a matter of rearrangement only, swapping this part for that one within his body. But to move a man to another place requires a conversation with the world and the world prefers not to change unless soundly convinced. Six men is a much longer conversation."

"But you can do it?" Emily said.

"Mm." The witch touched her chin with a finger. "If I am to help you, you must help me." She pulled her hood back, revealing gray eyes in her lined face. They fixed on Elizabeth as the witch pulled her hair back over her shoulders. "You are powerful. I can feel it. But you will not act for yourself and you fear to do what you propose. I will tell you, you are wise to fear. The rules of magic are not the same here as they are in your homeland.

"In Arcadia, magic has a price, always. Each spell requires sacrifice. Magic without sacrifice too often goes astray... Oh, Emily Sledge, put that face away. I do not speak of blood and flesh. Listen to my words. I will make this bargain with you. To work this spell I require power, which you have in plenty, Elizabeth Pendragon. Lend me your Gift. I will make the spell you desire and after, I will return your Gift."

"There's no way—" Emily started, but Elizabeth cut her off.

"Give me a moment." She turned away in thought. The witch promptly busied herself around the hut, straightening and dusting as though she didn't care what Elizabeth's reply would be.

Emily stood waiting as the two magicians made their decision. Actually, she wasn't sure that was quite right. Bronwyn Queen had told her once, when they were locked in the white dungeon by the dragon's mercenaries, that Gifted were only born on Earth. Assuming Valeria Tall and Gray wasn't a transplant from Earth like them, if she had been born here in Arcadia, she couldn't have the Gift of the Arcane the way Elizabeth, Michael, and Marlow did. Well, if magic worked differently here than on Earth, it was reasonable to think that the requirements for spellcasters were different, too. The witch was obviously the real deal.

"I agree to the bargain," Elizabeth said.

Valeria Tall and Gray turned away from her small wall mirror and flipped her hood back up.

"Excellent," she said. "Let us begin."

CHAPTER 5

She moved along the wall, plucking various implements off hooks and shelves: a stone bowl, a knife, a length of fine-linked silver chain. There was a certainty, a confidence, to Valeria Tall and Gray's movements, one that Emily recognized from her long hours in the training ring. The witch knew exactly what she was doing and why. She was unburdened by doubt.

Valeria Tall and Gray balanced everything in one hand, kneeled down, and used her free hand to smooth the dirt floor inside the circle of candles. She stood, examined her work, and knelt again to touch up a few spots. Satisfied, she set the bowl in the center.

"Come." She beckoned to Elizabeth, who entered the circle and knelt across from the witch. Valeria Tall and Gray laid the knife across the bowl, then gestured for Elizabeth's left hand. She extended her own to meet it, touching them wrist to wrist, then tied them together with a few deft motions of the silver chain. She took her hand away. Elizabeth winced as the chain pulled itself tight, moving under its own power, digging into both women's skin.

The witch began to speak, yet another language Emily didn't know. She reflected, not for the first time, that magic sure seemed to involve a lot of memorization. There was power in the words, though, that was obvious. They grew louder, more forceful, and slowly Emily realized that she could understand them. Whether Valeria Tall and Gray had switched to English or something had happened inside Emily's head, she wasn't sure, but the meaning was clear.

Bound by blood are we, flowers of the same tree
Bound by gold are we, daughters of the same crown
Bound by fate are we, sailors of the same sea
Bound by magic are we, singers of the same spell

With a shriek, the witch plunged her knife between the women's bound hands. In the same swift motion she severed the silver chain and slashed deep into both of their wrists, spraying blood over the bowl as the chain slithered down into it. Elizabeth screamed and fell backwards into the dirt. Emily started forward, but a furious look from Valeria Tall and Gray froze her in place.

With this blade I release your power
With this chain I bind it
With this chalice I receive it

She grabbed the bowl and held it to her lips, gulping down the mixture of Elizabeth's and her own blood. There was a faint rattle as the chain slid out of the bowl and down the witch's throat. Then she also fell, landing on her back and knocking over a few of the candles, which went out.

Emily could move again and she dove to Elizabeth's side. The young queen was skeleton pale and sat on her haunches, rocking slightly, her right hand clamped tightly over her bloody left wrist.

"Let me see," Emily said. Elizabeth looked up at her with wide eyes, then slowly raised her arms. She unclenched her hand, which came away red. Emily felt her stomach unknot in a rush of relief. The cut on Elizabeth's wrist wasn't deep; it was perfectly aimed to bleed heavily then heal quickly and leave no lasting damage.

She threw her arms around Elizabeth. "You'll be okay. It's okay. It looks worse than it is. You're okay. You're okay."

"How do you feel, Elizabeth Pendragon?" Valeria Tall and Gray stood over them, as tall and straight as before. Her own wounded wrist was hidden within the sleeve of her cloak.

"Thirsty." Elizabeth's voice was barely audible; it could hardly even be called a whisper.

"Mm." Valeria Tall and Gray turned away and moved to the far wall of the hut. A moment later she returned with a clay jug and cup. "Drink."

Elizabeth took the cup and gulped down its contents. Emily could only hope it was water.

"Now?" asked Valeria Tall and Gray.

"Weak," said Elizabeth.

"Yes," the witch said. "There is little I can do for that. It was, after all, the intent of the working."

"So it worked?" Emily asked, standing.

"Yes. I have what I need now. I will send away your hunters and then we will talk."

Valeria Tall and Gray strode over to her mirror. She said a few words and nodded, then peered into the glass for a moment.

"Tell me," she said. "Where shall I send them?"

"Send them home," Elizabeth whispered.

"Their home," Emily added. "Not ours, *any* of ours. We need time to escape, not more trouble."

A smile flickered across the witch's face as she nodded, never taking her eyes from the mirror. She stretched her arms out and her sleeves fell back to reveal smooth, tan wrists unmarked by any cut. She took a breath, then began to speak again. This time it was the reverse of earlier—Emily understood the first few words, but then they slid into gibberish.

Powers of earth and air, I call thee!
Movers of sea and sky, I call thee...

Elizabeth got shakily to her feet. Emily put an arm around her, partially for emotional support and partially because she looked like she might fall over at any second.

"Are you okay?" she whispered.

"I feel... hollow," said Elizabeth. "Empty. Something that's been with me my whole life was taken out of me. Can you understand?"

Emily tried to imagine how she would feel if she suddenly lost her Gift of Combat. If instead of jumping ten feet straight up, she could only jump one. If she could only run six or seven miles an hour. If the couch in

Marlow's sitting room were an immovable obstacle rather than a handy weapon. She couldn't really do it.

"I'm not sure," she said.

"It's so quiet," Elizabeth said.

Emily's brow furrowed—the witch's chanting had gotten quite loud. In fact it almost sounded like she was having an argument with some invisible opponent.

"Is it?" Emily said.

"Magic has a sound, a song. It was a different song here in Arcadia than on Earth, but it was there. Casting spells was as simple as reaching into the song and pulling out the right melody. But... the song is gone."

Valeria Tall and Gray stopped chanting. She took a long, slow breath in through her nose and blew it out her mouth. Then she put her hood down and turned to Emily and Elizabeth.

"It is done," she said. "Your hunters are gone to their homes. It will be some time before they reconvene and the hunt begins again. Elizabeth Pendragon, your power is remarkable."

"I'd like it back, please," said Elizabeth. "That was our bargain. After you cast the spell, you'd return my Gift. What do we need to do?"

"After," said the witch, looking away. "After..."

"And that's now." Emily took a step forward.

"Is it?" said Valeria Tall and Gray. "Oh, is it?"

"Yes," said Emily.

"I am bound by our bargain," the witch said. "But our bargain was for *after*. *After* encompasses all of time from now until eternity, does it not? Why then shall I return your Gift now, when I might return it later?"

Elizabeth sat in the dirt and began crying softly into her hands. Emily opened her mouth then closed it again. She hadn't thought of that interpretation of the witch's words and apparently, neither had the queen.

"You can't do this," she said.

"I certainly can," replied Valeria Tall and Gray.

"No, you can't," Emily said in a sudden flash of insight. A decade ago her parents had both worked for the government of the Secret Commonwealth, so she'd grown up under the desks of lawyers and politicians. Every once in a while it came in handy. "You said you would return Elizabeth's Gift after sending the knights away. You promised to. Well, you could wait another fifty years and give it back then, but what if she dies before that? Being a normal person in the Gifted world isn't exactly the safest life." Emily thought briefly of Julian de Luna, driven to murder by his helplessness, and his heartbroken mother. She pushed the images aside. "You have to give it back at some point or you won't have kept your end of the bargain."

"Mm." Valeria Tall and Gray turned her back to them and flipped up her hood. She stood that way for a long moment, quiet and still. Finally she faced them again. "Very well. I will grant you a prophecy."

"A prophecy?" Elizabeth whispered. She opened her hands and looked up from the floor, her pale face streaked with tears, her eyes red.

"A prophecy," the witch said. "To tell the conditions of the return of your Gift. Thus the power to regain it is yours, but so is the burden of fulfilling the bargain."

"Agreed," Elizabeth said.

Emily was doubtful. It felt like they were just opening themselves up to more tricky treatment by the witch, walking into some new trap made from words. But Elizabeth had consented and Valeria Tall and Gray was already moving among her implements, picking up the gory stone bowl and filling it from her clay water jug.

She sat in the center of the ring of candles, where the dirt was still spattered with blood, then crossed her legs and placed the bowl in the little space they made. She dipped a finger of her right hand into the bowl and held it up as though testing the wind. Then she put her left hand gently into the bowl, letting the fingers rest on the surface of the water. Holding this pose, she steadied her breath and let her eyes roll back in her head until only the whites showed.

"The past echoes into the future," she said. She began to sway gently from side to side. "By knowing the song of the past we may know the future. Song of the past, grant us the sound of what is to come."

There was a rush of wind and the candles all went out, plunging the room into absolute black. In Emily's blindness, the witch's voice seemed magnified, booming all around her.

When no man's armor is broken
and Adam's daughter flees her throne
and the crown of iron turns to gold
and the queen returns home,
then shall thy spell be done.

As one, the candles flared to life, a hundred times brighter than before. Emily ducked her face into her elbow to shield her eyes. A circle of white spots burned in her vision, broken only by the shadowy outline of the witch. She felt the wind on her cheek and warmth on the back of her neck.

Cautiously, Emily took her arm away from her eyes. Bright, flat light pressed against her eyelids. She opened them and saw rich green grass under her feet, a broad blue sky above, and down at the bottom of a long slope, a stand of birch trees and a river winding from the eaves of an emerald forest. She took a long, slow breath.

"Come on," she said to Elizabeth, who was huddled on the ground with her arms around her knees. "Let's find our way back."

#

Coming back out of the painting was even more disorienting than entering it. There had been no sign of the Albian knights, to Emily's huge relief, and as Elizabeth led them to two alabaster columns that stood lonely by the river she was able to appreciate the beauty of Arcadia a bit more.

57

Still, they had to get out. The columns were carved with images of men and bears locked in battle and between them Emily could clearly see the river cutting between its banks of lush green, but Elizabeth told her to step through and she did. There was a wrenching feeling and Emily's stomach flipped over more than once before the world around her untwisted and she found herself staggering to her feet in front of Marlow's fireplace.

Aminah, standing in the middle of the room, dropped her teacup, which exploded with a crack.

"And I just got the bloody couch cleaned up," she said.

"Nice to see you, too," said Emily. "Come on, I'll give you a hand."

Elizabeth dropped into the squashed leather chair as Emily followed Aminah to the kitchen. They paused by the sink and the Albian woman put a hand on Emily's arm.

"What happened to her?"

"What do you mean?" Emily hedged, unsure if she had the right to divulge Elizabeth's new secret.

"Elizabeth is changed, that's obvious to anyone with eyes." Aminah cocked her head. "And you look like you got put through the ringer into the bargain."

Emily looked away, stung by the sudden thought that escaping to Arcadia had been her plan, but Elizabeth had paid the price. She grabbed a dish towel and headed back into the sitting room. The rest of the household, alerted by the breaking cup, had gathered around Elizabeth, who sat curled in a ball, almost swallowed up by the big chair. Michael half-knelt at her side, his arms around her, murmuring into her ear. Marlow stood gazing into the painting of Arcadia. Rigmaiden looked sour and awkward.

"Emily was just going to tell us what happened," Aminah said behind her.

Everyone looked at Emily, so she looked at Elizabeth, who gave her a faint nod. So Emily took a breath and launched into the story. She told it all, from top to bottom, forcing herself to recount every detail of Valeria

Tall and Gray's magic in case it might mean something to Michael or Marlow. When she finished, the room was silent, with all eyes on the queen who huddled powerless in Michael's arms.

Aminah was the first to move. She stepped around the broken teacup on her way to Elizabeth's chair, knelt, and put her hand on the girl's knee.

"Let me get you a bite to eat," she said. "'Food can't fix everything, but we should try it just to make sure,' that's what my mum always said. What would you like? Biscuit? Two biscuits? Bit of cold ham?"

Elizabeth nodded and Aminah patted her knee, then stood and headed for the kitchen. There was another awkward moment.

"Can you repeat the prophecy?" Marlow asked. "Are you quite sure you had it right?"

"Uh, sure," Emily said. Memorization had never been her strong suit. But Elizabeth saved her, speaking up in a tiny voice from her chair.

"*When no man's armor is broken, and Adam's daughter flees her throne, and the crown of iron turns to gold, and the queen returns home, then shall thy spell be done.*"

Marlow and Michael shared a long look. A look of raw pain passed over Marlow's face and he sighed. "Do you want to, or shall I?"

"Better you than me," Michael said.

"Better what?" Emily asked.

"Better sit down." Marlow gestured vaguely around the room. He lifted his chin and called into the kitchen. "Aminah, please put a kettle on."

"Already did!" she shouted back. Marlow nodded and made sure everyone was seated.

"Right then." He clasped his hands. "We need to tell you about Adam."

#

59

"Michael mentioned that we met at Starling our junior year. He'd come down from Killoke and pretty quickly found that the only place he fit in was in my little oddball clique. I'm glad he found us, but I reckon he'd agree that things were still… challenging."

Marlow looked up in thanks as Aminah put a steaming teacup in his hands. He blew on it and continued.

"Starling can be a cruel place. I can't fault the education I received, but the people there are rather hidebound, kids and teachers both. They don't care for anything that disagrees with their rather strict worldview. So those of us who saw things a touch differently, well…" He tried a sip of tea. "To say we were bullied would be the understatement of the year.

"I had the easiest of it, I think. For a mob of sixteen-year-olds from the Grand Kingdom, my accent was easy pickings, but I'd had a few years there before starting school and I could mostly keep my head down and fit in. They shoved me around some, but Teddy Chase was usually there to run 'em off.

"He had his own problems, of course. The Mentals were absolutely savage once he flunked out of his physics class. They can be quite creative with their insults, those geniuses. I still don't know what some of them meant. They took a special delight in disturbing his sleep, too. He told me once that he thought they were trying to get him killed in the practice ring, get him so tired he would make some mistake… I don't know."

Marlow sat with his tea for a minute, his eyes far away. Finally he looked up at Michael. "Care to tell some of your own horror stories?"

"No thanks."

"Don't blame you." Marlow nodded. "You can imagine how it was for Michael, having committed the triple crime of being poor, black, and an outsider. But I'm wandering. Avoiding the point, really… Adam.

"Adam was… it was difficult to be friends with him, sometimes. He was an Arcane like me and Michael, so maybe it was inevitable that he should join our little group. He was brilliant, a talented magician and near as clever as any Mental. But he was hard to like. He had… how would you put it, Michael? He built so many walls around himself. Everything was an affectation for him. The way he spoke, the way he dressed. I think he even believed some of the things he did as a way of pushing people away.

"Naturally, he got the absolute worst of it. The other kids were ruthless with him and I'll be honest, we weren't much better at times. It's no excuse, but I think he welcomed it. It was like a badge of honor for him, to be the most hated boy at Starling.

"Still... he was one of ours. It's hard to explain. We were hard on him—Mithras have mercy, we were only sixteen, seventeen—but I don't think it ever occurred to us not to be friends with him."

Michael nodded, his eyes on the floor.

"So one day, he got very interested in... there was a movement in Europe, in the nineteenth century, in the Gifted circles there. Painting. Specifically, arcane painting." Marlow's gaze flickered above the fireplace, where the painting of Arcadia hung. "Adam took it up. He started small: paintings that moved, paintings in three dimensions, just curiosities. But he got more and more absorbed by it. Soon he was doing portraits. You'd hear him talking to them at night. And then he painted Arcadia."

"And that was the last time we saw him," Michael said.

"Yes." Marlow nodded. "There was an inquest, of course. A student was missing, after all. But I don't think the school wanted to look too deep. It was easier to just wash their hands of their problem child. Well, of course we suspected he'd—he'd—*fled* in there. Into the painting, into the world he'd created. And I think I speak for everyone in our little clique when I say that we hoped it was true."

The sitting room was silent except the crackling of the fire, which did nothing to drive away autumn's chill. Each of the six occupants sat alone, staring variously at the hearth, the painting, the window, or simply at nothing. Emily wasn't sure how to feel. She'd done well in school, been happy. She'd been the best fighter there her last two years. Her teachers liked her. Everybody liked her. Her best friends were smart, funny, and kind.

But sixteen years old wasn't long ago at all and as much as she told herself it was true, Emily couldn't quite convince herself that she wouldn't have been one of the ones bullying a weird kid like Adam. Maybe not to his face, but in private… would she have stuck up for him, or joined in?

"This is all very sad, but what's it got to do with the prophecy?" Rigmaiden asked.

"I was getting to that," Marlow said. "Obviously I took the painting with me when I left Starling. When I moved back here to Barley Bright after my parents passed, old Arcadia came with me. I always wondered. If Adam had really gone in, what had become of him? I figured the most likely chance was that he'd died, but…" He sighed. "Well, with one thing and another, I never had a proper chance to investigate. Then Michael and Elizabeth showed up on my doorstep and the monsters started coming through the Veil. And we started to think, what if Adam had survived? Could it all be related? Maybe—" Marlow sniffed and cleared his throat. "Maybe he's still alive in there."

"So the prophecy—'Adam's daughter?'" Emily stood up, feeling the urgency to move return to her limbs.

"Yes, that's a riddle, I'll admit," Marlow said. "But I know it's no coincidence."

"If the prophecy is right, Adam's daughter needs dethroning." Rigmaiden's voice was low and gruff. "That is, if the queen wants her Gift back."

"I do," said Elizabeth. She pushed Michael's arms away and stood. "The witch tricked me. I should have been smarter, but I don't accept it as done."

"She'll need her power if we're going to survive," Michael said. He took Elizabeth's hand. "I'm sorry, but my Gift isn't enough to keep us hidden from King Arthur's court magicians forever."

"It's all right, my heart," Elizabeth said, and she smiled for the first time since they'd entered the painting. "I love the way you work magic. But this emptiness isn't right. This isn't who I am."

"Oh, it's not so bad being normal," said Aminah.

"Then we agree," Emily said. "We'll go back into Arcadia, smash up somebody's armor, figure out Adam's daughter and her throne, and get Elizabeth's Gift back." There it was. She was moving again, making plans, making things right.

"What if the knights come back?" Aminah asked. "We don't know where the witch sent them."

"Let them," Marlow said. "The queen won't be here. But you're right. Someone ought to stay behind in case of trouble."

"That'll be me." Rigmaiden lifted a creased hand.

"Wait," Emily said. "That'll be all of you. I'll take Elizabeth in and get this sorted out."

"Thank you, Rigmaiden." Marlow went on as though Emily hadn't spoken. "Aminah will get you settled properly. I hope you don't mind helping out with the sheep, they'll need shearing soon." He laughed. "Just do as Miss Mirza says and you'll be fine."

"Shear them yourself!" Emily said.

"I assume Michael won't be leaving Elizabeth's side," Marlow said. "Emily and myself make four. Sound right?"

"No!" Emily said and Michael put a hand on her shoulder.

"Yes."

The young magician indicated Elizabeth with a tilt of his head and Emily looked. There was a new light in the queen's eyes. It wasn't the same desperate glee that she felt in herself; it was warmer, softer, more tentative. It was hope, definitely, but Emily was sure there was something else there, too.

Chapter Six

The next morning found Emily, Elizabeth, Michael, and Rigmaiden gathered in the sitting room, staring at the painting of Arcadia.

The remainder of the previous day had been spent getting ready. Aminah and Rigmaiden drove back into Kennetsbridge to check the Free Stater out of his inn and fetch his things, along with Emily's duffle bag of clothing. Marlow took Emily into the forest to fetch her hammer, which she'd left behind in an attempt to forestall awkward questions when she'd thought he was a random non-Gifted farmer. They'd also found the spot where the slain monster had fallen—a patch of bright, golden moss, vaguely humanoid in shape like a police chalk outline, was the only indication of the thing that had almost killed them. Michael and Elizabeth went for a walk, returning long after the sun had set and everyone else had eaten dinner. They went straight to bed.

Now they'd done everything they could think of to prepare and the time had come. Emily's stomach was alive with familiar butterflies, a mix of excitement, anxiety, and adrenaline. She'd slept well, with no nightmares this time. She checked her weapons again—two knives in her belt and her hammer tied across her backpack—and nodded to Rigmaiden, who just stared at her from the leather chair he'd claimed.

Michael and Elizabeth were talking quietly by the fireplace, as ready as Emily if maybe not as eager. Occasionally one of them would indicate something in the painting, but mostly they just held hands. Michael was in his usual casual clothes, a hoodie over a black T-shirt and jeans, his hair bound back in a red band. Elizabeth had changed. Whether it was the ragged state of her dress after their flight through the painting, or just some change in taste, Emily couldn't say, but now the queen wore jeans, Wellington boots, and an oversized sweater of Aminah's that hung off one shoulder. Her bone-white hair was tied up with a red strip that matched Michael's.

Only Marlow was lagging and Emily watched through the doorway as he and Aminah hugged. Her hand lingered on his arm as they pulled apart. She stood on tiptoes to whisper something in his ear and his face was red as he came into the sitting room.

"Right, here we go," he said.

#

They came through the painting to a part of Arcadia Emily didn't recognize, stumbling out between two tall, fluted columns that supported a fragment of stone facing decorated with a relief carving of someone's legs. The river meandered by not far away and a line of small trees ran along it. They were sort of like upside-down pyramids in shape, spreading branches in all directions from low on their trunks, and their flowers looked like little spiders with deep red bodies and bright yellow legs.

"Oh, witch hazel," said Elizabeth. She moved to inspect the nearest tree, holding a flower gently between two fingers.

"Yes, but it's the wrong season," Marlow said. He held his hands up under the persistent sunlight. "Witch hazel blooms in winter."

"Anybody know where we are?" Emily asked.

"Arborea," Michael said, "but I don't think we ever came this far. I can't see the forest anywhere."

The first slopes of the hills rose behind them, but the land on the other side of the river was a broad, flat plain, as green as the hills but otherwise featureless.

"Arborea?" Emily repeated.

"*Omnia Gallia in tres partes divisa est,*" Marlow intoned.

"What?"

"Starling made us learn non-Gifted history," Michael said, as though that explained things. "What Marlow means is that Arcadia is divided into three regions: Arborea, Olympia, and Cantelon. All of this"—Michael gestured around him—"is Arborea."

"It's beautiful," Emily said.

"Let's have a look around," Marlow said. He whispered a few words, glanced up at the sky, and made a circle from his thumb and forefinger, which he held up to his right eye with the other fingers splayed out, forming a sort of impromptu monocle. He scanned the horizon, then paused suddenly, squinting. "Hello, who are you…?" He moved the three free fingers on his monocle hand, sticking the pinky out straight and crooking the other two into odd angles. He adjusted their positions a few times before he looked satisfied. "Ah, there we are… I'd say that's a castle. Bit run down by the looks of it. Maybe ten or twelve miles off."

"Well, we're looking for a throne," Emily said. "And a crown."

"It's as good as anything," Michael agreed. "Marlow, can you lead the way?"

"Certainly." He nodded, still peering through his fingers at the castle beyond Emily's vision. "I'll just toss up the old spyglass every now and again." He relaxed his hand and began to shake it out, then suddenly slapped it over his eye as he dropped to his knees with a gasp of pain. Michael rushed to his side as Elizabeth turned from her inspection of the witch hazel, her brow furrowed.

"What is it?" Michael asked. Marlow still had his hand clamped tightly over his eye and was rocking on his heels, hissing through his teeth.

Michael began to mutter something that sounded magical, but Marlow put his hand over Michael's mouth so suddenly it was almost a slap. His right eye was black and inky; something roiled just beneath the surface.

"What the hell is that?" Emily took an alarmed step back.

"I can't—I can't see." Marlow spoke through gritted teeth.

"Something happened with your spell." Michael gently moved Marlow's hand off his mouth. "It's all right, I won't try anything. Is it both eyes?"

"No," Marlow said. He took a few ragged breaths, which seemed to calm him down. "No, just the right. It's… it's all right. The pain is fading." His breathing slowed, but his eye was still just as black.

"A price," said Elizabeth. "A sacrifice."

"What do you mean?" Michael asked. He put his hands on Marlow's arm. "Can you stand?" Marlow nodded and they rose together, slowly. Michael was clearly doing most of the work, but Marlow seemed more or less steady once he was standing.

"Valeria Tall and Gray, the witch, said that all magic in Arcadia requires a sacrifice." Elizabeth turned to the river, her bone-white hair falling over her face like a curtain closing. "I apologize. I should have stopped you. It's such a small spell—"

Marlow put a hand up. "Don't. I'm all right. I can still see. Let's just get moving."

"Should we head back to Barley Bright?" Michael asked. "I might be able to heal it back home."

"I said let's move," Marlow said through gritted teeth.

A few minutes of silent walking brought them to the river's edge, where Michael paused to peer into the water with his arms crossed.

"I don't remember it being so deep," he said. "We were able to wade it last time I was here."

"So how do we cross?" Emily asked. "I'd rather not find out what happens to a flight spell."

"It's certainly inconvenient to have to think before casting," Marlow agreed. "Well, unless these ruins include a handy bridge somewhere, we'll need to look for a natural ford." He shielded his eyes and stared off to the left. "It's more likely to be shallow nearer the forest."

"Which way is that?" Michael asked.

"The river ran roughly east out of the forest, so if we assume it's morning here as well…" Marlow glanced and the sun, then pointed. "That way."

He set off and they followed. Emily was impressed by his confidence, as well as by his obvious woodsy knowledge. Most of the Arcanes she'd known in school relied almost exclusively on their Gift for all but the most basic tasks. Her friend Kayo had been notorious for disrupting study hall by floating books around her head and letting them drop on her desk as needed. Marlow, with all his outdoors skills, was clearly cut from a different cloth.

They walked along the river for about an hour before Marlow stopped them. "Here," he said, pointing. The river, which had been consistently smooth and unruffled as they walked, was different here. Wide teardrop-shaped humps of faster-moving water formed on the surface, making an uneven row from one bank to the other before they evened out again.

"There are some rocks here, just under the surface." Marlow knelt and put a hand in the river. "Not too deep. And quite pleasant, too. I'll go first."

He untied his shoes and pulled off his socks, which he balled up and stuck in a pocket, then stood and put a tentative foot into the water. Obviously satisfied that the rock beneath his foot was stable, he took a long step out to the next spot where the surface of the river was disturbed. He put his arms out for balance as he went, occasionally wheeling them around as he wavered or slipped while placing his next step.

He made it across the river without incident, though, and beckoned them to follow as he wiped his wet feet across the grass. Elizabeth went next, with a little more trouble than Marlow but no soaking disasters. Michael looked at Emily, who shrugged, so he crossed over and helped Elizabeth dry her feet before dealing with his own.

Emily pulled her sneakers off and stepped onto the first stone in the river. It was larger than she'd expected, based on how carefully the others had moved, and the water was warm and slow. She hopped from stone to stone, enjoying her own dexterity, and turned the last jump into a front flip that landed her neatly on the far bank.

Elizabeth, who had been watching her, turned and began to walk away from the river. Immediately a hot flush ran up Emily's neck and filled her cheeks. How could she be so thoughtless? Vowing to be less of a show-off in the future, Emily hurried to dry her feet and get her shoes back on. The rest of the group waited for her, except Elizabeth, who was already far out into the field.

"Emily—" Michael began.

"I know," Emily said.

"Not that," Michael said. "Well, yes, that, but there's something else. Elizabeth says these plants are all wrong."

"Wrong?" Emily asked as they caught up with Marlow.

"She's right, too. See that cypress?" Marlow pointed to a tall, straight tree standing alone in the field. It was surrounded by a dozen woody protrusions that stuck out like teeth all around it. "That's a swamp tree. Maybe it could grow right by the river, but out here in a meadow?"

"What does it mean?" Emily said.

"I don't know," Marlow said. "There doesn't seem to be a pattern. Did you notice the weeping willow we passed was just starting to flower?"

"That other tree was flowering, the first one," Emily said.

"That's a winter bloom." Marlow shook his head. "Willows bud in spring. You know, normally."

"And it's neither spring nor winter," Michael agreed.

"Is there a reason every Arcane in the world seems to know everything about plants?" Emily said. "Is that what you guys really did in class all day? Just memorize trees?"

"It's really just Marlow and Elizabeth." Michael laughed. "One of them runs a farm and the other had nothing but books for friends for ninety-nine percent of her life."

"Don't get Michael started on the bones in your body, though," Marlow added.

"What?" Michael shrugged. "You're born with more than you die with. It's cool. Come on, Elizabeth is waiting."

#

They walked toward the horizon until it got dark, and if the river hadn't disappeared behind them, Emily wouldn't have been sure that they'd made any progress at all. As varied and interesting as the landscape had been where they'd come out through the painting, this part of Arcadia was just a flat, endless field. Even the lush green of the trim grass grew boring after a while. Every now and then they passed a lone shrub or stand of trees and as often as not, Elizabeth or Marlow would comment on how out of place it was. They eventually stopped, though, leaving Emily uncertain whether the later plants were proper and correct or the wizards had just gotten tired of noting problems.

"I can't see a bloody thing," Marlow said in the gathering dusk. He snorted a bitter laugh. "Who'd have thought depth perception would be the least of my troubles?"

"As long as there's only one tree per mile you should be okay," Michael said. He unslung his backpack and dropped it on the ground. "Camp here?"

"You don't think we should push on? Try to find somewhere flat and grassy?" Marlow retorted. Michael rolled his eyes.

"Michael, is he always like this?" Emily asked.

"Only when he's been half-blinded by wild magic."

Emily smiled. She set down her own backpack—much heavier than Michael's, as it contained most of their gear—and knelt to unzip it, then froze as a deep, threatening sound carried over the still night air.

She put her hand up for silence and raised her chin. "What's that?"

"What's what?" Michael asked.

"That sound. Something is roaring."

"Roaring?" Elizabeth repeated.

70

"She's right," Marlow said. "Is that a bear?"

It was hard to imagine anything so big as a bear could escape their notice in that flat land, but as Elizabeth led the way toward the sound, Emily had to admit Marlow had hit the nail on the head. They approached another cypress tree—Emily had gotten pretty good at recognizing them by now—with a knotty pyramidal tangle of roots thirty feet across showing aboveground, as though the whole tree had been pulled twenty feet straight up by a giant. Somewhere within the mass the muffled roar of a bear continued to sound.

Marlow stepped forward and put his hand on the roots. He shut his eyes for a moment, then looked at Elizabeth. His right eye was like a roiling pool of tar.

"I reckon it's worth it, don't you?"

Elizabeth nodded. Marlow closed his eyes again and took a long breath, then reached into a pocket and pulled out the white stone charm he'd used when he talked to the fox. He murmured a few words, his hand still on the roots.

"Hello there," he said gently. The bellowing from within the roots stopped immediately. "That's right... there's a fellow. No need to worry. I'd like to help you, please."

Emily blinked, thinking her eyes were tricking her. But no—Marlow's fingers were changing. Either they were getting absorbed into the root system, or it was growing to engulf them, as flaky bark grew up his fingers and over the back of his hand.

"Is great, thanks," said a deep voice from within the roots.

Marlow jumped back like a startled cat, snapping his woody fingers free from the tree. Michael raised his eyebrows and Elizabeth laughed as realization dawned.

"Marlow, did you—" Emily started.

"No! No." Marlow waved his hands; the one that had touched the root system looked to have sprouted a few twigs of its own. "At least, I don't think so. Elizabeth?"

Elizabeth had just opened her mouth to reply when the voice came again.

"Hello? Are helping us?"

"Just a second," Emily called back.

"Is fine!" boomed the voice. It sounded like it would be rather loud if it weren't muffled by the roots.

"Okay, what's happening?" Emily said.

"Apparently he speaks English," said Michael. "Marlow, your hand—"

"It's fine," Marlow said, "if perhaps unnecessary."

"Okay, we're gonna get you out!" Emily yelled. "Just hang tight!" She grabbed two thick roots and began to pull. They were tough, clearly old and buried deep, but in the end they were only wood. They tore away from the body of the tree and Emily broke them off near the ground and tossed them away.

She went on like this for a few minutes, tearing, snapping, and throwing, until there was a small pile of broken roots all around her. Every now and then the bear would check in with her—"You are coming? Is going good?"—and she would reassure him that yes, she was on her way. Apparently he was a fairly anxious creature, though Emily had to admit that she didn't really know much about bears' personalities. Soon she had made a gap in the root structure large enough to crawl into, which she did. Deep within the roots, back near the center of the mass, she could just make out a large, furry body.

"Okay, I can see you!" she called. "Can you move?"

"Can't!" the bear shouted back. Within the shelter of the roots, his voice was an echoing boom.

"Okay, just stay where you are," Emily replied. "This might take a while."

"Are staying," the bear rumbled.

It was fully dark by the time she reached the stuck bear. Luckily they'd brought flashlights, buried deep at the bottom of Emily's bag since they'd expected to rely on magical light during their explorations, but the animal was still a huge shadowy bulk when she finally put her hand on its back

72

paw. It took another half hour of breaking on Emily's part and twisting on the bear's to get it facing forward, out the tunnel she'd made. Then it was just a matter of squeezing their way back out, which the bear did with aplomb, snapping twigs as he went.

Finally they were free, stretching their cramps out under a star-spattered sky. The bear stood on two legs as soon as he was out from under the roots and gave a bellowing roar that shook the ground beneath Emily's feet.

"Is good!" he cried. "Is good. We thank."

"You're welcome," Emily said. "How'd you get stuck in there, anyway?"

"We not know," the bear said. "Was sleep under tree. Night is come, we wake. Tree is all around."

"We?" Emily began stretching again, telling her tired muscles they might have to get back to work sooner than she'd thought. "Are there others under there?"

"No, no," said the bear. "Just us."

"I'm sorry, the tree grew that much in a single day?" Marlow interjected. "That's just incredible."

The bear shrugged, which looked like a mountain having an earthquake. He was as big as his voice, nearly as round as he was tall. Under the faint light of the stars, Emily could see that he was actually wearing a sort of crude, old-fashioned armor. A metal chestplate was strapped around his barrel-like torso with thick leather bands and a simple pot helmet sat on his head. Emily tried to imagine facing down a line of charging bears dressed like this one and couldn't.

At least he likes us… I think.

"We should do introductions," Michael said. He stood with an arm around Elizabeth, who was absolutely dwarfed by the towering animal. "I'm Michael. This is Elizabeth and Marlow. And you can thank Emily for getting you out."

"Thank," the bear said. "Are Utros. Please to meet."

"You too," Michael said. "We were about to have some dinner. Care to join us?"

"Is good," said Utros, so they headed back to the spot they'd picked for camp. The others had been busy while Emily broke Utros out; their little tent had been pitched and a campfire made from the torn-up roots she'd left behind her. It was quite cozy, not to mention lovely under the warm summer stars.

Marlow got a meal going—canned beans and ground beef, not exactly gourmet fare but perfectly suited to Emily's mood—as Utros settled heavily to the ground and the others made a circle around the fire. Soon they were digging in happily, forgoing conversation by natural agreement.

Utros finished first and belched noisily as he put down the tin of beans that he'd eaten with remarkable dexterity.

"We thank," he said. "We help."

"Help?" said Marlow. "How's that?"

The bear took off his helmet, scratched his head, and replaced it. "Not know. What you are need?"

"Well, information, mainly," Marlow said. "Do you know this land well?"

Utros waggled his forepaw in a *so-so* gesture.

"Do you know Adam?" asked Elizabeth.

The bear sat straight up and his helmet fell off his head. It landed with a noisy *thunk* that would have been funny if it hadn't been so alarming. "Adam? Adam?" He put a paw over his heart. "We know Adam."

"How? Where is he?" asked Michael, leaning forward. "Have you met him?"

"Met Adam?" Utros laughed, a terrifically noisy rasp. "No, no. Chieftain maybe has? Chieftain's sire maybe has?"

"Then how do you know him?" Emily said.

"All bears know Adam," said Utros. "Adam make us free. Give us castle and castle."

"Castle and castle?" Emily couldn't make sense of that one.

"And castle and castle," said the bear. "All castle. All for bears. All for us."

"Adam gave you all the castles in Arborea," Michael translated. "For what? In return for what?"

"Bears make blood of humans run. Slash, bite, stomp. For Adam. And Adam give castle and castle."

"You... killed for him?" Marlow's face was ashen in the firelight. Emily put a hand out and touched the handle of her hammer which lay on the grass near her backpack.

"Not us." Utros waved a paw. "Chieftain maybe killed. Chieftain's sire maybe killed. We are young."

"How long ago was this?" Michael asked softly.

"Not know." Utros shook his head. "Long and long." He went to scratch his head, realized his helmet was missing, and turned to retrieve it.

"Okay, *what* is going on?" Emily hissed as soon as the bear's back was turned.

"If this is true—" Marlow began.

"Adam wouldn't," Michael said.

"Wouldn't he, though?" said Marlow.

Michael sat back, his face a mask of worry.

Marlow tossed another torn-up root onto the fire, which flickered red over his face. "To play the king..."

"We help!" said Utros, making them jump. He'd replaced his helmet and sat smiling as though nothing had changed. "We take to chieftain. Chieftain will tell. Tell where is Adam."

#

They spent the night arguing. Between Utros's terrible snoring and the shock of his words, nobody but the bear could sleep. So they sat up as the fire died between them and bickered over whether or not they could trust the bear.

"They killed humans," Emily said for the dozenth time.

"*He* didn't, though," said Michael.

"I *know* that," Emily whispered. "But still, he said the bears killed people. For Adam. He might be nice, but how do we know the others are?"

"Speaking frankly, what choice do we have?" Marlow said. "Right now, we need information more than anything. If Utros's chieftain can tell us more, well, there you are. Otherwise we're just wandering."

"There's still the castle," Emily said.

"The castle?" Marlow shook his head. "If Utros is to be believed, we'd end up among bears anyway. Better to show up in the company of friends."

Emily sat back, frustrated. She knew she'd lost the argument; she just wasn't ready to admit it. Despite the bear's friendliness, something, some fighter's instinct, was telling her not to go with Utros. She forced herself to take a slow breath, in and out. Michael and Marlow were all for it, eager to chase any hint of their missing friend. Only Elizabeth hadn't spoken, just sat and listened, her pale face gleaming in the dying firelight.

"Elizabeth, what do you think?" Emily asked.

The queen closed her eyes and it was like candles going out. "I would rather fail for being too trusting than too suspicious."

So the next morning, when Utros awoke with a crashing yawn, they told him that they would go with him to his chieftain. He leaped to his back paws with surprising quickness and set out immediately, not even checking to see if the humans were following. They scampered around the camp, grabbing their things and repacking hastily, then ran to catch up with the bear.

He led them in roughly the direction they'd been going already, which was somehow a relief. A few hours of steady walking brought them in sight of the castle that Marlow had spotted the day before.

"See?" Marlow nudged Emily in the ribs. "It's bears all the way down."

The castle was a few miles away and they were still a ways off when its great front door opened. A horde of bears spilled out, dozens of them, black and brown against the faraway blue sky. They moved on four legs in a sort of loping, humping gallop that ate up the distance and the humans weren't much closer to the castle by the time the bears reached them.

Marlow stepped forward and raised a hand in greeting, but the bears showed no interest. Their armor was strapped tight to their bodies, their helmets pushed low on their heads. Each carried a long iron-tipped spear on its back and they began to unsling these as they made a rough circle around the humans. Utros was soon absorbed into this circle and lost to sight. The ring complete, the bears leveled their spears, making a bristling fence of iron that penned the humans in on all sides.

"You will come," said one of the bears.

Emily punched Marlow on the shoulder. "See?"

Chapter 7

"The humans will come," insisted a black bear even bigger than Utros, with a black-and-white plume on his helmet. Emily took one look at the glittering ring of iron and admitted to herself that, yes, they would come.

The bears stripped them of their weapons and gear, then set out for the castle, only a few miles in the distance. The bears made an arc as they marched, prodding the humans on with their spears and constantly threatening to close the circle at anything they took as a sign of trouble. Their armor rattled and a few removed their helmets as the sun warmed the air, but the overall effect was still quite intimidating.

As the castle drew near, a new shape appeared over the horizon. At first Emily thought it was a second, bigger castle, but it just went up and up as they approached. It was a mountain, the biggest she'd ever seen, with rocky gray slopes and a jagged top looming over the castle despite its obvious distance from them. It was strange to see something so bleak and dead in this bright land of Arcadia.

"What is that?" she whispered to Michael, who shrugged. His eyes were locked on the rising mountain as well, his face a mask of concern. A look at Marlow showed the same fear. Only Elizabeth seemed unfazed, but it was hard to tell if she had even noticed the mountain.

"What is that?" Emily said again, louder, so the bears could hear. She looked around at their captors, but none of them would meet her eyes. "Come on, one of you has to know."

"Is Olympia," said the bear with the plumed helmet. "Not go there."

"Why?" Emily said. "What's there?"

"Walk," said the bear, emphasizing his point with a jab of his spear that made Emily jump to avoid being impaled. "Almost home."

The castle was closer than Emily had expected, low and gray against the backdrop of the mountain called Olympia. They stopped at a double door twice Emily's height, made from wide wooden planks and iron rivets. The castle itself was small, little more than a square wall with four towers at the corners. A bear's head appeared over the crenelated wall, helmet at an angle.

"Who is going?" it called.

"Skaros and our warband," called up the bear who'd been doing all the talking. "We find Utros and humans besides."

The doors creaked and groaned as they swung open, pushed from inside by two bears. Skaros shoved Emily forward and she stumbled through the doors into a large, square courtyard. Bears lazed everywhere, mostly asleep. They lay seemingly at random between refuse piles and burned-out campfires. Bones, broken spear tips, bits of armor, scraps of rotten cloth, and other assorted junk made the ground a minefield of careful stepping. The whole place stank like an abandoned fish-canning factory overtaken by feral cats.

The structure of the castle itself wasn't in any better condition. The stone walls were falling apart; the mortar was cracking and flaking and entire chunks of wall had fallen away in places. The stairs that led up to an inner walkway were worn and crumbling and sections of the walkway itself had fallen into the courtyard. Each of the four towers had a doorway leading in, but only one still had its door and that hung skewed from a single rusted hinge.

They weren't given any time to wonder, though, as Skaros and his warband prodded them across the yard toward the back left tower. A few bears raised lazy heads or opened a single eye to watch them pass, but mostly they were ignored. The archway leading into the tower was in gray shadow despite the sun now high overhead.

Emily led the way in. Inside the tower was cool and dim. As her eyes adjusted, she made out maybe a dozen large, humped shapes arranged like a half-melted royal court. On a huge pile of stone at the back of the circular room sat a great bear, his fur more white than brown, with a circlet of beaten iron on his head. A dusty shaft of light from the cracked ceiling twenty feet above fell on his face, showing white, hairless lines marking a dozen or more scars. Emily was immediately reminded of Durgan dun Raven—the animal's hunched shoulders and scar-slumped face made him seem like her mentor's lost brother or funhouse mirror reflection. He was eating a hunk of raw meat off a thick white bone.

On either side of the chieftain sat more bears in attendance, filling the room except for an aisle that led from the doorway to the throne. Emily, Marlow, Michael, and Elizabeth were nudged into this space by Skaros, who then took up a spot just inside the door. The rest of his warband stayed outside, except for Utros, who had reappeared and now stood with Skaros.

"Our Skaros," rumbled the chieftain. "Who brought?" He tore off a last bit of meat with his ragged teeth, then tossed the stripped bone into a corner.

"Humans, great Arcturus," said Skaros. He kept his eyes on the floor as he spoke.

"In Arborea?" The bear called Arcturus seemed to raise an eyebrow.

"Yes, Chieftain."

"Hrmmmmmm…" Arcturus scratched his chin. The chieftain's yellow eyes were milky and they roved over the four humans before the he spoke again. "Can fight?"

"Yes," said Emily. "I can."

"Good," said Arcturus. "Good. We welcome. You eat?"

"No thanks," said Marlow. Emily was hungry, but she wasn't sure about eating raw meat off the bone.

"Fine. Now." Arcturus leaned forward on his makeshift throne. "Why here? Arborea not for humans. Arborea for bears. Why here? Where from?"

Emily wasn't sure what to say and apparently nobody else was, either. Arcturus was being much more polite than she'd expected given their initial reception at spearpoint. Perhaps the bears weren't so bad after all— misunderstood, maybe, or just wary of strangers. She was just debating telling the truth when Utros spoke up from the back wall.

"Seeking, great Arcturus."

The chieftain turned his scarred head to look at Utros and his iron circlet slumped to one side. "Seeking?"

"Seeking for Adam," said Utros, his head down.

"Adam!" Arcturus boomed. "Adam!" He shook his huge head, sending a cloud of flies buzzing from his fur. "How many winters ago was Adam?"

"Many and many," said a new voice. From the shadow of Arcturus's throne, a bear stepped forward. Compared to his kin, this one was small, barely taller than Emily and probably only three hundred pounds. His fur was tawny, his face painted with bone-white chalk. He wore no armor, just a string of bones around his neck.

"Aidos, you are teller of the story," said Arcturus. "Tell us well of Adam."

Aidos shut his eyes and touched a small bone that hung over his heart. The room fell silent as he took a long breath. He opened his eyes and took in the room, catching the glance of each human for a moment.

"So."

"When Adam came, humans ruled Arborea. We bears lived in our woods and our caves and did not go out. When we went out, the humans hunted and killed us. We lived in the shadows beneath the trees and the dark corners of the caves.

"You might ask, did Adam came to be among other humans? He did not. He came first to the forest. When he was in the forest, he met us, the bears.

"At once he saw our strength and rather than hunt us and kill us as humans always did, Adam joined us. He joined the clan that found him. He learned the ways. He could not fight as we fought then, before we

81

took the armor and the spear, but he had magic and his magic was strong. He lived as bears lived and was one of ours.

"We did not know then that Adam was of the divine.

"In time, Adam became our leader. First he led the clan that had found him. Then he bound the clans together into one army under his rule, in the shadows beneath the trees and the dark corners of the caves. He told us that we were stronger than the humans. He told us true.

"At a meeting of the clans, Adam spoke. He said to us that the things the humans had that we wanted could be ours. They had armor: we could wear it. They had spears: we could wield them. They had castles: these could be our new dens when we took the place of the humans in the castles. He promised us these things if we killed for him. We said to him, yes.

"We soon smelled that Adam was of the divine. He walked among us, touching bear and bear and bear. When he touched, bear grew. Grew thoughts, plans, ideas. Like humans. Like Adam. Now we spoke, not only listened. Each and each carried a piece of the divine, the gift of Adam.

"For one thousand days we waged war on the humans. We killed them and killed them. They could not resist us. They were small, weak. We are strong. We killed them all and took their armor, their spears, their castles. It was as Adam told.

"We knew then that Adam was of the divine. We knew because when we had killed all his enemies and done all that he asked, he turned on us in fury. He said to us that the land called Arborea had been fouled and was worth nothing to him now. He said to us that we were animals only, not his clan. Only one of the divine would think in such a way, to make a thing and to discard it. To be given a gift and to refuse it.

"Still, he had mercy. He did not want Arborea, so he gave it to the bears. The armor is ours, the spears, the castles. We took his gift. These things are ours. The land is ours. This was Adam's gift to us to repay our service. And he went on to Olympia, leaving us to rule here.

"This is the story as it was told to us, Aidos, teller of the story."

"Who told you the story?" asked Michael, breaking the silence that had followed Aidos's recital.

"Oumeros, who was teller of the story when we were a cub," said Aidos.

"Who told him?" Michael said.

"Ellos." Aidos shook his head. "But we did not know him."

"Did Ellos know Adam?" asked Marlow, picking up Michael's thread. "Was he there? How long—how many winters ago was Ellos the teller of the story?"

Aidos was silent for a while. Finally, he looked up at the ceiling of the tower, where cracks of age let in slanted hints of the sunlight outside.

"You are seeking for Adam," he said at last. "When it is night, we will show you where is Adam."

"Among the stars," said Elizabeth quietly.

Michael turned at the sound of her voice, as though he'd forgotten she was there. "What do you mean?" he asked gently.

"Can't you feel it?" Elizabeth said.

"Feel what?" said Emily.

Elizabeth sighed, a sound not of frustration but of sorrow. "The river we crossed near the forest… Where we first met it, it ran slowly. It was wide and calm. At the ford, rocks blocked the path of the river, changing its shape. Around the rocks, the water flowed more quickly. It was still the same river, heading in the same direction to the same end, but in that place it moved differently."

"Time," said Marlow. "Time flows differently here, is that it?"

"Yes," Elizabeth said. "More quickly. I felt it before… I felt it."

"So that means Adam is—" Michael began.

"Among the stars, yes," said Elizabeth. She took his hand and looked him in the eye. "I am sorry, my heart."

"Mithras have mercy," said Marlow. He looked at the ceiling, his eyes narrowed. "An entire life in ten years."

"That can't be right," Michael said.

"Is so," Arcturus rumbled. He raised his huge head from his fisted paw, where he'd supported it as he watched the whole exchange through narrowed eyes. "Many and many winters ago was Adam. Trees grew since his time."

"Did he…" Michael looked back at the great bear. "Did Adam have a daughter? A cub?"

Arcturus gestured to Aidos. "Tell the line of Adam."

"Adam was king of Arborea," said Aidos, "and of Olympia, and Cantelon besides. He ruled from Cantelon at Beverlay and married the queen called Noone. They became stars. His daughter was Danae and became queen at Beverlay and married the king called Nobody. They became stars. Her son was Adama and became the king at Beverlay and married the queen called Nothing. They became stars. His daughter is Adae, who married the king called Zero. They rule at Beverlay."

"Four generations," said Marlow. "But Adam's daughter."

"Close enough," Michael agreed. "And her throne must be at Beverlay."

"Wherever that is," Emily said.

"Not go!" Arcturus boomed, making them all jump. "Arborea for bears. Olympia not. Cantelon not. We will stay."

"Uh, don't worry about it," Emily said. "We'll go alone."

"No," said Arcturus. "We will stay. Later stars will fall."

Emily looked at her friends. Michael spread his hands and Marlow raised his eyebrows; Elizabeth was watching Arcturus as the great bear went on.

"When stars fall, Adam returns. Leads bears again." He gestured to a few bears around the room. "Now. Fetch armor. Fetch spears." The animals he indicated passed by Emily on their way out the door.

"We really need to get going," Emily tried. Arcturus ignored her. The bears returned, one carrying a clattering pile of armor and the other with an armful of spears. They dumped it all on the floor between the humans and the bear chieftain.

"Good!" Arcturus leaned back on his pile of stones and indicated the gear with a wave of his paw. "Take."

"I'm sorry, I'm not sure I understand," Marlow said. "You're giving these to us? Why?"

"All bears use," Arcturus rumbled. His eyes narrowed. "You are bears."

"We're not," said Emily.

"You can fight?" asked the chieftain.

"Yes, but—"

"You are bears." He nodded decisively. "Take."

"No," Emily said, stepping forward and raising her chin. "We won't. Let us go."

"Go?" Arcturus's eyes narrowed. "Go?" He waved his paw again, a gesture hardly different from the others he'd made, but his men clearly understood. The bears who held spears lowered them to make a new circle of iron around the humans as a few moved between them and the door. From the shadow of the rubble throne, Aidos spoke up.

"Adam joined the clan that found him," he said. "All other humans, we killed."

"Join or die?" Emily said. "Seriously? Come on, guys, let's…" She looked behind her. Marlow, Michael, and Elizabeth had their hands in the air.

Emily couldn't blame the others for surrendering—Elizabeth was powerless and Marlow had learned firsthand the price of magic in Arcadia. The massive firepower the Arcanes should have brought had been all but entirely neutralized… meaning it was up to Emily to get them out.

She took a quick glance around her. Eight bears held spears and another three, including Aidos and Utros, stood ready but empty-handed. Arcturus on his stone pile made an even dozen. How strong was a bear? Fighting Earth animals wasn't really part of Emily's Harkness education—and that assumed that Arborean bears weren't stronger as well as smarter.

"Take," Arcturus repeated, so Emily complied. She grabbed a spear in both hands and spun in a quick circle, making sure all the bears saw her weapon. A few of them stepped back reflexively, but most seemed unintimidated. The bears near the door raised their spears over the heads of the other humans. All eyes were on her.

"Run!" Emily shouted.

"Emily, don't!" Michael said.

"Run, dammit!" A bear took a step toward Emily and she jabbed her spear at him, forcing him back. "I'll catch up!"

Their spears leveled, the bear warriors along the walls closed in, making a wall between Emily and her friends. They were trapped, too, blocked from leaving by more animals that were surely turning their attention back to the helpless magicians. Emily ducked to the side, but couldn't see past the mass of muscle and fur that now ringed her in completely.

Skaros, the bear who'd brought them in, loomed on her right hand. His battered, black-and-white-plumed iron helmet covered nearly his entire face and gave him an extra eight inches of height. To Emily's left was another bear, smaller and shorter than the others, though still a head taller than Emily and twice as wide.

She flung her spear at Skaros, then spun and grabbed another from the pile. A glimpse of Skaros slapping it out of the air flashed across her vision as she turned to face the smaller bear. She took a few quick steps, planted her new spear on the ground, and vaulted.

A huge paw on her back caught her mid-leap and pulled her to the ground with a teeth-rattling crash. The spear clattered down beside her. Blinking, Emily saw the wavering plume of Skaros's helmet above his wide yellow eyes, which peered down at her.

"You can do better than that," Emily said, pushing up to her elbows.

The huge warrior set a paw on her left shoulder and pushed her back down to the ground. Emily's muscles creaked as she strained against Skaros, but he was as strong as she was and far heavier. He pinned her down with incredible force, but it was almost a gentle motion, as though her resistance meant nothing.

Emily twisted, trying to wiggle her pinned shoulder clear. Skaros slammed his other paw down, trapping her under his incredible weight.

Her legs were free and she bucked, arching her back, but only succeeded in making the bear press down harder. Next she tried a few kicks aimed at the bear's huge belly beneath his armor. He growled and flexed his paws. Inch-long claws dug into both Emily's shoulders and stayed there. Now every twist and wrench of her body sent lances of pain down her arms and she stopped fighting, keeping still other than the rise and fall of her heaving chest.

"A bear fighter," said Skaros. His voice shook her thoughts and his stinking breath was hot on her face.

"A good fighter," agreed Arcturus, somewhere above and to her right. Emily turned her head slightly, squinting at the pain, to watch the chieftain as he sat up straight on his stone pile. His head broke the scant light from the cracked ceiling, sending dust whirling. He looked down at her. "A bear fighter. Human?"

"Yes, human," she grunted. "Not as easy to kill as you're used to?"

"Kill?" The chieftain actually looked offended. "Kill? No. You are bear. Take spear. Take armor. You are bear now. Arborea is home. Castles for den. Eat, sleep, kill. A bear fighter with bears."

"I'm not a bear!" Emily shouted. "Let me go, dammit!" It was humiliating to be pinned down like this, as helpless as any of non-Gifted she'd walked past in Deseret, as doomed as she had been in the wyverns' den. But Durgan dun Raven hadn't followed her into the painting, just waiting to leap out from a shadow and save her.

Skaros leaned down, his face close to hers, and laughed.

Emily grabbed his helmet by the nosepiece and yanked. The bear immediately pulled his claws from her shoulders and scrabbled to right the helmet that was now tilted over his eyes. The room shook as he fell back onto his haunches. Emily scrambled backwards. Her hand landed on something—the hilt of a spear. She grabbed it and used it to lever herself up to a standing position, her legs shaking under her.

She jumped, clearing Skaros's twisting body, and landed on Arcturus's stone pile. The rubble underfoot shifted and slid as she landed, forcing her to catch herself, but after a desperate moment she stood with her feet solidly planted and the tip of her spear at Arcturus's throat.

"Everybody freeze!" she shouted.

The chieftain's eyes were bloodshot up close and they crossed slightly as he looked down at Emily's spear. His large patches of white fur were yellowed and a bit mangy. His lips pulled back in a slow snarl, showing broken teeth and clinging drool.

"Okay," said Emily. "Let's talk."

"No!" In a rush, Arcturus stood, knocking the spear from Emily's hands. He was huge, so much bigger than he'd seemed seated on his throne. His head brushed the ceiling as he gave a roar that shook the room and brought dust and debris pattering down. The bears below the throne cowered at their chieftain's wrath.

Emily looked up at the towering chieftain as paws the size of dinner plates grabbed her roughly by the arms. Arcturus lifted her bodily into the air until he held her straight out from his body. She twisted and kicked, trying to get free, but she couldn't break the bear's grip.

He drew her closer, his eyes locked on hers, rage twisting his face. As she came near his matted, stinking fur, Emily wondered if she was about to be crushed to death. But Arcturus had another plan in mind. As suddenly as he'd grabbed her, he threw her, out and away into the open space where the spears and armor had been scattered during the fight.

The broken flagstones of the tower floor came rushing toward her much faster than she expected. She barely had time to throw her arm over her face before she hit the stone. Her elbow went first, with a crack like a gunshot and a lightning bolt of pain that lanced up to her torn shoulder. Her neck twisted in a last shot at survival. Then her head met the ground, stars exploded everywhere, and the world went black.

CHAPTER 8

It was still black, with stars. They swirled when she moved her head and disappeared when she shut her eyes. There was also a drum playing, faintly, somewhere far away.

"She's awake." That was a voice, human, male, soft. Michael.

Memories came wobbling up uncertainly like tipsy partiers heading home in three a.m. darkness. She could smell Jack's auburn hair, feel the smile behind his eyes. She could still feel the cold lines of the tower floor on her cheek—no, that was real. Her face pressed against bars of iron or steel, cool in the warm night.

"Are you quite sure?" Marlow, a bit past Michael.

"I'm up," Emily said. "I'm up." She pushed herself off the metal bars, overbalanced, fell to the dirt and caught herself on her forearms. Another memory rushed up, of her right elbow popping like a dropped lightbulb, and Emily bounced up in alarm.

"You feel okay?" Michael asked.

Sitting on her haunches, Emily extended first one arm, then the other, then bent them both. There was no pain, no grinding or looseness or any other feeling than her well-toned muscles sliding beneath her skin. In fact, she wasn't even sore. No headache. It was impossible, unless…

"You healed me," Emily said.

In the darkness Elizabeth sat in the dirt with her back against the wall of their pen. She turned her face away into a stripe of shadow.

89

"Michael, you shouldn't—" Emily's breath caught in her throat. "What did it cost you?"

Michael, who stood with his back to her, turned and raised his hands. No—he raised one hand. His left arm was missing from what looked like the elbow down; half the sleeve of his hoodie dangled empty.

"Michael, I'm so sorry." Emily's voice was a whisper.

"Another spell, another sacrifice," said Elizabeth.

There was no way to respond to that. Emily stood, stretching her back, which also didn't hurt, and took in the situation. They were outside, under the stars, in the courtyard of the tumbledown castle. The bars around them, some fifteen feet high, made a sort of pen that might have once been used to hold animals. They were as thick as Emily's arm and forged from solid steel.

The four of them were alone in the pen and their gear was nowhere to be seen. Outside the cage, the humped forms of sleeping bears lay scattered around the courtyard, making Emily wonder if they ever woke, or if they just slept here forever under some fairy spell.

"We were tossed in here after your escape attempt," Marlow said. "I'm not sure Arcturus knows what to do with us. I think he really expected us to join the cause."

"I'd rather not," Emily said.

"Then get us out of here," the magician replied.

Emily turned back to the bars of the cage and gave them an experimental tug. They seemed securely seated in the ground, either run deep into the earth or set in stone or concrete under the dirt, and had no give. Emily grabbed two adjacent bars, one in each hand, and set her feet. Then, with an effort that bent her back and tested just how healed her arm was, she bent them.

At first they didn't respond, but Emily persisted, her teeth bared in an unconscious snarl. With a loud metallic squeal, the bars gave in and bowed away from each other, changing the gap between them from a narrow rectangle to a slightly wider oval.

The snoring of a nearby bear cut off suddenly at the noise. Emily back-pedaled away from the bars as though she could retroactively silence them if she looked innocent enough.

The bear grunted, rolled a quarter turn onto its stomach, and resumed snoring.

"Well, that's no good," Marlow murmured. "Can't escape if we wake the whole place doing it."

"Is loud," said a low voice, making Emily jump. A bear stood at the bars, poking its nose through the little gap she'd made. Her heart leaped in terror; then she realized it was Utros. The bear chuffed. "Stay."

Utros lumbered around the cage, moving in and out of shadows cast by moonlight through the battlements of the half-tumbled castle walls. He came around a corner and stood on his hind legs at a gate where a huge padlock hung. Drawing a key from somewhere within his shaggy mass, he unlocked the padlock and opened it with a soft click.

"Come," he said.

Emily bounded to the gate and gave it a push; it rattled but did not open. She blinked in momentary confusion, then hissed to Utros, "You need to pull the lock out of the hasp."

The bear stared back at her for a long moment, then turned its slow eyes to the padlock, which hung open with the shackle still holding the gate closed. He reached out a paw and drew the shackle free noiselessly, then dropped the lock in the dirt with a thump.

"Come," he repeated.

Emily went first; behind her, Marlow hustled both Michael and Elizabeth through as they huddled together in a sort of mutual shock. They followed Utros as he picked his way among his sleeping clanmates with surprising grace. Emily had no trouble keeping up with the bear and silence was easy on the soft earth of the courtyard, but the three magicians kept stumbling over chunks of rubble and bumping against each other. Emily was torn between wanting to shush them and hurry them along.

Eventually Utros brought them to a spot where the castle wall had all but completely collapsed, leaving only a low mound of rubble to be scaled before they were free of the bears' camp. Utros paused at the base of the pile as Emily helped Marlow, Elizabeth, and finally the one-armed Michael over it.

"Are you coming?" she whispered to the bear.

"No," Utros rumbled. "Are home."

"Won't you be in trouble?" Emily was surprised to find how attached she'd grown to Utros in their short time together, considering that he'd led them nearly to their deaths by bringing them to the castle. He'd come through for them when it counted, though; she was willing to bet that the bear's heart worked fine even if his brain didn't.

Utros shook his shaggy head. "No, is secret. Will go to sleep, wake in morning, pretend is mystery and mystery."

Emily frowned. "If you're sure." She stuck out a hand. "Well, thanks for the assist. I hope we see you again."

Utros shook with both his paws, which dwarfed her hand and made her feel like a little doll. The bear showed his teeth in something that Emily thought for a moment was a smile, then realized was actually a grimace of concern.

"We warn," Utros said. "Olympia is bad and bad. Do not go."

"I'll try," Emily said and she turned and leaped over the rubble pile into the waiting darkness beyond.

#

They walked through the night, striking north on Emily's suggestion that the bears' obvious fear of Olympia would make them less likely to search thoroughly in its direction. The truth was that they still had no idea where exactly to go. Queen Adae ruled from Beverlay in Cantelon, but where exactly that was or how to get there was, as Utros might say, a mystery and mystery.

As dawn broke in what Emily assumed was the eastern sky, she forced herself to slow her habitual brisk trot and let her trailing entourage of magicians catch up. For three accomplished Arcanes, they were a sad bunch, she reflected as they stumbled to a weary halt. Marlow seemed to be holding up the best despite his eye, which was still a swirl of inky black, but the loss of Michael's arm had made both him and Elizabeth more withdrawn. The need to apologize burned in Emily's chest, but she couldn't decide whether she would be doing it for Michael's sake or her own, so she kept her mouth shut.

They camped in the shadow of a boulder about Emily's height, a gray rock that loomed incongruously amid the flat green of Arborea's endless meadow. At midday, after an unsatisfying nap, they set out again. There were no more plants, Emily reflected as they went, seasonally inappropriate or otherwise. Even the grass, so lush for so long, was yellowing and thinning. They passed another boulder, then another, and soon the ground itself became a crumbly clay as gray as the rocks.

Through it all, the mountain called Olympia reared higher and wider until it filled Emily's field of vision entirely. In the long, silent hours that they walked, her focus on their unspoken goal became an all-consuming fixation that only ended when Elizabeth made her jump by whispering her name.

"Emily!" The young queen had already said it once or twice.

"Yes! Yes, sorry." Emily shook her head. "What is it?"

"Something is coming," said Elizabeth. "Up ahead."

Emily looked, but all she could see was gray ground dotted with gray rocks. It was certainly possible for something to pass among those boulders invisibly, though, and Elizabeth had heard Utros from far away when the bear had been stuck beneath that overgrown tree.

"Okay, let's hide," Emily said. She stood watch as the others darted for the nearest boulder, putting it between themselves and Olympia. She stood for a moment after her friends reached safety, watching the path ahead, until a faint scraping sound reminded her that she needed to find cover as well.

Emily reached the shielding rock just as something appeared from between two huge boulders about fifty yards ahead. Branches came first, high up, and Emily thought for a moment that it was some sort of walking tree, but then her breath caught in her chest as the creature revealed itself fully. It was eight or nine feet tall, with antlers like a buck, and its face was like a horse's skull, green with moss and lacking a few teeth. Its body was slender and lacked all the little details of a proper human; instead, its bark-like skin made it look more like a tree roughly carved into the shape of a man. Long talons of horn curved down from its hands, which hung at its waist, shackled with black iron manacles. Matching cuffs around its ankles reduced its gait to a shuffle and it wore a thick band of iron around its waist like a belt.

It was a twin to the monster they'd fought in the forest near Barley Bright.

Following after the creature came a pair of soldiers. They wore heavy armor made from what looked like plates of gray ceramic, segmented like an insect's shell; their matching helmets, which covered their faces almost completely, bore antlers like a beetle's which swept up a foot or more from the crowns of their heads. Over the gray armor, they wore tabards of white stitched with a symbol of three stars whose multicolored rays were inter-twined, making a sort of Celtic knot of green, gray, and gold.

Broad, flat-tipped swords like splinty blades hung from their belts; at first Emily thought they both held long spears pointed at the monster's back. As they came out from between the boulders, she realized that one of soldiers did have such a weapon, but the other was holding an iron pole that connected to the monster's belt with a single link of thick chain. This soldier was forcing the creature along ahead of him and whenever the thing seemed to balk or disagree with the path it was being forced down, the spear-wielder would jab it into submission.

"The poor thing," Marlow breathed at her shoulder. His face was crin-kled with worry.

"I'm not so sure," Emily whispered. Around the boulder, Elizabeth peered out for a look of her own, then ducked back suddenly when the monster turned its head.

The path of the soldiers and their captive took them past the spot where Emily and the others hid and as they drew near, she could hear the soldiers chatting quietly. Their voices were muffled by their huge helmets, but they sounded human, and before long she was able to make out their conversation.

"…got more fight in it than the last one, wouldn't you say?" the soldier with the spear was saying. "I've lost count how many times I've had to use this thing."

"That's only because it's more than you've got fingers," said the one holding the pole. "Now shut up, Edrag, I need to focus. You're right about this one. He's a proper fidgety bastard."

"Ahh, but let's take a break," said the soldier called Edrag as they neared Emily's hiding place. He swung the tip of his spear up and jammed the butt into the gray earth, then leaned his weight on the spear and stretched his back. "This damn thing weighs a ton."

"Care to switch?" retorted the other. "I bet you'd—ho! Easy there! Easy, you!" The monster, apparently unwilling to pause for a break, had attempted to dart off the moment the soldiers stopped walking. It dragged its captor a few stumbling feet through the clay before he was able to brace his feet and yank against it. Edrag forgot about his spear and leaped forward to help his comrade, grabbing the iron pole a bit farther down and hauling on it as though he was playing tug-of-war. Together they forced the monster to a standstill, though it wasn't clear to Emily whether they'd really overpowered the thing or just convinced it that any further resistance would be too much bother at the moment.

"Curse of Adam," gasped Edrag between ragged breaths. "If this thing decides to go bear hunting, I quit. Mark the day, Jermone."

"Noted," replied Jermone. "The sooner we pack the beast off to Earth, the better."

The hair on the back of Emily's neck stood up as surely as if it had been hit with an electrical charge. Beside her, she could feel Marlow tense and the others perk up. Elizabeth moved with painful care to bring the soldiers back into view.

"Better slow than sorry," Edrag was saying. "Plenty of breaks, that's what I suggest."

"Convenient," said Jermone.

"Adam's truth," Edrag said, holding up three fingers in what looked like a sign of sincerity. "You didn't hear what happened to Elfric and his team? He was in a hurry just like you, made them march overnight. Well, next morning, what do you expect but theirs got loose. Killed all three of 'em."

Jermone eyed the monster warily, his gaze roving up from its long claws to the antlers high above his head. "Maybe," he admitted. "Still. I'll be a lot happier once we kick it through."

"If only we didn't have to take the shackles off first," Edrag agreed. "Hey, what's it doing?"

The monster had raised its head, pointing its skull-hole nostrils to the sky. Little clouds of vapor appeared from them along with a puffing sound, as though the thing were breathing heavily in cold air.

"Beats me," Jermone said. "You think we'll get a reward if we get back quick?"

"Get off that." Edrag shook his head. "Old King Zero is short on rewards, you know that. Best we can expect is a pat on the back for doing our duty."

"I'd take a pat from Adae—"

"Don't you talk like that," Edrag cut him off. "King Zero'd have your hand if he heard you."

"Who'll tell on me, you?" scoffed Jermone.

"Besides," Edrag went on, "the queen's no bleeding heart either. She's as obsessed with Earth as he is, don't forget."

Emily ducked back around the boulder as Edrag and Jermone began to stir from their break. It wouldn't be easy to keep out of their sight entirely, but if she could get the others to keep the rock between them and the soldiers, and if they could do it reasonably quietly, they might avoid detection all together.

"Come on, you bastard," came Jermone's voice. "Put your head down and get walking."

"Don't make me use the spear, eh?" added Edrag.

A quick glance showed Marlow, Michael, and Elizabeth all watching Emily with wide eyes and held breath, clearly waiting for her direction on what to do next. She put a finger to her lips and was about to motion them to slide around the side of the boulder when a noise froze them all where they stood. It was the same puffing they'd heard earlier, the sound of the monster breathing, and it was louder—closer.

"Come on!" grunted Edrag, followed by the soft *thunk* of him jabbing the creature with his spear, once, twice, three times. "Move it! Push him, Jermone, use your back!"

The ground shook with a sudden screech, louder and longer than any Emily had heard during the fight in the forest. She shared a look with Marlow, wondering if her fear was showing as clearly as his, then dared a peek at the scene on the other side of the boulder.

The antlered horror was stalking straight toward her, only a few feet away, dragging Jermone and his pole behind it.

Emily ducked back around the boulder and pressed herself flat against it, feeling a shot of adrenaline pour into her veins like liquid lightning. There would be no hiding, that much was clear: the monster knew they were there, even if the soldiers didn't.

The creature grunted in annoyance as the sound of scraping and cursing suggested that Jermone had dug his feet in and gotten the thing under control for the moment.

"Okay, big fella, let's all take a breath, let's just take a second and all calm down…" Edrag was close to babbling, but he kept his voice even as he pleaded with the monster. "That's a fella, there we go, nobody wants to hurt you. See, I'm putting the spear away, see? There we go, there we—ah, no, no, no no no—look out—Jermone!"

Something scraped against metal, the creature screeched again, and a desperate scuffle could be heard between a few strained grunts and the sound of boots on earth. There was a crack like a rifle and a broken link of chain whizzed past Emily's head.

Something loomed over top of the boulder where they hid, a pale-faced shape coughing blood: Jermone, rising in a slow arc. The soldier who had held the iron rod latched to the monster's waist was now impaled on it; it pierced the armor over his stomach, passed fully through him, and showed two bloody feet out his back. He slid a few inches down its length with a sound of metal on metal, retching, a look of surprise stamped on his features.

The monster stepped around the boulder; it held Jermone's long pole, which had broken free from its belt, like a spear with the soldier transfixed on the end. Jermone gave a last twitch and fell still. The beast looked down its long skull face at Emily, its cat's eyes unblinking, and puffed from its nostrils. Jermone slid another few bloody inches down the spear and the monster tossed it away; it landed with a thud in the gray clay a dozen yards from them.

Edrag came pelting around the boulder, spear at the ready in a shaking grip. He skidded to a halt when he saw Emily and the others.

"Who in Adam's name—"

The beast rounded on him and he immediately realized his mistake. He jabbed at the thing with his spear, forcing it to flinch as he retreated a few hasty steps.

"Hide!" Emily hissed.

"Where?" Michael retorted.

"Anywhere!" Emily said and then she leaped, clambering up the boulder and over the top. She slid down the far side to where Jermone lay in a pool of blood. She hooked his body with her foot and rolled it over to reveal his sword, still in its scabbard. She pulled it free and gave it an experimental swing. It was like the swords they used for the dangerous game called splinty back at Harkness, wide and flat with a blunt tip and razor-sharp edges, but lighter and better balanced.

"That'll work," she said to no one in particular and charged into the fight. Edrag barely had a glance to spare her as he worked desperately to keep the looming monster away from him. It was still shackled hand and foot, which limited how fast it could advance, and only this kept the soldier alive as he stumbled backwards while jabbing the spear desperately into the thing's bark-like hide again and again and doing no apparent damage.

"Hey, asshole!" Emily shouted, swinging the big sword two-handed. The thing twisted and screeched at her as her blade thunked into its side like an axe striking a tree. Emily wriggled it free and was gratified to see a bit of black, syrupy stuff leak from the wound she'd made.

To his credit, Edrag was stabbing the beast gamely with his spear, though he didn't seem to have the strength to do any real damage. Keeping its slitted eyes on Emily, the creature whipped its hands up in an almost lazy motion just as Edrag's spear came in. Its tip tangled in the thing's manacles and the antlered beast grabbed the spear with both hands and wrenched it from Edrag's grip, then flung it away, sending it twirling off into the distance.

"Shit," said the soldier.

Emily brought her sword around in an overhand chop, aiming for the thing's left shoulder. It brought its hands up and caught the blow with the short chain between its wrists, which split with a bang. The creature shrieked and raised its freed hands.

"You've got to be joking—" Edrag gasped as the beast slammed a fist into his chest with a whirling backhand. He staggered a few feet back and sat down heavily in the clay, his eyes wide, his breath coming in ragged wheezes.

The monster turned back to Emily, now free to focus all its attention on the girl with the sword. The black goop seeping from the cut she'd made had hardened like old sap, making a thick, crusty scab over the wound.

Emily raised her sword. Behind the monster, she could see her friends, who had all decided to ignore her orders and step into the open to watch the fight. Not wanting to give away their presence, she forced herself to keep her eyes on the creature shuffling toward her with its talons extended and its slender chest heaving. Breath came from its skull-nostrils in white puffs. Its ankles were still chained.

Emily darted forward, her sword trailing, then juked to the side just as she came within claw range. The creature turned to track her and she bounced back the other way, forcing it to twist to keep her in sight. Her feet barely touched earth before she jumped again, backwards this time, just outside its reach. The thing lurched forward, swinging a clawed hand much quicker than she'd expected, just close enough that the gleaming talons could rend her chest.

It screeched as its feet tangled in its shackles and it overbalanced, toppling forward to crash to its knees and pitch face-first into the clay. Emily swung her sword like a woodcutter, putting all her muscle into the blow as it came down in a neat arc to sever the monster's head from its neck with a loud *whock* and a spray of black blood.

The sword bit another six inches into the earth and stuck there.

"Good heavens," said Marlow. "Well fought."

Emily wrenched the sword from the ground and raised it again, watching for any sign of movement from the beheaded creature at her feet. A still moment passed as the adrenaline began to ebb from her limbs. The sword became suddenly heavier and she flipped it around and jabbed it point-first into the clay at her feet.

"He's gone," said Michael. He knelt by Edrag, who was still sitting with his legs outstretched like a doll that had been set down for a moment then forgotten. The armor over his chest had been crushed like an eggshell. The color was gone from his face and his jaw was slack.

"Dammit," Emily said. "I didn't realize... dammit." She shook her head, trying to clear her thoughts.

"Who were they?" Marlow asked.

"Soldiers from Cantelon," said Elizabeth. "They spoke of Queen Adae and King Zero."

"She's right," Michael agreed. "Which means the monster came from there as well."

"But they came from Olympia," Emily said. Olympia, where Utros had warned her not to go. Still... "There must be a way from Olympia to Cantelon. Actually, there must be a quick way, because these guys weren't about to take the scenic route."

"What are you suggesting?" asked Marlow.

"It makes sense," Emily said. "Retrace their steps and we'll find Cantelon."

Elizabeth murmured something in Michael's ear and he frowned. "There must be another way," he said.

"What's the problem?" Emily said.

"Utros warned you not to go to Olympia," Michael said. "We heard him. Maybe we should listen to him."

"Are you serious?" said Emily. "He's a bear. I get that they're scared of the mountain, but for all we know it could be because it doesn't have enough salmon."

"I just have a bad feeling about it," Michael said.

"Do you have a better idea?" Emily put her hands on her hips. "Or maybe a map or something?" Michael looked away, chewing his lip. Emily snorted. "Look. For Elizabeth to get her powers back, we have to dethrone Queen Adae. We also just found out that she's the one responsible for the monsters back in Albion. It's a two-for-one deal here, a win-win. The sooner we get to Cantelon, the quicker we can get this whole thing sorted out and go home."

Emily tugged Jermone's sword from the earth and gave it a few test swings.

And tell the Sabre & Torch I finished the mission... without help from Durgan dun Raven.

CHAPTER 9

Olympia stood alone. It had no foothills, no lesser peaks, just a single great mountain that rose from the green plains of Arborea in an endless gray sweep. Far, far above, Olympia ended with a jagged tor like the tip of a knife, around which the dim stars of early night spiraled as though the reaching peak pierced the very center of the universe, itself a slowly turning pinwheel.

Emily stared up at it, contemplating infinity as she trudged across the sloping dead earth below, until she stubbed her toe on a rock.

She cursed and kicked the rock away; it skittered through the dust and disappeared between two of the looming boulders that had become more and more prevalent as they'd neared the foot of the mountain. Behind her, Marlow, Elizabeth, and Michael froze at her sudden motion like a trio of nervous fawns. They were only a few yards back, but the persistent haze that hung in the air on the mountain slope like unwelcome cigarette smoke made them indistinct in the bluing evening. Emily wiped her hands on her pants every few minutes, but they still felt clammy.

The rock she'd kicked clattered to a stop and Elizabeth cocked her head. Emily caught on a second later—the rock had stopped moving, then started again. Which seemed unlikely, to say the least.

"Did you hear that?" Emily whispered.

Elizabeth nodded and murmured something in Michael's ear.

"Animal?" Emily asked. "More soldiers?"

"We're being followed," Michael replied softly.

"How does she know?" Emily asked.

"She knows." Michael gave her a half-smile.

"Okay," Emily said, then raised her voice. "Hey, whoever's out there, we're onto you!" Her only answer was her own echoes, bouncing off the boulders until they receded into silence. She shrugged and set off again, heading further up the long, slow slope.

#

"Yeah, but what *is* it?" Marlow said again.

"It's a statue, I dunno," said Emily. "Come on." She moved to continue, but the magicians didn't follow.

It was more than a statue, even Emily could see that, despite not wanting to admit it. It was a colossus in the shape of a man; it probably would have been forty feet tall if it were standing, but instead it sat on the mountain slope with its knees tucked up to its chest and its arms around them. Its head was down, resting on the knees, face hidden. It wore the full panoply of an ancient Greek warrior, done in exquisite detail from the hairbrush crest atop its helmet to the greaves guarding its shins. A huge round shield, carved with a stylized mountain that closely resembled Olympia itself, leaned against its left shoulder. All this was sculpted in weathered gray stone and covered in a pale greenish-white moss and small needly bushes. A few stray birds sat pecking at the moss but fluttered away as soon as they noticed Emily watching them.

A face appeared over the statue's right shoulder, peering down at them with wide, unblinking eyes. A boy of maybe fourteen, apparently human, clambered the rest of the way up to sit near the colossus's lowered head, swinging his feet in the air. He was skinny, too skinny, with ashen-pale skin and bland gray clothes that hung off him. Emily stared at him and he stared back.

"Hello there!" Marlow called. The boy glanced at him, then went back to watching Emily. Marlow pursed his lips in a moment of thought, then tried again. "Can you understand me?"

"Can you understand *me*?" the boy retorted without taking his eyes from Emily.

Marlow looked at her, too, then shrugged. "Your witness, my learned friend."

Emily gave him a doubtful glance then turned back to the boy. "Hey there!"

The boy waved.

"I'm Emily," she tried. "What's your name?"

"You're not from here," the boy replied.

"No, I'm not," Emily agreed. "Can you help us? We're a bit lost."

"What are you looking for?"

Emily glanced at the Arcanes, who seemed content to let her take the lead with the boy; she had to admit that he only seemed interested in her anyway.

"Cantelon," Emily called back. The boy's eyebrows went up. He slipped silently back over the statue's shoulder and for a moment Emily thought he had fled, until he reappeared at ground level from behind the colossus.

"Where are you from?" The boy stood a few yards away, looking like a skittish deer that hadn't yet decided if he should run.

"We're from Earth," Emily said. She took a few steps toward the statue and the boy. "I'm Emily, this is Marlow, and that's Elizabeth and Michael."

"You're all from Earth? Is it nice there? Warm? Plenty to eat?"

"Yes, it's fine." Emily looked back at the others uncertainly. "Are you hungry?"

Something decisive crossed the boy's face. "I'll take you to the Counselor. I'd like to answer your questions, I really would. Maybe I can."

"That would be great, thanks," Emily said. The boy turned and set out instantly, moving quickly among the rocks and rubble of the slope.

He headed roughly west, in a path that would go all the way around the base of the mountain if they gave it enough time, and didn't look back. Emily hustled to catch up with him.

"Where are we going?"

"To Barbary Cross," said the boy. His voice dropped to a conspiratorial whisper. "I shouldn't tell you this, but I live there, and the Counselor does, too."

Emily was about to ask who the Counselor was when a grinding noise from behind made her turn. The others were hustling toward her; just beyond them, the colossus was moving. As she watched, amazed, it turned its head toward her. Then it lifted its arm, tearing through sheets of moss and the roots of a few bushes to do so. Soon its hand was extended, palm out, in a gesture that clearly meant *stop*.

"We should hurry," said the boy and there was no doubting the urgency in his voice. Emily let him lead on as Marlow, Michael, and Elizabeth caught up.

"What is that thing?" Marlow puffed as he drew even with the boy.

"You're also from Earth?" the boy asked. Marlow nodded. The boy frowned for a moment. "I'd like to tell you, really. We'll see what the Counselor says."

#

Another colossus guarded the gate into Barbary Cross, which hung rusted and permanently open. This statue, which crouched on one knee with a leaf-bladed sword plunged into the ground at its side, looked much like the one on the slopes, and was equally furry with moss and small plants. But its details were unique and it was marked with chips and gashes that looked to Emily's eye like real scars of battle.

As they passed under the gate into a wide plaza of cracked cobblestones, Emily was reminded immediately of the Castle Forlorn: crumbling, dejected, and echoingly empty. Just as the Irregulars had been unable to fill the castle's many dormitories or command more than one or two tables in its Great Hall, the population of Barbary Cross seemed entirely inadequate to the size of the city.

The buildings that faced the square had probably once been grand; the remnants of friezes clung to their walls, and white marble showed here and there beneath a layer of grime and the same pale green moss that covered the colossi. Their windows were open and black, staring out like skull's eyes. Against the backdrop of the mountain, it was hard to tell where a building ended and the slopes began.

The boy led them across the square toward a broad avenue that seemed to run the length of the city. As they passed by a dead, dust-filled fountain at the heart of the plaza, Emily saw the first signs of movement around them. Two women, their hair covered by scarves the same drab color as the boy's clothing, stood talking at the door to one of the great buildings. They'd blended into the background all but completely and Emily only realized they were there when one adjusted her scarf and revealed a momentary flash of bright red hair. The color disappeared when the woman's companion said something that made her laugh and cover her face. She put her hand on her friend's shoulder in a familiar gesture, then glanced up at the sound of Emily and the others moving past her.

She froze, her mouth half-open in an aborted smile. Her face was lined and ashy, with sharp cheekbones, and her expression settled back into a cautious neutrality as she turned away. She murmured something to her companion and they disappeared together into the nearby doorway.

"Friendly," said Emily. The boy didn't respond, so she tried again. "Is your home around here?"

The boy looked at her with his wide eyes, which she realized probably seemed bigger than normal due to his malnourishment.

"Not right now," he said.

"Do many people live in the city?" They'd reached the avenue that led off from the square and Emily felt the uneven street beneath her feet begin to angle upwards as they headed up the side of the mountain. The avenue ran more or less straight, aimed like an arrow toward a low, wide building that sat half-nestled in the cradle of Olympia's slopes.

To Emily's utter unsurprise, the boy didn't respond, but led them up the street in silence. Before long they reached the far end, where the way terminated in a small square before the colonnaded entrance of a squat temple-like structure that appeared to be built mostly into the side of the mountain. Even compared to the faded grandeur of the buildings near the city gate, this one had a distinctly shabby-splendid air; the white marble was clean enough to show some of its old glory, reminding Emily of some ancient Greek or Roman ruin. As they approached, a hooded man scuttled out from between the columns, his head down, and disappeared down a side street.

The boy stopped halfway across the square and gestured to the temple. "You can ask the Counselor all your questions in there."

"You're not coming in?" Emily asked. He gave her one last lingering, wide-eyed stare before fixing his eyes determinedly on the ground and heading back the way they'd come.

"Lovely chap," said Marlow.

"He's scared," Michael said.

"Certainly," Marlow agreed. "But of what?"

"Let's find out," Emily said and set out for the colonnade without looking back. The others followed after a moment and they soon found themselves passing under marble eaves into the cool dimness of the mountain.

The interior of the temple was no less tumbledown than the rest of the city. Illegible frescoes of flaking, peeling paint covered the walls of a large tiled foyer where a few doors faced in green copper hung at angles from rusted hinges. Only one was still seated properly in its jamb, at the back of the room, and after a moment this opened to reveal a hooded man like the one they'd seen leaving. He raised his gaze to them, his face hidden in shadow.

"You are here to speak with the Counselor?"

"Yes," said Emily.

"Wait here," he replied. "I will return for you in time." He returned the way he'd come in, shutting the door behind him with a decisive click.

Emily found a seat on a pile of rubble that had cracked away from one wall. She leaned her stolen sword nearby, stretched her back, and watched as the Arcanes explored the room. Michael and Elizabeth slowly examined each of the frescoes, discussing the fragmentary images in low voices that Emily couldn't make out. Marlow peered through each of the open doorways and even went a little way down a hall behind one of them, but returned with a shrug and sat near Emily.

Eventually Michael and Elizabeth also ran out of things to catch their interest and sat against the wall across the room. Emily frowned, trying to guess how much time had passed. Half an hour at least, maybe more. She found her mind wandering and her thoughts bounced back and forth between images of Jack and, unaccountably, Sir Maximilian. She stood, stretched, walked the perimeter of the room, sat back down in the same spot where she'd started, and immediately stood up again.

"Let's go."

"What?" Marlow glanced up at her from his spot on the floor.

"They're wasting our time on purpose," Emily said. "Whatever they're hiding, it doesn't have anything to do with our mission. So come on, up and at 'em. We can find Cantelon on our own."

Elizabeth whispered something into Michael's ear then settled her gaze on Emily, her chalky hair falling in a curtain over one eye.

"You have a better idea?" Emily said. "I'm open to suggestions."

Michael stood up. "Let's be patient."

"That was me being patient for the last half an hour," Emily replied. "This is me getting sick of it."

Elizabeth swiped her hair over her face, hiding it completely.

"Emily," Marlow said carefully, "maybe Michael is right. Every time we've been hasty here in Arcadia, we've been punished for it."

"Is that what they teach at Starling?" Emily said. "Fine. You're all welcome to sit around here and rot. I'm going solo."

Behind her, the copper door clicked open.

"The Counselor will see you now," said the hooded man, his voice a blank.

Emily sighed and crossed her arms. Her stomach gave a sudden noisy rumble as a pang of hunger stabbed her in the guts. Michael reached out his remaining hand to help Elizabeth up and Marlow stood and brushed dust from his pants. The three Arcanes followed the hooded man through the open doorway. Emily wrinkled her nose, picked up her sword, and went after them.

The room beyond was illuminated in a warm, red glow lacking an obvious source. It was longer than it was wide and empty other than a throne of gray stone where a humanoid shape sat in the dimness. Emily couldn't even guess at its gender and as she approached she realized that the shape was made of the same stone as the throne and almost featureless. Beyond the throne, hidden in shadow, there seemed to be some sort of pit that spanned the width of the room and reached its back wall.

The hooded attendant stepped to one side and the figure on the throne raised its smooth head as though looking at them one by one.

"You are seeking answers," it said. Its voice was as neuter as its shape, but carried an unexpected warmth. When it spoke, a patch on its chest glowed red in time with its words, looking almost like a beating heart.

Emily was about to ask how to find an entrance to Cantelon, but Marlow spoke first.

"What happened to this city?"

The Counselor angled its head in a gesture of sorrow. "Adam came."

The effect of those two words was electric; Michael grabbed Elizabeth's hand and Marlow stiffened, straightening his back. A little thrill even ran down Emily's spine, though she knew it couldn't compare to what the boys from Starling were feeling. Their friend had come this way and apparently brought tragedy with him.

"Did he destroy Olympia?" Marlow asked. "Was it like Arborea once?"

"No." The Counselor straightened and set its gaze on the Albian. "Olympia has always been gray. Adam did not conquer us."

"Why not?" Emily stepped forward.

"The people of Olympia created defenses against him," said the stone figure. "The Paramounts guarded them. They drove Adam away."

"You mean those statue things?" Emily asked.

The Counselor inclined its head in a nod. "Cronos guards the lower slopes. You saw Crius at the city gate."

"So if they beat Adam, what's the problem?" Emily spread her hands in a sort of half shrug. "What's everybody afraid of?"

"They are not afraid," said the Counselor. "They are cautious."

Emily snorted and crossed her arms. She was getting tired of the people here refusing to answer simple questions. Still, this was their only shot at moving their mission forward and she wasn't going to waste it.

"Where's the nearest entrance to Cantelon?"

The Counselor's blank face stared at her. "There were many entrances, once. They are all closed now. You cannot go there."

"But—" Emily started, but the Counselor cut her off.

"It is time for you to leave," it said. "Return down the mountain to Arborea. Do not come back."

The hooded attendant stepped forward, putting himself between Emily and the Counselor's throne. "I will show you out."

"Look," Emily said, "we just need to know how to get to Cantelon. Point us that way and we'll be out of your hair."

"That is not possible," the Counselor said. "You will leave Olympia now."

Emily took a step forward, rolling her shoulders. "Sure. By way of Cantelon."

"Do not threaten us," said the Counselor.

"Emily—" Michael tried.

"They obviously know where it is," Emily said. "Let's get some answers and get going." The hooded man put up a warning hand and Emily pushed it down.

"Let's—" Marlow started, but his words were lost under a sudden rumble that shook the chamber, shaking dust from the ceiling like a gray

110

snowfall. Behind the Counselor's throne, something moved in the darkness of the pit. A hand as big as Emily appeared over the lip of the hole, then another, and then a massive head appeared as a colossus—a Paramount—twice the size of the others they'd seen levered itself up from the shadows.

Its head came first, a plumed helmet like the one on the first Paramount they'd seen, its stone bristles brushing the ceiling of the room. Its eyes glowed with misty blue pinpricks that left trails against the ruddy light of the room. Next came shoulders nearly as wide as the room itself and a chest like the face of a skyscraper, in ornate stone armor where decorative carving intertwined with countless battle scars.

The Paramount stopped, because there was no more room for it.

"Go back," it said.

Emily stumbled as she turned to obey and saw that her friends had already run.

#

Emily was far out in front when she hit the street moving at a full sprint. She'd gone about a hundred yards past the square when she realized how ridiculous she looked. The avenue was empty and she was alone, unless the sense of being watched from the dead windows of the crumbling buildings lining the boulevard was instinct and not just imagination. A glance back up the street showed her friends also running, crossing the square in front of the Counselor's temple. Nothing was following them.

Emily sauntered back up the street to meet them, shaking her head as the Arcanes came to a puffing stop in front of her.

"That was maybe not our finest moment, guys," she said.

Marlow leaned back, his hands on his hips, and took a few gulps of air with his eyes on the sky. "Maybe not."

"That thing was incredible," Michael breathed. Elizabeth clung to his good arm, her face paler than usual. "You could feel the power flowing off it."

"Did the Counselor say they *made* those?" Marlow shook his head. "What kind of civilization was this?"

"Whatever it was, Adam ruined it," said Michael. "Even if he never conquered them."

"I wonder what happened," Emily said.

"I can tell you."

Emily turned in surprise to see that the boy who'd led them to the temple had silently returned. He looked up at her anxiously, his huge brown eyes looking black in the gathering dusk. His gaze flickered to a side street, then he straightened up and raised his chin.

"We'd love to hear it," Emily prompted gently.

"My great-grandmother told me stories," the boy began. "She was here when Adam came. Olympia was a place of builders." His eyes roved over the grand facades of the buildings all around them. "Food doesn't grow here, so we built everything we could and traded with Arborea for the rest. Things were good until Adam came, or at least that's what great-grandma said. She said he had an army of bears who walked and fought with weapons like people. We needed something to fight back, so we made the Paramounts."

The boy glanced at the temple, looking like he expected the Paramount inside it to come smashing through the colonnade to crush them all at any second.

"What is it?" Marlow asked.

"No... nothing," the boy said. "I'm fine. The stories... they made the Paramounts and it worked. Adam couldn't conquer Olympia. He gave up, moved on to Cantelon. But the Paramounts... my great-grandmother's people told them to defend Olympia. To keep invaders out. They kept Adam out, but after, they didn't understand the difference between an invader and a friend."

"So they kept *everyone* out," Marlow said softly. The boy nodded. Marlow blew out a long breath, his eyes soft. "Why are you telling us this?"

"I had to tell someone," said the boy.

"So the Paramounts guard the ways to Arborea *and* Cantelon?" Emily asked.

"Yes," the boy nodded. "Arborea is all around us and Cantelon is underneath." He shrugged. "Enemies in every direction."

"It must be hard to be a Paramount," said Elizabeth, the first words she'd spoken aloud in days.

Emily ignored her. "Then there must be an entrance to Cantelon in the temple."

"You want to tangle with that thing?" Marlow looked at her with eyebrows raised.

"Do you have a better plan?" Emily asked. Marlow held her gaze, but said nothing. Emily cracked her knuckles, first one hand, then the other. "Then leave that *thing* to me."

Marlow turned to the boy, concern lining his face. "Can Paramounts be beaten?"

"Everything has its weakness," the boy said.

"But you're not gonna tell us what it is, are you?" Emily said. The boy looked away, his head down, his shoulders slumped.

"No."

#

Under cover of night, sneaking into the Counselor's temple was surprisingly easy. Whether it was depopulation, ignorance, or sheer apathy, the people of Barbary Cross apparently couldn't spare a guard. The foyer was still as Emily moved silently across its tiles, the three Arcanes in tow. They crossed to the copper door and Emily eased it open.

113

The room beyond was the same lurid red as before, but the Counselor's throne sat empty. The pit behind it was featureless black. Emily crept forward in a half crouch, sword slung over her back with a strip of cloth, eyes scanning the room for motion or any sign of traps. Her breath caught in her throat as she passed the throne, but nothing moved.

The pit gaped beyond, opening into who knew what, but Emily was confident that she'd guessed correctly. The pit would lead them to Cantelon, where King Zero, Queen Adae, and their monsters waited. All she had to do was figure out how to beat the Paramount that blocked the way.

"What's your plan?" Marlow asked, peering into the pit at her side.

"I used to fight mechs that size at Harkness," Emily said. "Well, almost that size. Whatever, it doesn't have a lot of room to maneuver in here, so…" She shrugged. "Shouldn't be too bad."

The first time the Paramount had come up, it had done so slowly, shrugging its great bulk over the edge of the pit in an intimidating display of power. It had moved deliberately, one piece at a time, rising foot by foot, staring them down.

This time it moved quicker than Emily ever could have guessed. One second there was nothing, no movement, just an empty black space of unknown depth. Then there was a fist, a great mass of gray stone filling her vision for a terrifying instant before it crashed into her at speed and sent her skidding back to slam into the throne, which cracked with a sound like a gunshot as everything went blank.

CHAPTER 10

The dragon's jaws sheared Sir Maximilian in half and Emily woke up. That wasn't the sound of foot-long teeth rending steel armor; it was the Paramount's huge fist smashing the tiled floor where Marlow had stood just a moment before. She'd only been out for a moment, hardly longer than a blink.

Emily bounced to her feet, hands itching for the weight of the hammer the bears had taken from her, but her looted sword would have to do. She unslung it from her back and charged at the Paramount with a yell. The colossus turned its massive head, staring her down with its glinting blue eyes. It was only half out of the pit, unable to come any farther into the throne room, but easily able to reach far with arms the length of full-grown trees.

The Paramount swung a fist at Emily and she jumped straight up, aiming to land on its arm with her blade in wood-chopping position. Instead the massive hand shifted direction at the last second and slammed upwards into her as she came down, breaking her rhythm and sending her tumbling up and back. She turned the fall into an arcing backflip that she just barely landed without falling over as she threw her huge sword out for balance.

The Paramount's other hand swept in from behind her like an oncoming train; it was trying to crush her like a fly between its palms. She threw herself flat, hoping to get under the blow, but the colossus adjusted its aim. As the hands bore in, Emily shoved her sword up to wedge between them lengthwise. The broad blade bent with a screech, then snapped, sending the upper two feet of the blade twirling up to stick in the ceiling as the hilt and lower blade spun away into the pit. The colossus's palms clapped closed with a bang, clipping Emily's heel as she sprang toward the cracked throne and away from the blow that would have surely turned her to paste.

"Shit!" was the best she could manage between gulping breaths as the Paramount renewed its attack. It had clearly settled on her as the number one threat, ignoring the Arcanes who had retreated to the door after Emily had drawn the thing's attention. Some magical support would have been nice, but given what had already happened to Michael and Marlow, Emily couldn't blame them for hanging back.

The colossus's eyes flared, changing momentarily from pinpricks to blazing lanterns, and bright beams of blue-white fire lanced out like the plasma-rifle bolts Emily had dodged back on Finalhaven.

"That's not fair!" Emily gasped as she leaped forward over the sweeping beams and tucked into a roll that brought her skidding up to the opposite wall. The Paramount immediately swung its head in the other direction, bearing down on her with its searing light. She jumped straight up and kicked off the wall, but the colossus was just as quick as she was, and when she hit the tiles behind the throne, the eye beams sheared the back off it almost before she could duck.

Someone stood on the other side of the throne, between Emily and the Paramount. It was Elizabeth, empty-handed, her white hair unbound, Aminah's sweater hanging off one pale shoulder.

"Lizzie, get down!" Emily screamed, but the young queen didn't move.

Instead, she spoke.

"Let us talk," she said.

Emily watched, tensed to spring out and pull Elizabeth back, as the blazing beams from the Paramount's eyes blinked out and it turned its focus to the little white shape in front of it.

"Let us talk," the colossus agreed, settling its person-sized hands to either side of Elizabeth.

"Seriously?" Emily breathed.

"I am Elizabeth I Pendragon, rightful queen of Albion," she continued. "I am headed to Beverlay in Cantelon on royal business. I request safe passage for myself and my companions."

Emily straightened up to watch over the cut-down remains of the throne. The Paramount angled its head in a decidedly sorrowful gesture.

"Kings and queens," it murmured, if it was possible for a voice like breaking thunder to murmur. "Greetings, Pendragon and rightful queen. I am Hyperion."

Elizabeth stepped forward, moving to the lip of the pit where Hyperion loomed, and reached up to place her slender hand on its great stone face.

"Why are you awake when the others sleep?" she asked.

The Paramount blinked slowly. "I woke to my brother's cry. Astraeos called for help and I heard, but could not act."

"Your brother?" Emily said. "Another Paramount?"

Hyperion fixed its gaze on her and cocked its head, then turned away.

"You cannot leave here," said Elizabeth, "but you ache for your brother." The colossus nodded once. "Where has he gone?"

"To Cantelon," said Hyperion, "dragged down by those who rule there."

"King Zero and Queen Adae," Elizabeth said, and Hyperion nodded again.

"So I wait," said the Paramount. "Hoping that some agent of Cantelon will come with answers."

"Have they come?"

"No." Hyperion's voice was heavy. "They come and go from other entrances. Secret entrances that the Counselor has not closed. I can feel them. But they do not pass this way."

"They fear you," said Elizabeth and suddenly the colossus reared up so its shoulders struck the ceiling and chips of stone fell around the room like a hailstorm.

"They *should* fear me!" it roared and the room shook from its voice. Then it slumped forward again. "But they do not come this way."

"We are going to Beverlay," Elizabeth said softly. "Our hope is to turn Queen Adae out from her throne. Will you let us through?"

"Will you find Astraeos?" the colossus asked.

"We will try," said Elizabeth.

"We'll get your brother back," Emily said. "Don't worry. The king and queen are going down."

This time, Hyperion didn't even bother to look at her. Instead it kept its gaze on Elizabeth, who also hadn't acknowledged that Emily had spoken.

"Come," said the Paramount. "I will bring you to Cantelon. I cannot guide you through its many halls, but I will warn you: it is a place of soldiers and spears. They will not like your coming. If you go to Cantelon, go there to fight. Otherwise you will go there to die."

#

Hyperion made a staircase from its own limbs, bending and angling them so Emily and the Arcanes could descend into the pit by following them down in a spiral around the Paramount's body. As they went, the colossus was so totally still that Emily would have sworn it was just a statue if the bruises flowering all over her body weren't there to remind her otherwise. In the rush of the fight she'd forgotten that Michael couldn't just heal her if anything went wrong and a prickle of embarrassment crept up the back of her neck until she pushed the thought away.

"Go there to fight," Hyperion had said and Emily had every intention of doing so. Her scuffle with Hyperion itself had been cut short by Elizabeth before it really got serious, leaving Emily frustrated, amped up, and

118

eager to find out whether the beetle-antler helmets that Cantelon soldiers wore would crack when you banged them together.

Emily hopped off Hyperion's foot at the bottom of the pit and found herself in a wide, echoing cavern with a soaring ceiling where stalactites dripped in the darkness. Easily the size of a football field, the chamber extended deep into the mountain; the pit they'd come down was just a little notch cut into one end to allow access to the Counselor's temple. Far off in the darkness, there was a source of light, like a faint white circle painted on the distant cavern wall.

They headed for the light in silence and soon Emily realized she was looking at the mouth of a tunnel, lit from within by glowing crystals that crowded the ceiling and walls. A shadow moved across the light, roughly human-sized, and then another. Emily stopped short and put a hand out to tell her friends to do the same.

"Someone's there," she whispered. "Two—no, three at least. Guards, I think." Another shadow had crossed the tunnel mouth and Emily was pretty sure she'd recognized the curious helmet of a soldier of Cantelon.

"What should we do?" Marlow asked.

"Stay here. If I can get the drop on them, this'll be over quickly."

Emily crept forward, keeping away from the fringes of the light from the tunnel. Soon she found her questing fingers brushing a damp cavern wall; the glowing opening gaped maybe ten yards away. She pressed herself against the stone and listened, but heard nothing. The guards must have heard them coming down—maybe even heard her brief fight with Hyperion—and would do nothing to give away their position. Clearly they hoped the intruders would come to them.

Emily was only too happy to comply.

She sidled along the wall until she was only a foot from the tunnel mouth. Now she could hear them: the scuff of a boot, the scrape of segmented armor, the rattle of a sword handle in a gauntlet. She yearned momentarily for the sword Hyperion had snapped, but put the thought away. She'd have a new one soon.

"Where are they?" said a male voice within the tunnel and the tiny distraction of the question was Emily's cue. She took the corner into the crystal-choked corridor as tightly as she could, keeping her back to the glowing wall as she entered the light. The corridor stretched a few feet and then, across from Emily, widened into an area of what looked like worked stone. Around the curve of this new opening she saw a slice of a soldier's armor—just his back, from his heels to the crown of his helmet—and watched him shift his weight from one foot to the other.

Emily slipped across the tunnel so she was now on the wall that opened into the little space that was probably a guard post. She took a deep breath, held it for a moment, blew it out silently, and leaped out to bull rush the soldier whose back she'd glimpsed.

They went down together, the soldier dropping his sword in surprise; Emily snagged it from the air before she hit the ground. She bounced back to her feet and aimed a wild chop downwards at the soldier beneath her. It caught him in the shoulder as he tried to stand and bit through his gray armor to scrape against bone. Emily wrenched it free as the soldier fell back to the stone floor, clawing at the shattered pauldron where blood was welling up.

There were two other soldiers in the guard post, just as she'd guessed, and they had their swords at the ready. A quick glance showed that one of them was just slightly off balance, leaning a bit forward, perhaps from a hasty drawing of his blade, and Emily sprang for him with her free hand leading the way. Unable to pull back in time, he caught her fist on the jaw, and Emily followed up by slamming the blunt tip of her sword into his chest. The soldier fell backward onto a low wooden table, which snapped a leg, scattering hexagonal playing cards and tin plates of half-eaten food across the floor.

The third soldier came at her swinging, but he clearly lacked her superhuman speed and strength, and the sword moved as if in slow motion. She slapped it aside with her own blade, ducked inside the soldier's guard, and hooked her foot behind his back heel. He crashed to the ground in a tangle of armor and she kicked him in the head before leaping clear.

Two of the armored men lay gasping on the ground; as for the one she'd just kicked, his chest was moving with the shallow, even breaths of unconsciousness.

"Thanks for the fight, boys," Emily said. She pulled over one of the wooden chairs the soldiers had pushed aside in anticipation of a fight, picked up the plate with the most food left on it, and helped herself to some dinner.

Marlow, Michael, and Elizabeth joined her eventually and found her just cleaning off the last of the third plate of food.

"There you are," Emily said, licking a bit of a tangy brown sauce from her fingers. "I was starting to get worried."

"You were worried?" Marlow said, his eyebrows high. "Mithras save me, we thought you were dead. We heard a fight, then you never came back for us, so we figured..." His gaze took in the beaten soldiers, one of whom was acting as a footrest for Emily during her meal. "Well. It looks like you had things in hand."

"Yep," Emily agreed. "I was about to ask these guys the way to Beverlay."

#

They caught a few hours of sleep at the guard post before moving on. Emily argued against it, but the fact was that they were all exhausted, and when she finally let her guard down, she fell instantly into a deep black sleep unworried by dreams.

She snapped awake a few hours later, but found the three Cantelon soldiers still stripped of their armor and safely tied up. After a moment of deliberation, she shook Marlow awake. He woke Michael and Elizabeth as Emily gathered their gear and tried on the stolen armor. None of it fit her quite right—she was shorter than the guards—so eventually she tossed one suit and gave the other two to the boys.

They spent the better part of the day walking. There seemed to be a main thoroughfare, a wide, straight corridor of smooth stone that headed deep into the mountain and seemed to trend inevitably downward. They stopped just once, in a cavern where the only source of light was a crystal-floored pool that stretched farther back than Emily could see, to rest and eat what was left of the guards' food. They set off again as soon as possible, following the beaten guards' directions. Emily was just starting to worry that they'd been lied to when a city came into view that could only be Beverlay.

The tunnel they'd been following opened onto a narrow shelf above a sort of interior crater, a miles-wide bowl that formed the floor of the largest cavern Emily had ever seen. It stretched so far above her head that the ceiling was invisible and she could only judge its breadth by the receding lights of the city that filled the caldera entirely.

They glowed in every color imaginable, a star-spattered rainbow of crystal pinpricks in the eternal night at the heart of the mountain. For sheer square mileage, Beverlay was easily the equal of Boston and if the lights were any indication it was just as densely populated.

"Emily." Marlow put a hand on her arm. Emily glanced over to see the magician pointing along the shelf, where two soldiers in the familiar beetle armor were approaching with a strange, glowing creature. It moved like a lizard, with its head low and a long tail swishing behind it, but it was easily larger than a komodo dragon and made entirely of pinkish crystal.

"Time to go," Emily said and stole one last glance back at the patrollers as she herded Marlow ahead of her. About thirty yards along the shelf, a ramp curved out and down towards the city, making almost an entire circle before reaching the cavern floor half a mile below. Michael and Elizabeth started down it as a shout came from the guards.

"Stop, there!"

"Run!" Emily ordered and they did, pounding down the spiraling ramp with the soldiers close behind. It was agonizing for Emily to keep pace with the Arcanes, who moved as slowly as normal humans, but she forced herself to stay behind them in case of the worst. Luckily, it seemed that the crystal lizard, for all its intimidating size, couldn't move very fast.

Soon they reached the base of the ramp, at the outskirts of the city. Buildings of piled stone and glowing crystal rose ahead of them as they sprinted toward their promised shelter. The four Gifted ducked between the nearest two buildings, which looked like warehouses, as the guards made the cavern floor. Emily pushed past the Arcanes and sprinted ahead to check out their options; the city seemed to be laid out like a spiderweb, with broad avenues radiating out from a central point, streets connecting these, and alleys cutting at random among it all.

Emily dashed back to her friends and pulled them along behind her down a zigzagging path that cut left and right down random streets in what she hoped was an unpredictable pattern, but that led eventually toward the city's heart at the center of the spiderweb.

Where, she hoped, they would find the palace.

The few people they passed in the streets watched with dull-eyed disinterest as they sprinted past. Elizabeth stumbled and Michael caught her, pulled her arm over his shoulders, and half dragged her as she gasped for breath. The guards were nowhere to be seen and Emily dared hope that they'd eluded them when another breathless turn brought them suddenly face-to-face with a high wall of black crystal.

They'd reached the palace. A narrow street curved away in both directions, running the perimeter of the circular wall. Emily picked a direction at random and set off again, sparing only a second to make sure the magicians were following. Another hundred yards brought them breathless to a gate where two guards with tall halberds stood at rigid attention. Emily forced herself to breathe, willing her pounding heart to slow as she gulped down much-needed air. She strode toward the guards at what she hoped was a casual pace.

"Hello, we—"

"There they are!"

Emily spun to see the two soldiers and crystalline lizard puffing their way up a broad boulevard that ran from the palace gate to a plaza maybe a hundred yards distant where a single huge crystal glowed red.

The guards at the gate swung their halberds down into fighting position, clearly aiming to pin the four Gifted between themselves and the approaching soldiers. Emily darted forward and grabbed the shaft of the nearest halberd, set her feet, and wrenched it around so the guard holding it slammed into his companion and they both tumbled to the street empty-handed. The two soldiers and their lizard had nearly reached her, so she hurled the halberd at them like a javelin, but it wasn't made to move that way and wobbled off to the side to clatter off the wall of a nearby building.

"Come on!" Emily barked and dashed past the fallen guards. Marlow followed and Michael and Elizabeth came after him, the queen still leaning on the magician for support.

Beyond the gate was a ring-shaped garden that followed the wall and within that, like the smallest of a set of nesting dolls, was the palace. It was carved from what looked like a single cyclopean outcropping of crystal, hollowed and worked by human hands, with every color imaginable gleaming from its black depths.

Another pair of surprised-looking guards stood at the nearest door. Emily led the charge toward them and when they lowered their halberds and set themselves she didn't slow or change direction. Instead she let them attack, dropping into a feet-first slide as the long blades flashed over her head by an inch. The halberds clattered together and Emily popped up to put her fist into the jaw of one guard as a blind backwards kick took the other in his chest. They hit the ground as the three magicians caught up, the original two soldiers and lizard still hard on their heels.

The palace doors swung open at a shove and the four Gifted piled into a long hall of shifting crystal colors. The floor was a parquet of white wood, loud under their running feet. Heavy wooden doors, hanging in openings cut into the crystal walls, ran along either side.

"Throne room?" Emily asked as they ran.

Elizabeth, hanging from Michael's arm, said something faintly, and Michael pointed to a large double door at the far end of the hall.

"That way!"

Two side doors crashed open simultaneously as they passed, ejecting two more sets of guards. These were accompanied by pinkish animals not unlike the lizard thing behind Emily, but standing on two legs instead of four.

"Go!" Emily shouted, shoving the magicians ahead of her. As they stumbled toward the double door, Emily turned to face the newcomers. There were six in all, armed with swords instead of polearms, plus the original two patrollers and three crystal creatures.

"Who's first?" Emily said.

"Emily, come on!" Marlow shouted. Emily dared a glance over her shoulder and saw the magicians hurrying through the open double door into a bright chamber beyond. A look back at the assembled guards suggested that they weren't going to come at her one at a time politely, but were instead gathering their courage for a massed rush that would bury her under their combined weight. Almost an unfair tactic, but she had to approve.

So she ran, pelting through the door with the soldiers close behind. Elizabeth had been right—this was the throne room for sure, a tall circular chamber lined with columns of gray Olympian stone that ran some thirty yards to a raised dais where two huge thrones stood. They were roughly made from a strange mixture of crystal and iron, color and black in a swirling mixture like ink stirred into water.

A young woman, dressed all in black, sat on the larger throne, her dark face a perfect mask of surprise. Another half dozen guards, swords drawn, stood between her and Emily.

"Stop!" commanded Queen Adae. Her voice was like thunder in the great chamber. The guards from the hall skidded to a halt only a few yards from the intruders. They were surrounded.

"Emily—" said Michael.

"*When Adam's daughter flees her throne*, right?" Emily said. "She runs, Lizzie gets her power back, we walk out of here."

Michael started to respond, but Emily ignored him, dashing out between the stone columns with her sword up and ready for the first swing. Behind her, soldiers swirled around the three Arcanes, leveling their weapons to make obvious the price of resistance.

"No!" shouted the queen of Cantelon.

The guards between Emily and the queen weren't afraid to meet her. They charged her with their swords high, making a loose curve to try to flank and envelop her. Instead, she jumped, clearing the beetle-antlered helm of the central soldier with six inches to spare. Twisting in the air, she hit the ground facing the guards' backs.

A slash of her sword brought the nearest one down, shattering the backplate of his armor and driving him to the floor. She hit the next in the side as he was turning, striking with the flat tip of her blade so he flew a few yards through the air before slamming into a column.

The third came at her from the left, swinging his sword two-handed, but Emily caught it easily with her own and twisted it from his hands. As he stumbled forward in surprise, she drove her heel into his knee; the armor buckled, the knee inverted, and he fell.

"Stop! Stop!" Queen Adae was yelling. Her voice didn't sound so thunderous now, just scared.

The fourth and fifth attacked together, one low, the other high. Normal humans were just so sluggish in their movements, creeping along like a slow-motion movie. Emily kicked the sword from the hand of the lower soldier and crushed the face of his helmet with her heel on the backswing; the higher attack went over her rolling shoulder and she turned the dodge into a throw that sent the guard crashing along the floor, skidding on his back like an overturned insect.

The sixth guard froze in place.

Emily brushed past him and stalked up the steps of the dais to where Queen Adae sat paralyzed on her throne.

"Please, no," she choked. Tears glistened in the corners of her eyes. "Wait."

Emily raised her sword.

Chapter 11

Marlow was there, shouting, and Michael was behind him waving his hands frantically, and the remaining guards were coming toward her not understanding how slowly they moved and how much time she had to kill the queen, but it was Elizabeth who stopped her.

The queen of Albion stepped in front of the queen of Cantelon. Her face was still, her green eyes placid, and Emily saw that there was a smattering of freckles on her bare shoulder.

"Emily, don't."

"The prophecy," Emily said, her sword high, but it was starting to feel heavy. Incredibly, Elizabeth smiled, and some of the old light was in her eyes.

"Prophecies are complicated things," she said. "I've read many of them. Often enough we must throw away our first interpretation, and our second, and our third, before we can understand how our first was in fact correct."

Emily lowered her sword. "But the monsters." It had all seemed so clear, so simple, a moment ago. "We have to stop the monsters."

Elizabeth put a slender hand on Emily's arm. Behind her, Queen Adae watched the exchange with wide eyes. A silent moment passed and then Adae stood and gently pushed Elizabeth to one side, stepping forward to look Emily in the eye. She was nearly Emily's height, with skin the color of burned umber with a flush like rose quartz beneath it; Emily thought immediately of the crystal walls of the palace with their many hidden colors. Her hair was black, wavy, and incredibly long, tied up with broad ribbons of black-and-gold checkers. She wore a circlet of black iron around her head and a black gown with gold stitching at the seams so fine as to be almost invisible.

"This is all a misunderstanding," said Adae. She had fine lines around her eyes. "I'm sure Emily didn't really mean to hurt me."

On the floor of the throne room, the soldier who'd bounced off a column groaned, stood up, and sat down again.

"No, of course not," agreed Elizabeth.

"Right," said Emily.

"And for our part, allow me to apologize for your treatment by my guards." Adae spread her hands. "Of course, we would prefer if you made an appointment, but there was no cause for such a response. You are guests in Cantelon and we welcome you."

"Thanks," Emily said. Her adrenaline had ebbed away, leaving her tired and hungry.

"Excellent." Adae nodded. "Emily, would you introduce your friends?"

"Oh, sure," said Emily. "I'm Emily Sledge, from Earth. Actually, we're all from Earth. This is Elizabeth, she's—uh, and that's Marlow Bright and Michael Fletcher."

Michael and Marlow approached. They wore matching expressions, looking like they'd both just been electrocuted and were waiting for their brains to reset. Marlow actually seemed to be trying to say something but failing.

"Pleased to make your acquaintance," Adae said. "Now, where is my majordomo?" The queen clapped her hands and a curtain in the back wall opened. Through it came a tall, slender crystal lizard that stood on two legs like the ones Emily had faced off against in the hall. It was a deeper color than the others, more purple than pink, and carried a simple iron rod.

Adae smiled. "There you are, Eneph. We have visitors from Earth. Give them a tour of the palace, please, then show them to the guest quarters so they might freshen up. Alert the kitchen; we'll have a formal supper tonight."

"I don't suppose you could show us around," said Marlow. His voice sounded like his tongue had swollen to twice its usual size and he still seemed a bit dazed.

"I've much to attend to," Adae replied. "Come, Eneph, our guests are waiting."

The thought of touring the palace, with its heavy walls of crystal, made Emily's head hurt. She needed fresh air, or what passed for fresh air in an underground cavern, and she needed time alone.

"Your majesty," she ventured, "would it be all right if I explored Beverlay a bit?"

"Certainly." Queen Adae cocked her head, her eyes locked on Emily's. "I think you'll find it quite lovely. Explore all you wish; my people are quite friendly. Just don't bother them if they are busy with work. Oh, and be sure to return in time for supper."

#

Queen Adae was right, Emily had to admit: when she wasn't being chased through it by armed guards, the city of Beverlay was beautiful. Most buildings were a mixture of stone and crystal and the streets were wide and clean. A glittering river meandered through the streets, crossed and recrossed by stone bridges and occasionally ducking down into the stone to tunnel beneath a shop or apartment then reemerge a few blocks away.

The city folk who'd stared blank-faced at their chase scene seemed just as disinterested now, though whenever she caught one's eye, the person would unfailingly light up with a smile before looking away. It was cheery the first few times, but the consistency started to unnerve Emily as one after another smiled and turned their back. Still, compared to the gray misery of Barbary Cross, Beverlay was positively joyful.

She turned a corner and discovered a square where a throng of people milled around, chatting, yawning, and eating the last few bites of sandwiches and other portable meals. There were maybe two dozen of them, men and women ranging from her own age to elderly. Emily took up a post along the wall of a facing building, trying to make herself inconspicuous as she watched.

As the minutes passed, the mob sorted itself into a neat line that snaked around the perimeter of the square, passing by Emily and nearly looping back on itself. In the open center of the plaza was a large rectangle cut from a single flat stone, which the people avoided. Emily's curiosity got the better of her and she reached out to tap a nearby woman on the shoulder. She was rewarded with the same smile-and-turn she'd come to expect, so she tried again.

"Hey, what's going on?"

"Off to work!" the woman said chipperly. She had ruddy cheeks, long, straight hair, and wrinkles at the corners of her eyes and mouth.

"Oh, where do you work?" Emily asked. The woman's smile faltered a little, then returned.

"You know how it is," she said. "Busy busy!" She shrugged. "But you have to get by."

"Yeah," Emily persisted, "but doing what?"

If the woman intended to reply, she was cut off by a sudden grinding noise from below their feet. In the center of the square, the rectangular slab was angling up to reveal a gaping entrance into the ground. With a final *thunk*, the slab locked into place at about a forty-five-degree angle, and the line of people began to move forward. One by one they shuffled down into the mouth of the opening that had been revealed.

"Hey, doing what?" Emily called as the long-haired woman walked away. She didn't look back. Soon the square was empty except for Emily herself and the slab lowered back into place. The people were gone as though they'd never been there, swallowed up by the earth itself. Somewhere in the distance, someone laughed, then fell silent.

Eventually her wandering brought Emily to another small plaza between four tall buildings that looked like housing. Crystal poles as high as Emily's waist lined its borders, shedding a soft pastel light over a square that was empty except for a familiar rectangular slab at its center. She sat on a bench carved from crystal and watched people hustle by with their heads down. Aside from the curiosity of the entrances into the underground, Beverlay had started to lose its charm—too many straight avenues, identical structures, briefly smiling people—and was no longer working the magic of occupying her mind. As Emily's interest in the city waned, the dark thought coiled beneath her consciousness reared up and demanded attention, and as she sat in hunger and exhaustion, she let it rise.

If Elizabeth hadn't stepped between them, Emily would have cut down Queen Adae.

She sighed as though letting out a single breath she'd held all afternoon. There it was, the cold, hard truth that had been itching at Emily since Elizabeth's green eyes stayed her hand in the throne room: she'd gone too far.

Or had she? All signs pointed to Queen Adae as the author of all their current problems. The prophecy called for Adam's daughter to leave her throne and a crown of iron to be replaced, and Adae fit both lines perfectly. And the queen of Cantelon was responsible for the monsters invading Earth, that had been confirmed by the soldiers they'd met in the wilds of Arborea as well as the Paramount Hyperion.

Emily kicked at a chipped stone near the foot of the bench, sending it skittering across the square. It wasn't crazy to kill an evil queen. That was the kind of work the Sabre & Torch did every day. What would Durgan dun Raven or De Soto Rigmaiden have done? Emily had a hunch neither man would have hesitated.

So why had she?

"Is it a boy?"

Emily nearly jumped at the voice. There was a girl sitting next to her on the bench, maybe thirteen. She had the same jeweled brown skin as Queen Adae, though her pin-straight brown hair reminded Emily more of Elizabeth's. Her simple shirt was cut from some rough tan cloth but clean and well-fitted and her white skirt was the same way. A single turquoise stone shone in the lobe of her left ear.

"What?" Emily said.

"You've got this face on," explained the girl. "My dad says I always get that face when I'm thinking about boys. So I asked if it's a boy."

"No."

"Oh." The girl screwed up her mouth in thought. "A girl?"

Emily laughed. "No, not a girl either. Just… grown-up stuff."

"You're what, twenty?" The girl looked doubtful.

"Eighteen."

"Really? You look—" A noise across the plaza distracted the girl from the pressing question of Emily's age. She pointed and Emily saw a few people shuffling into the square. "It's almost time!"

"Time for what?" Emily asked.

"Work," said the girl. "I meet my dad here after school. He's got the evening shift, so he's always asleep when I leave in the morning."

They watched people enter the square, milling around like Emily had seen before, until the girl jumped up with a yelp of joy and ran to a tired-looking man in gray clothing who emerged from one of the apartment buildings facing the plaza. A smile appeared on his face like the sun from clouds and they shared a deep hug. Emily had to smile watching, but it was also impossible not to think of her own dad. They'd been like that, once, when Emily's parents had worked for the Prime Minister of the Secret Commonwealth. Then Mom had died and Dad had lost his arm and suddenly the space between them had become a chasm.

Across the plaza, father and daughter chatted animatedly, until he put his hand on her shoulder and said something with a serious face. The girl hung her head—she was remarkably incapable of hiding her feelings—and the man hugged her tight for a long moment. The others in the plaza were already making a line and the man moved to join them. Shoulders slumped and hands in pockets, the girl mooched off across the square as the rectangular slab in the center began to rise up.

Her angle brought her close enough that Emily could see the tears in her eyes.

"Hey!" Emily waved. The workers began shuffling down into the mouth of their underground passage. There was something about her tears—Emily's heart went out to her, but it was more than that. This girl was the only person in all of Cantelon she'd seen display an attitude other than polite cheer. Nevertheless, despite being obviously less interested in chatting now that her father had come and gone, the girl slouched back to Emily's bench.

"Yeah?"

Emily racked her brain for something to say to cheer the girl up and settled on the first thing that came to hand. "Why do you think I look twenty?"

The girl's brow furrowed. "Seriously?"

"Seriously," Emily said.

"Well, uh…" The girl scratched her neck. "You're kinda muscly."

"Muscly?"

"This can't be news to you."

"I'm a lot smaller than a lot of kids I know," Emily said.

"Then you know some big kids." The girl dropped onto the bench and Emily's mouth quirked up in a half-smile of satisfaction. "Where are you from? And don't say Cantelon, I'm not an idiot."

"You're right," Emily allowed. "I'm from pretty far away."

"Where everyone is muscly?"

"Sort of."

"Could you lift this bench?"

Emily snorted a surprised laugh. "Wanna find out?" She stood and gave the bench a look over. The crystal looked lighter than solid stone and the kid couldn't weigh more than a hundred pounds…

The girl shrieked with incredulous laughter as Emily bent her knees, aligned her back, and deadlifted the whole thing with a satisfied grunt. It was a bit lighter than she'd guessed, so she curled the bench and girl up to her chest, paused for a breath, got her hands in position, and pressed the bench straight up over her head.

She was about to let the load crash back to the ground like they'd always done in the gym at Harkness when she remembered the girl on top. Instead, she dropped to her knees and gently lowered the bench back into something roughly like its original position, if slightly askew from the glowing crystal poles on either side.

The girl's eyes were like dinner plates and her mouth hung open like a cartoon of amazement.

"Guess so," Emily said.

"That was incredible," the girl breathed. "You're so lucky."

"Lucky?" Emily dropped back onto the bench, shaking out her arms. She'd never thought of it that way, not really. She knew that most people weren't Gifted, of course, but she'd grown up in the Gifted world, where the superhuman was commonplace and the incredible merely average. Her parents had been just as strong as she was and they'd been thrown out like yesterday's garbage when their employer was voted out of office. She snorted. "No, I've just spent my life training."

"For what?" The girl's admiration shone on her face.

"Oh, uh…" Emily didn't know how to answer that. For what? She knew the official answers down pat: to keep the Gifted community, not to mention humanity at large, safe by sending back anything dangerous that came through the Veil between the worlds. To coach the next generation of Combat Gifted. To serve her government or another one like it. To fight, and fight, and fight, until they didn't need her anymore.

Of course she'd nearly killed Queen Adae. It was what she was trained for.

"To lift benches, obviously," Emily said at last.

"You're weird," said the girl.

"Thanks," Emily said. "Hey, what's your name?" It hadn't even occurred to her to ask until now.

"Mere," said the girl. "What's yours?"

"Emily."

"That's pretty," said Mere. "It's dinner time. Want to come? You can meet my mom."

"Dinner?" Something turned over in Emily's memory. "Oh, shit! I mean—uh—shit! What time is it?"

"Dinner time?" Mere shrugged.

"Mere, I gotta go." Emily jumped up from the bench. "Thanks for chatting with me."

"Wait!" said the girl. "If you come over tomorrow you can meet my dad."

"Tomorrow?" Emily blinked. "When?"

"Breakfast time."

"Shouldn't you be more specific?"

"Shouldn't you be on time to dinner?"

"Unbelievable." Emily sighed. "All right, Mere, I'll see you tomorrow."

#

For the second time that day Emily found herself running through the streets of Beverlay, though at least this time nobody was chasing her. It was hard to say why she cared so much about being on time to dinner, but eventually she settled on not wanting to embarrass her friends.

Emily jogged through the palace gate, where the halberd-wielding guards flinched away from her, and into the front hall of the palace. There she skidded to a halt, realizing she had no idea where dinner was, or the three Arcanes, or their guest rooms. Luckily, she wasn't alone: Queen Adae's majordomo, the slim purple crystalline lizard, stood with his iron rod as though he'd been waiting for her. Eneph, that was his name—but did he speak English?

The majordomo pointed to a side archway with his rod. Emily blinked, then followed the command, pushing through the heavy wooden door with the lizard at her heels. It opened into a long, curving hallway lined with more doors along both walls. Eneph pushed past her and moved swiftly along the hall to a door about halfway down, which he opened with a bow. Emily hustled through it.

There was a table, lined with chairs which were filled with people, and behind every chair was an attendant standing with a cloth napkin and a crystal ewer of water, and the table stretched a hundred yards down a long, long hall so that at least two hundred people sat and another two hundred stood and every single one of them was looking at Emily.

There was silence except for the slap of her feet on the stone floor as she walked the length of the table. She passed a dozen doors as she did and it occurred to her that Eneph easily could have let her into the hall much closer to her seat. Finally she reached the head of the table, where Queen Adae sat in a tall wooden throne, with a matching chair empty at her side. Elizabeth sat at the queen's left hand, with Michael across from her and Marlow next to him. The seat next to Elizabeth, one down from where Adae waited with a blank expression on her face, was empty.

"Excuse me," Emily said. The scrape of the chair on the stone floor was like a scream in the silent hall and it was just as loud when she pulled it back under her to sit. Across from her, Marlow gave her a look that hinted at just how long the assembled diners had been waiting for the fourth guest of honor.

Behind him, a door opened. The hallway beyond was bright, making the figure that stood in the crystal archway little more than a black smear that cast a long shadow across the floor of the hall. At first, Emily thought he was wearing one of the beetle-antlered helmets that she'd seen on all the soldiers of Cantelon, but as he moved toward the empty throne she saw that his armor was different.

It encased his entire body, leaving only a vee open over his face to show his dark eyes wandering over the assembly and his thin lips arching in a frown. It was made in the same fashion as the cyclopean thrones in the throne room, crystal and iron swirled together like liquid, but the crystal of the armor was a uniform smoky gray that revealed nothing of what was beneath. Instead of antlers, his helmet bore three twisting horns that made a fan across his head. It clattered as he walked, much louder than Emily's own worst moment, and he seemed to enjoy being the only source of noise and focus of all attention in the room.

The armored figure lowered himself into the throne beside Queen Adae. He raised his hand and lowered it again and behind the diners, the rows of neatly arrayed servants began to pour drinks as the guests slowly struck up conversations up and down the long table. Across from Emily, Marlow blew out a long-held breath.

King Zero had come to dinner.

CHAPTER 12

King Zero removed his helmet. His lank black hair spilled around his face as he placed the helmet on the floor beside his throne. He straightened up in his chair and swiped a few greasy strands from his eyes. He was like a drawing in black ink on white paper; under the jet hair his face was as pale as a skull. Even his eyes were the gray of erased pencil. He was older than Queen Adae; deep lines on his face pulled his mouth into a permanent frown and made his eyes look sunken and shadowed. His hairline was receding, though the hair itself spilled down to his armored shoulders, and his nose jutted out like a hawk's beak over thin lips. He was the most evil-looking person Emily had ever seen.

"Ladies and gentlemen, if I may make a toast." Marlow stood, a crystal goblet in his hand. A wave ran down the table as the guests' faces turned. Marlow raised his goblet in a sweeping motion that covered his entire place setting, which was empty except for a glass of water, and said, "The queen."

Adae and Zero sat still-faced as the assembled company repeated the toast and drank. The liquid that slid down Emily's throat was like fire, with a hint of blackberry, and if there was alcohol in it she couldn't taste it. Marlow sat and the guest next to him immediately stood. He was a portly, ruddy-faced man in a three-piece suit, with thinning, slicked-back black hair. He swayed a bit as he raised his own goblet.

"Well toasted, sir," he said, glancing down at Marlow, "well toasted. Then, as ambassador to Cantelon and the official representative of the

First Baron Wasteland of Deseret, let me make a toast to the royal lineage. The queen, her ancestors and her descendants, Adam first of all."

Emily blinked in surprise at the unexpected mention of Jack Twelve-Fingers' home, Deseret, and his father the Baron. Nobody else seemed to think anything of the presence of another person from Earth in the hall, though; the diners drank the strange toast as the first course was placed in front of them by the rows of straight-backed servants. At first Emily thought it was a geode, with a rocky crust and a jeweled interior, then her stomach did a backflip as she realized she was looking at a slab of meat from some sort of crystalline creature, maybe even one of the lizards she'd seen around the city.

She picked at the food half-heartedly as Elizabeth struck up a conversation with Adae.

"What a lovely set of toasts," she said. "I would enjoy hearing more of your lineage, your highness, if you don't mind."

"It would be my pleasure," Adae replied. "My ancestry is pure. My father was King Adama, who married Queen Nothing. His mother was Queen Danae, who married King Nobody. Queen Danae's father was, of course, Adam." She gave Elizabeth a smile. "So you see that there we have no confusion over the line of secession in Cantelon and no pretenders. And as for descendants, well." She glanced at King Zero, who was fully engaged with his dinner. "That is a question for the future to answer."

"King Zero is an interesting name—" Emily started, but Elizabeth gave her a short, sharp shake of the head that cut her off as surely as a punch to the throat. Emily coughed awkwardly and the servant behind her leaned forward with a napkin that she pretended to need as she prayed the conversation would hurry up and move on. Fortunately, the ambassador from Deseret was eager to grill his fellow Earth-born humans. He looked at Marlow as he spoke, but he was loud enough for their entire end of the table to hear.

"Tell me, friend, what brings you to Cantelon?" He smiled, making his cheeks look like gleaming apples. "Marlow Bright, was it? Is that an Albian accent I detect, Mr. Bright?"

"It is," Marlow said.

"Elizabeth is here on behalf of the Albian government on Earth, Mr. Lopez," said Queen Adae.

"Is she!" Lopez's eyebrows went up. "Is she indeed!"

"Yes," said Elizabeth, watching Lopez from beneath lowered eyelids.

"No," said King Zero. He gestured at Emily with his fork, where a chunk of crystalline meat hung quivering. "Don't cover for them, Adae. You missed quite the show this afternoon, Grant. This one tried to kill the queen."

Emily opened her mouth, but no sound came out. Marlow choked momentarily on his food and Michael thumped his back. Even Elizabeth seemed lost for words. The long table was silent.

"It was a misunderstanding, dear," said Queen Adae. "And no harm done."

Something moved behind Emily, making her stiffen, but it was just her servant removing her untouched crystal meat and setting down a bowl of spicy-smelling stew. There was no telling what it was made from, but at least it had the color of Earth food, and Emily was ravenously hungry. She dug in, grateful that everyone at the table had something to do with their mouths other than ask questions.

That excuse ran out eventually, though; Emily wasn't surprised to find that King Zero was the first to finish his food after her. His gaze caught hers and he pointed at her with his spoon, his sunken eyes narrowing.

"You asked about my name," he said. It wasn't a question.

"Oh, I just..." Emily's mouth was suddenly dry.

"It's a tradition," said King Zero. "Nothing more. When King Adam took a wife, he called her Queen Noone. The convention stuck around and when Queen Adae chose me as her consort, she gave me this name." He laughed suddenly, a bark that echoed in the high-vaulted hall. "I like it! But make no mistake, I am no puppet. I am as much king as Adama or Adam himself. The queen and I rule Cantelon together. Isn't that right, Adae?"

"We rule together," the queen agreed, her eyes on her food. "Nobody commands King Zero."

Zero sat back, looking smug, as a servant set a sort of gelatinous dessert in front of him. He dug in immediately and Emily looked down to confront her own serving. Another brief period of quiet fell. Rather than being sweet, the gelatin tasted like it had been spiced with cinnamon, cumin, and something smoky that she couldn't identify.

"Someone tell a story," said King Zero. His glance fell on Michael. "You there. How did you lose your arm?"

"Michael is a magician on Earth," Elizabeth interjected. "Strange ailments are their stock in trade."

"And your eye." Zero pointed to Marlow. "The same?"

"Yes, your majesty." Marlow held the king's gaze steadily, but Emily could see the tightness around the Arcane's jaw.

"I see." King Zero set down his dessert spoon. "Well, I am finished. Allow me to give the final toast of the night." He stood, goblet in hand, and all along the table the other diners stood as well. Emily joined them, grateful for any excuse to get out of her chair and one tiny movement closer to leaving the dinner entirely. A subtle change came over the king's face, a crinkling around the eyes that could have been humor or suspicion or both.

"To the Curse of Adam," he said. A murmur ran down the table like a wave and heads turned in anxious glances, but the guests recovered and raised the king's toast in voices that almost matched their enthusiasm at the start of the dinner. Zero waited until every one of them had repeated his words, then, with a satisfied smile, grabbed his helmet from the floor and stalked off with it under his arm.

#

Eneph, the crystalline majordomo, chaperoned the four Gifted and the ambassador from Deseret back to the section of the palace where the guest quarters lay. The circular building didn't really have wings per se; instead it seemed to be composed of a series of concentric rings with the throne room at the center and short halls connecting each layer. Emily was reminded of old medieval depictions of labyrinths that she'd seen in her Arcane friends' magical texts. It would be easy to hide, sneak, and spy in this palace and even easier to get lost.

Eneph bowed his goodbye when they reached a short, curving section of the outermost hall given over to guest chambers and Elizabeth led Emily to the small suite they'd be sharing, which was adjacent to Michael and Marlow's own set of rooms. Elizabeth opened the door, which was unlocked, and Emily was about to follow her in when a quiet cough behind her made her turn.

"You missed the formal introductions," said the Deseret ambassador. His face was still red and he'd loosened his tie and unbuttoned the collar button of his shirt. "Had better places to be, I imagine?"

"Something like that," said Emily.

"Well, allow me to introduce myself properly." The ambassador gave her a half bow, making his tie swing momentarily as it dangled free. "Grant Lopez, ambassador plenipotentiary to Cantelon, serving the First Baron Wasteland, First Father, Layer-On of Hands—"

Emily held up her hand. "I know the rest."

"—Beloved Giver of Laws," Lopez continued, "Bringer of Miracles, and Wise Administrator of the Gifted Nation of Deseret." He smoothed his tie and adjusted his vest. "Hm. You are?"

"Emily."

"Pleased to meet you, Emily," said Lopez. "Did you really try to kill Queen Adae?"

"It was a misunderstanding," Emily said. "Look, I'm pretty tired—"

"I don't mind." Lopez waved a hand in dismissal. "Your friend Elizabeth is here on behalf of Albion, isn't that right? Smart move. Deseret was the first of the Gifted Nations to reestablish relations with Arcadia following the coup, you know. Surprised it took so long for another ambassador to arrive."

"Other Nations know about Arcadia?" Emily asked.

"Certainly," said Lopez. "One of the easiest worlds to reach through the Veil, you know. Bit tricky to manage the time difference, but it's all to our advantage on Earth. I can spend a year here getting to know the locals and only a month's lost back home."

"So Deseret and Arcadia have an alliance, or…?"

"Nothing so formal." Lopez rolled his eyes. He still seemed a bit drunk. "A friendship, let's say. All the Nations are looking for friends these days. Things are changing, you know. Borders are shifting. Especially down south. You're from the Secret Commonwealth, aren't you?"

"How'd you know?" Emily had to admit, she was a bit impressed.

"You've got that Harkness look about you." Lopez shrugged. "The American Nations aren't all so stable as the good old Commonwealth. There's that business between the Grand Kingdom and Sabine, for example."

"Business?" De Soto Rigmaiden was from the Sabine Free State, Emily remembered. Though of course as a member of the Sabre & Torch Society he'd given up any attachment to his old home, just as she had.

"Oh, just a little border thing." Lopez shrugged again—it was starting to seem like an affectation. "I'm sure they'll sort it out soon enough."

"Well," Emily said with what she hoped was polite finality. "It's very nice to meet you, Mr. Lopez."

"Please," Lopez said, "call me Grant. And—may I give you another piece of advice?"

"Sure," Emily said.

"Keep an eye out." The ambassador tapped his own cheek near his eye. "A royal line as young as Adae's is an unstable thing. Still working out the kinks, you know. They'll either expand or implode, that's how it goes with these new royals. Make sure you don't get caught in the blast radius."

In the brief delay of Emily's conversation with the ambassador, Elizabeth had already gotten in bed. Emily sighed and followed suit, crawling between the scratchy sheets of the strange bed with her clothes on, steeling herself for a night of wrestling with her conscience despite her physical exhaustion.

She was nearly asleep when Elizabeth spoke.

"You are not well, Emily."

"I beg your pardon?" Emily sat up and her sheets slipped down to her waist.

"You are different from the girl I met on Finalhaven."

"Sorry to disappoint you by growing up," Emily said.

"Please," said Elizabeth. "I mean no insult. I'm worried for you. I saw death in your eyes today."

Anger swelled in Emily's chest like irritation around a splinter. Something in the queen's tone, all sensible and concerned, the way she was restarting an argument Emily had already had with herself earlier, made her feel like a child being spoken down to. What right did Elizabeth have to judge her—Elizabeth, who'd lived in two rooms her entire life, with her food brought on a silver cart and nothing to worry about except which book to read that day?

"You have no idea what you saw."

Morning came eventually, as crystals set into the walls of their suite faded into rainbow-hued brightness at whatever hour the people of Cantelon thought guests ought to be waking up. Elizabeth was already gone, which suited Emily just fine.

Pulling on yesterday's clothes, Emily resigned herself to not being able to find a shower and set out into the curving halls of the palace, hoping to avoid her friends entirely on her way out to the city. Her actions in the throne room sat on her shoulders like a too-heavy squat bar that she couldn't push off, and Elizabeth's solicitousness still rankled. What else was she supposed to do? Queen Adae was sending monsters to Earth and stood between Elizabeth and her magic. She was the perfect target for the Sabre & Torch brand of justice.

A series of friendly guardsmen—presumably none of the ones she'd kicked around the day before—guided her to the front hall and she set out into the city to keep her promise to meet up with Mere. The girl's home was easy enough to find; Emily recognized the bench she'd lifted, still at an angle to the light poles on either side, and the image of Mere running to greet her father as he stumbled from their front door was seared into Emily's memory. Soon she found herself knocking on a plain wooden door that hung in walls of stone.

It swung open instantly, revealing Mere wearing a stained apron and a wide smile.

"You came!" the girl said. "Come in! Mama is just finishing up breakfast."

It smelled delicious, Emily had to admit as she followed Mere into the house. The inside was cozy, far homier than an apartment with walls of stone had any right to be. It reminded Emily of Marlow's house at Barley Bright, with a sort of rustic farmhouse charm that was far from the urban austerity she'd grown up in.

She was about to shut the door behind her when she heard a familiar grinding noise. The stone rectangle in the center of the nearby plaza began to rise, despite the lack of any workers queued up in the square. Emily paused, her hand still on the doorknob, and Mere came up behind her impatiently.

"What are you—oh," the girl said, her eyes following Emily's gaze. The slab thunked into place and for a moment, all was silent again in the plaza.

Then a monster marched out of the darkness. It was draped in chains that weighed down its slumping head, held its arms against its body, and reduced its footsteps to a clanking shuffle, but Emily's heart still leaped to attention in familiar terror as she realized she was looking at another of the skull-headed, great-antlered beasts she'd fought twice before.

"What is it?" she whispered.

146

"That's the project," said Mere. "The one everyone's working on."

"Mere, breakfast!" a woman's voice called from another room. "Is your friend joining us?"

"Coming, Ma!" Mere shouted back. "Come on."

Emily followed the girl through the cozy sitting room into a cramped dining room, just large enough for a round table and four chairs. Mere's mother came through a swinging door on the opposite wall a moment later, carrying two plates of steaming pinkish meat and what looked like brown scrambled eggs.

"So nice to have company," she said, putting the plates on the table as Emily and Mere pulled up their chairs. Emily shut her eyes and took a sniff—as long as she ignored the colors, the food actually seemed delicious.

"Thank you," she said. "It smells great."

Mere's mother stood expectantly by as they ate. Every now and then Emily tried to catch her eye and give her an appreciative smile or make a little noise of enjoyment, but the woman kept the same expression of bland contentment on her face. Finally, it was too much.

"Aren't you hungry?" Emily said.

"Ma always waits until we're done," Mere said.

Emily fixed her eyes on her plate and tried to hurry. Soon enough she was finished and pleasantly satisfied, her belly properly full for the first time since they'd come to Arcadia. Mere's mother cleared their plates and didn't return.

"Shouldn't you be going to school?" Emily asked as soon as they were alone.

"I could," said Mere. She raised her eyebrows. "Or..."

"Or what?"

"Or I could show you the project."

"The project." Emily sat up straight. "The one underground? Where the monsters are coming from?"

"Yup." Mere's mouth quirked up, betraying her pleasure at having an interesting secret.

"How?"

"We'll just say we're going to visit Dad at work."

"Will that work?" Emily spread her hands. "Aren't you forgetting someone?"

"Nope." The girl chewed her lip. "I used to have an older sister. She died. We can just say you're her."

"Wait, she *died*?" Emily blinked. "There's no way that would work. Whatever guards they have would know she died, right?"

"What?" Blank confusion crossed Mere's face. "Why?"

"Why?" Emily stumbled for the words. "Why? Because... you can't just pretend someone's still alive!"

"Sure you can," said Mere. "It took a year for my aunt to find out Tish was dead and that was only because Ma started crying during dinner. Then my aunt told us that my uncle wasn't actually just busy with work... it was a weird day."

"So nobody tells anybody when someone dies."

"Nope."

"So the guards could really believe I'm your sister."

"Yep. We can't bring your friends, though."

"My friends?" Emily blinked.

"I saw them with you when you were running around last night. Looked fun."

Emily buried her face in her hands. Here she thought she'd finally found a nice, normal family... but maybe there *was* no such thing as normal when it came to families. There was another problem, though. For all her moxie, Mere was just a kid. Emily hadn't even started at Harkness at her age. However nonchalant she was about visiting her dad underground, Emily had a feeling it wouldn't be so simple, or so safe. Could she really put a kid in danger like that?

Memories of her own childhood flicked across her thoughts like photos in an album. She hadn't been at Harkness yet, but she'd certainly been a troublemaker. Scampering through the prime minister's offices with Clea Coates, dodging guards and politicians as they played made-up games. Defending Clea when a group of older boys picked on them… and returning home with the inevitable black eyes and bloody lip afterwards, Clea bouncing all around her as she told an only slightly embellished version of the fight to the concerned grown-ups looming above them. The twinkle in her father's eye as he pressed an ice pack to her face.

"Let's do it," Emily said.

#

They waited in the plaza until the next shift gathered and went underground behind them. Nobody stopped them; nobody even bothered to give them more than a polite smile when their eyes accidentally met. They shuffled down the exposed ramp into the lamplit shadows of a short stone corridor that quickly split in three directions.

Guards posted at the intersection did question them, briefly, but they bought Mere's story that Emily was her sister Tish and that was that. The girl led the way down a twisting series of tunnels with their walls brightly whitewashed and doors spaced evenly down their lengths. It was almost cheerful compared to the gray stone and dim colors of the city above and Emily said as much as she trailed behind Mere.

"They had to paint it over," Mere explained. "My dad said these tunnels used to be a museum or an archive or something. I guess the walls were all covered with paintings. King Zero had them all painted over."

"Any idea why?"

"It was all old stuff, from before Adam. When I was little they brought up piles and piles of books and papers and burned them all. It took forever for the smoke to clear out."

"What was it?"

Mere shrugged. "Just junk. I dunno. Hey, we're here."

Rather than a door, the tunnel ended at an ornately carved stone archway that opened into a large chamber with smooth whitewashed walls and a hardwood floor that was incongruous after all the rocky tunnels they'd

149

walked. Its ceiling rose thirty feet overhead in chambered arches of brick like a medieval cathedral. The floor was marked with rectangular discolorations at even intervals, maybe every ten feet, that had Emily baffled until she realized they reminded her of the rows of shelves in the Harkness library stacks.

Whatever had once been here had all been stripped out and now the room was a laboratory. Dozens of gray-clothed technicians bustled around low wooden tables covered with all sorts of inexplicable implements. If she had to guess, Emily would have put the ratio at about half scientific and half magical, but it would have taken at least one of the Arcanes, plus her mechanically minded friend Chris McLeod from Harkness, to be sure.

Emily was about to ask Mere if the girl had any idea what they were looking at, when a pair of techs rushed by pushing a rolling cart bearing something large under a purple cloth. Intrigued, Emily trailed them at what she hoped was an inconspicuous pace, making sure to keep them in sight as they pushed their way through the crowded lab.

They stopped at a long metal bench where glass bulbs full of various colored liquids hung like IV bags connected via glass piping to a tall, headless humanoid shape that looked to be made from stone and moss. It was familiar, but Emily couldn't place it as the technicians with the cart had a hurried conversation with their counterparts around the body.

A decision was made and the two cart-pushers rushed back to pull the purple cloth off their burden as the others hastily locked chains over the stone body. The cloth came off, revealing a grinning white shape underneath: another long, toothy skull with huge antlers spreading like branches. The two techs locked eyes, counted to three in unison, and heaved the skull from the cart to the metal table, dropping it just above the body. There was a flurry of activity as all half dozen people did something that seemed to attach body to skull. Then, almost as one, they stepped away from the metal table.

Faint blue pinpricks of light flared up in the eyes of the skull. A tremor ran down the body and at the end of its left arm, a finger moved, and then another.

CHAPTER 13

"Hey! Kid!" One of the lab attendants pointed at Mere, who froze. "Yeah, you. What's your name?"

"Mere," stammered the girl, as Emily glanced around for something to serve as a weapon.

"Mere, that's right." The technician waved. "And you must be Tish. Haven't seen you down here in years. Your dad's not in yet."

"I was just showing Tish around," Mere said. "But we were just—"

"Wait." The tech raised a gloved hand, then hooked a finger at them. "Want to see something interesting?"

"Sure," Emily said, moving forward and dragging a reluctant Mere with her. The technician stepped aside, giving them a better view of the operating table where the monster stirred feebly, the lights in its eyes fading in and out as it rocked its skull-head back and forth.

The tech looked at them expectantly. "Incredible, isn't he?"

"Viktor!" Mere said, snapping her fingers.

"Yes?" said the tech, a bemused smile growing on his face.

Mere looked at her shoes. "I'm sorry, I forgot your name for a minute."

"Viktor," Emily said. "You... made this?"

"We did, yes." The tech nodded. "Almost makes all this worth it."

"Makes what worth it?" Now that her initial rush of fear was passing, Emily was burning with curiosity.

"Viktor is from Olympia originally, isn't that right?" Mere said.

"Yep," Viktor said, scratching the back of his neck. Behind him, the creature groaned and gave a little dusty puff from its nostrils. "A bunch of us are. My grandma worked on the original Paramounts, you know."

"We know," said Mere.

"So what happened?" Emily asked.

"King Zero happened." Viktor's tone was hushed and he glanced around the lab before continuing. "His soldiers came up from Cantelon and took us to work on his little projects down here."

"That's terrible," Emily breathed.

Viktor shrugged. "He's the king, after all."

"Wait, I thought he was the king of Cantelon."

Viktor glanced at Mere with a raised eyebrow. "She new here?"

"My sister is, uh…" Mere laughed nervously. "Yeah."

Emily's breath caught. Clearly she'd done wrong to reveal her ignorance about the political structure of the world within the painting.

"Whatever," said Viktor. He looked at Emily, his mouth quirked to the side. "Zero calls himself High King and usually he's got the soldiers to make the rest of us play along. But back in my grandma's day there was a *proper* High King, until Adam came."

"The High King ruled Cantelon, and Olympia, and Arborea?" Emily asked.

"And people actually wanted them there." Viktor shrugged. "Or that's what Grandma said."

"But that changed when Adam took over."

"Yeah. He conquered Arborea first, but I guess he gave it to the bears. They're still waiting for him to come back, poor idiots. Then he tried to do Olympia, but we made the Paramounts and fought back. They've caused their share of problems, but it worked. So."

"And then he came down here?"

Viktor nodded. "Cantelon was always the real prize. Still, I think it wouldn't have fallen if they hadn't given the princess away."

"Princess?" Emily shook her head. There were always so many moving pieces to keep track of in royal politics.

"Princess Anne," said Viktor. "The High King's daughter. They married her off for some alliance, I don't know. But then there wasn't really an heir, so there was nobody to resist Adam after he killed the High King. You know how it is."

"I guess so," Emily said. "What alliance—"

"Hey!" Viktor shouted, spinning around as the monster on the bench began to thrash against its chains. A few of the glass pipes leading into its body snapped, spraying colored fluids over the panicking technicians. Viktor shouted directions as the techs rushed to reconnect the broken lines and tighten the thing's chains.

"Get me a syringe," Viktor snapped to an attendant who promptly slapped a long steel needle into his hand. He shoved his way past two struggling techs and grabbed one of the woody slabs that covered the thrashing creature's body like armor. Tugging it up, he revealed gray flesh underneath, into which he promptly jabbed the metal syringe. The creature roared once, shaking the laboratory, then fell still. For a moment Emily thought it was dead, until she saw its chest rise and fall in a long, shallow breath.

Viktor turned back to Emily and Mere, his face pale and shining with sweat. "Sorry about that. You kids should probably move on, wouldn't you say?"

"Nice meeting you," said Emily, but Viktor's back was already turned.

"Anyway," Mere said, "that's what my dad does for work. He's not from Olympia, but he has his own team, just like Viktor."

"He's chattier than the other Olympians I've met," Emily said.

Mere shrugged. "They're all a little cold when they first get down here, but they're really pretty nice people." Her eyes lit up. "Hey, wanna head back? We could tell my mom I came home for lunch. She likes making lunch."

"Sure, I guess so—hey, what's that?" Something at the far back of the lab had caught Emily's eye: a wide iron door, painted a bright warning red. It looked like the entrance to a bank vault, with a huge geared lock and thick metal bars holding it shut.

"I don't know," said Mere, but she paused by Emily's side to watch. A lab tech in a long red coat, pushing a rolling metal cart that was like a steel box on wheels, stopped by the door. A moment later, two guards in full armor, the first Emily had seen in the lab, appeared from behind a partition and removed the bars. The lock turned, grinding around in almost a full circle, then the door opened about an inch with a puff of air. One guard stood watch, peering into the chamber beyond the door as often as he gazed around the lab, as the other dragged the door the rest of the way open with a squeal of metal.

The red-coated tech nodded his thanks, then pushed his cart through the opening, into a deep darkness that swallowed him up even as the guards were reversing the process of opening the door, until it slammed shut and the heavy bars fell back into place.

"We have to get in there," Emily breathed.

"I've never been in there," said Mere. "Dad works out here."

"Still, there has to be a way." Emily grabbed Mere's hand and pulled her deeper into the lab, ducking around busy tables and behind equipment to get a closer look at the red door without giving them away.

From behind a shelf of glassware, they watched as the same guards went through the same routine to unlock the door and swing it open. A different technician than the one who'd gone in, though wearing a matching red coat, rolled out a matching metal box. By the curve of his back and the set of his steps, Emily judged that this one was much heavier than the box they'd seen go in. In all likelihood, the carts went in empty and came out full.

"Oh good," she murmured to Mere. "This'll be easy."

They found an unguarded store of the rolling boxes in a small room off the main lab. There was no sign of the tech who'd recently exited the red door, suggesting that once full, the carts didn't return here. Emily left Mere to watch the door as she examined the boxes, which stood in a neat row along one wall. They reminded her of old-fashioned mining carts, but completely closed, just big metal shells with hinged tops. A knock on the lid of the nearest one suggested the box was hollow, but when she went to open it, Emily found it was locked.

"Mere, anybody coming?" she whispered.

The girl shook her head.

"Okay then," Emily muttered, turning back to the cart. She hooked her fingers under its flanged lid and pulled. The lid resisted and Emily squared her feet and put her back into her work. As she shifted her weight she noticed a spot where the resistance felt strongest and she moved her grip to put all her force where the lock seemed to be.

"Emily!" Mere hissed. "Someone's coming! One of those red guys!"

Shit. Whatever was holding the box closed was proving to be much stronger than the simple metal deadbolt she'd expected. She strained against it, sweat prickling her brow.

"Emily!" Mere scampered to her side. "He's coming!"

Suddenly and silently, the lock simply gave way and the lid of the crate swung open to reveal an empty space. A quick glance showed Emily what she'd been fighting against: two long, black magnets dangled from the lid, one that was meant to be there and the other that she'd pulled out of its housing in the body of the cart.

"Get in," she ordered and Mere complied. Emily leaped in after her and let the lid fall shut, plunging them into black; her last glimpse of the lab included a sliver of red fabric in motion.

Ten seconds passed, then twenty, then thirty, and Emily had just managed to convince herself that she'd picked the wrong cart when they were jostled into sudden motion. They moved slowly, backing, turning, then rolling forward, as Emily prayed silently that the lab tech wouldn't notice the extra weight of two human bodies crammed together inside the rolling box.

They bumped against what Emily guessed was the door jamb, then moved slowly in the direction of the red door. There was another long wait as a faint clunking suggested the vault-like door was being unlocked, then the cart turned and rolled on. It turned again, moved for a while, turned again, and bumped solidly into something and stopped.

There was silence, or at least there was inside the metal box. No matter how she strained her ears, Emily couldn't make out anything outside their dark prison. She counted to sixty, then forced herself to do it again, but after that she couldn't wait any more.

"Stay down," she whispered to Mere. Then with painful slowness she pushed the lid of the cart open.

The room beyond the red door was an extension of the larger lab, with the same vaulted ceiling and brick arches. The technicians here, all dressed in long red coats, moved more slowly and spoke more quietly than their counterparts outside, creating a regal hush in the chamber. The sight that revealed itself to Emily as she raised the lid a few more inches explained why entirely.

The body was absolutely colossal, at least fifty feet tall from its mossy feet to the head that hid among the high shadows of the ceiling, and half as wide. It lay upright on an angled slab of pockmarked gray Olympian stone, which would have been impressive enough for its sheer size if it weren't supporting a dead titan. At least, Emily would have sworn it was dead—its stillness was somehow different from that of the others whom she'd met in Olympia and, besides, huge chunks were missing from its arms and legs and its chest was splayed open like a patient on an operating table, revealing a heart the size of a car. A wooden scaffold had been erected around the corpse, allowing the red-coated technicians access to its heights, and as Emily watched a few clambered off the superstructure and onto the body itself.

"Astraeos," Emily breathed.

The Paramount's heart beat.

Now Emily noticed the iron shackles that held Astraeos's wrists to the stone beneath it and the great pile of chains wrapped around its ankles. One of the techs on its chest clambered down into its open organ cavity and prodded its heart with a metal rod that arced with purple lighting. The colossus stirred feebly, then was still. The tech glanced up at his counterpart and gave him a thumbs-up.

157

"Go ahead!" the second technician called, waving to someone at the Paramount's feet. A mechanical whine filled the room as the worker fired up what looked like a crystal-tipped buzz saw, then he was lost in a shower of blue-white sparks as he applied the saw to a plate of stone armor on Astraeos's leg. The shriek of the saw rose to fever pitch and then died away suddenly, leaving the man with the saw wrapped in a thin white smoke that drifted off across the floor of the lab.

Two more techs hustled up and there was a tearing sound as they did something in the haze that Emily couldn't quite make out. They marched out of the smoke with a man-sized chunk of stone—one of the Paramount's greaves—held unsteadily between them.

With a bang and a clatter, Emily and Mere's cart began to move.

"What's happening?" Mere asked from somewhere around Emily's feet. They were grinding slowly forward under no obvious power—the cart had to be on a track, or hooked to the one in front of it, or something.

"Stay down," Emily whispered, but as soon as she said it, their cart slammed to a stop as the line ahead of it halted. A matching cart had appeared on the far side of the chained Paramount and a technician stood filling it with a yellow-brown liquid from a segmented metal hose.

"That's the guy who brought us here," Mere said, and Emily glanced down in alarm to see the girl peering over the lip of their cart, her nose pressed to the metal.

"Get down!" Emily hissed.

"Why?"

"Then be quiet!"

The techs carrying the plate of Astraeos's armor had reached the liquid-filled cart, into which they unceremoniously dumped their burden. There was a splash and a sizzle and oily black smoke poured out from the bin, much thicker than the off-gassing from the buzz saw. One man backed away, coughing into his elbow, but the other stayed peering into the cart. A few seconds later, he raised his hand.

"All right!" he called and stepped away from the smoke, which was thinning and sputtering. The tech with the hose hung it on a hook on the back wall, then slammed the lid of the cart shut, cutting off the last few wisps of smoke with a final bang. Wordlessly he began to roll the cart toward the red door; when he reached it, he left the cart and banged three times on the door. A minute later, it swung partway open and he pushed his burden past the waiting guards and into the lab.

"What the hell are they doing…?" Emily had stared transfixed as the gruesome procedure played out and now she watched the guards with equal fascination, any pretense at stealth forgotten.

The guards turned to shut the door and one of them locked eyes with her.

"You there!" He pointed and every head in the room turned to look at Emily and Mere, hunched under the lid of the cart, their mouths hanging open in dumb surprise.

Red-coated techs scattered out of the way as the guards sprinted toward the intruders, their halberds raised. Emily shoved the lid the rest of the way open and leaped out, shoving Mere down into the relative safety of its interior as she did so. There were only two guards; surely she could take them and a few scientists.

She started toward the door, then skidded to a halt as, from the shadows around the Paramount, a dozen more soldiers appeared, hefting their flat-tipped swords.

"Where—" Emily glanced back to see the original two guards advancing on her and the technicians crowding around a wooden crate from which they were pulling spears of their own. "Shit."

How many had she taken on in the throne room? Half a dozen? That had been easy, but Emily wasn't so sure they'd really been fighting back. She shook off a sudden stab of guilt. King Zero and Queen Adae were clearly up to no good down here and as both a member of the Sabre & Torch and a good Gifted warrior, it was her job to stop them.

The guards closed in, making a half-ring to pin her against the back wall where the carts, and Mere, waited. Emily glanced around in a half-panic, looking for something to even the odds a little. Her gaze settled on the biggest weapon in the place: Astraeos.

159

She dashed toward the guards, just a few steps. One jump took her high over their heads; they watched in shock as she twisted to keep them in sight, but to their credit, had recovered by the time she hit the ground on the far side. The next jump got her halfway up the scaffolding, only a few feet from the iron shackle that held the Paramount's left hand bolted to its slab. She scrambled across the sloping stone and stood by Astraeos's tree-thick wrist.

The Paramount, perhaps sensing Emily's presence, stirred in its chains and let out a thick-tongued moan. On the floor of the lab, the guards were advancing with weapons raised, their upturned faces flashing in the gloom. Beyond them, the line of carts showed no sign of movement— Mere had obviously let common sense win and hidden herself away until it was all over.

A sudden pang of doubt pierced Emily's chest. When *would* it be over? What would unleashing the Paramount actually do? Would it know the difference between friend and foe? Would it smash its way out the red door and find Viktor on the other side?

Would it find Mere?

They hadn't noticed the girl, that much was clear. If Emily could just distract the guards, draw them off, Mere might have a chance to sneak away unseen. And if she didn't want to get killed in the process, her options for causing a distraction were pretty limited.

"You've probably heard of me," Emily called down to the mass of soldiers and scientists. "I almost killed the queen, no thanks to you!"

A murmur ran through the fighters on the floor and a few of the less hardy-looking techs shuffled their feet and shifted their grips on their spears.

"Let's be honest with each other," Emily went on. "There's a lot of you and only one of me." She shrugged, hoping it looked nonchalant. "Maybe I could take you all. Maybe not. To be honest with you, I don't really feel like trying my luck today. So I'll tell you what: I surrender. Take me to your leader."

CHAPTER 14

They threw Emily in a dungeon, an old-school one, with dank, dripping stone walls, rusty iron bars, and a foul smell. It reminded her of the lowest levels of the Castle Forlorn, where she'd found the Sword That Cuts Both Ways, which had ended the dragon's and Sir Max's lives in one blow. That time, she'd ended up under a hundred feet of stone because she'd been so certain of her plan to fetch help before the dragon and its army came that she'd gone against direct orders, risking everything on the gamble that she was right.

It had been so simple on Finalhaven. When someone ordered you not to do something, it was a safe bet that that was the thing to do. Being the one making the decisions was way worse. All the pieces were there—King Zero, Queen Adae, the captive Paramount, the stag-headed monsters—but Emily couldn't quite put the puzzle together. She'd had her chance to flip the table over and quit the game entirely by freeing Astraeos and she hadn't taken it. It was an open question whether or not she'd live to regret it.

Time passed uncertainly and eventually King Zero came to speak with her. He was dressed in his full armor, with the three-horned helmet on his head, and he carried the huge plate of Astraeos's armor as though it were a tower shield.

King Zero leaned in to peer at Emily through the bars of her cell, then turned to pull a wooden stool from the corner of the room. He sat, his legs splayed open, and settled the stone plate between them, leaning it

161

against his thigh. Finally, he removed his helmet much as he'd done at dinner, letting his lank black hair fall around his face as he set the helm on the floor at his feet and rotated it so its empty faceplate stared at Emily.

"I'm not going to tell anyone you're down here," he said.

Emily made herself hold his gaze. "Your wife won't be a little curious where her guest went?"

Zero snorted. "What's a marriage without a little mystery?" He leaned forward, one hand on the armor plate. "Would you like to know a secret?"

"Sure."

"I know who your friend Elizabeth is," he said, showing a smile like a knife wound that just hadn't started bleeding yet. "My poor, dear wife doesn't know exactly whom she's invited into our home, but I do."

"Who's that?" Emily knew the answer and she knew King Zero knew, but she had to say it, had to play the king's game.

"I wasn't certain at first." Zero sat back on the stool. "I'd expected to feel much more power from her. But it's no matter. Elizabeth the First Pendragon, first-born child of Arthur the Twenty-Ninth. I imagine she feels entitled to the Albian throne, as well. Shame she'll never see Albion again."

The king stood, leaning his slab of Paramount stone carefully on his vacated seat. "Tell me, Emily. Do you know of the Curse of Adam?"

"I've heard of it," Emily said, trying to estimate how long it would take her to tear one of the iron bars from her cage, slip through the gap, and twist the thing around Zero's neck.

"But do you *know* it?" Zero hissed.

"No."

The king began to pace, five steps forward and five back in the little dungeon chamber. "When Adam slayed the High King and took the throne of Cantelon, he set a curse on all of Arcadia. None but the royal line, his line, could work magic without paying the price. Imagine my surprise when two Earth magicians show up with a missing arm and a ruined eye." He stopped and turned to stare at Emily. "Add a warrior who fights like ten and tries to kill my queen. Now you have what looks like three people sworn to protect a fourth, who is powerless."

"Cool story," Emily said, trying to keep her face neutral.

"Ah," said Zero, "but it has a twist ending. You see, when your little queen walked right into our kingdom, she saved us the trouble of having to kill her on Earth."

"The monsters?"

"I understand you've met them," Zero said.

"And killed them both," Emily replied. Technically Marlow had killed the first, but the king didn't need to know that.

"Hm." Zero smiled. "Then I'll be happy to put an end to you, too. I have just the thing, as it happens. But first, tell me one thing: where has your little queen's power gone?"

"She's not the queen," Emily said. "She's just a regular girl."

"Don't play dumb," said Zero. "Not now, not here, not with me. For my entire lifetime we believed that the stories of an Albian queen in exile, a female heir, were just rumors. Imagine my surprise when our agents on Earth carried back word of sightings, whispers that the queen had returned to Albion. And it all began with a great burst of power, like a burning lamp for all my little moths."

The image of Elizabeth rising from the wreckage of the Castle Forlorn in a great wheel of flame and smoke flashed across Emily's thoughts.

"So you see," Zero continued, "I know what Elizabeth Pendragon is capable of. So tell me: where has her power gone?"

"I'll never tell you," Emily said. "And if you kill me, you'll never find out."

Zero shook his head in mock sorrow. "I'm afraid you have it wrong," he said. "I'll kill you and I'll find out anyway."

#

They stood in front of another door, smaller than the red door to the Paramount but just as heavy, with the same complex set of locks and bars. Emily was ringed by guards, their halberds inches from her on all sides, and just beyond them stood King Zero with his slab of Astraeos's armor, which he'd carried along with him.

They'd come here through a series of disused tunnels lined with slumping shelves of rotting books that suggested the remnants of the old royal family's archives hadn't been totally cleared out. Emily had done her best to keep track as they prodded her through the twisting catacombs, even trying to make a song out of the turns as Jack Twelve-Fingers had done once, but she'd lost her way almost immediately.

The door was shiny, if dented, and clearly a recent addition to the ancient halls. It sat in the middle of a long, straight hallway as though dropped there at random. It fitted neatly into a freshly plastered wall that was equally out of place in the crumbling tunnels.

"I've made something new here," said King Zero, as though reading her mind. "Isn't it wonderful? To take old, broken things and repurpose them for my own use. To give them new life in my image. All this space was being wasted before me, filled with useless memories."

Emily said nothing.

"Well," the king said. "It takes quite a bit of effort to shape the world." He drummed his fingers on the armor plate, then leaned it against a wall of the corridor. "And quite a bit of sacrifice." He looked at Emily. "Not by me, of course. Emily, you're going to help me. I have a friend who needs exercise and he's grown rather bored with normal people. You're quite special—only humans born on Earth can be Gifted, did you know that? Imagine my disappointment. Well, I expect you'll give my friend a good workout."

"I've already killed two of your *friends*," Emily said. "Why would I be afraid of a third?"

Zero laughed. "Oh, no. Not a staghead. My friend is something much, much worse." He gestured to one of his guards, who advanced with a pair of iron manacles. "Still, we can't run the risk of his exercise program getting out of hand. Derenk, would you, please?"

The soldier called Derenk stepped forward with the manacles, moving a bit warily despite the dozen ready men at his back. Emily took a final glance at their steady faces and leveled weapons, considered King Zero in his massive armor, and admitted to herself that she was probably outgunned. Better to take her chances against whatever waited beyond the door and hope she'd get a chance to break free.

Keeping her face neutral, Emily stared into Derenk's eyes as she raised her wrists and allowed him to clamp the manacles around them with two solid clicks. They were connected with about a foot of iron chain, enough for her to use her hands but certainly not enough to fight with them.

"There, now," said Zero. "That wasn't so hard, was it? I appreciate your obedience. Derenk, the door, please."

Derenk and another guard went through a process like the one that had opened the red door in the laboratory and soon the dented metal door swung out toward them, revealing a wide rectangle of gloom beyond. A light flickered to life in the darkness, showing a glimpse of the crumbling stone walls Emily had come to expect down here, then went out again.

"Go ahead," said King Zero. Emily squared her shoulders, set her jaw, and marched into the black. Immediately the soldiers swung the door shut behind her; the sound of the lock being reset was almost lost in the echoing boom. The same light, a nauseous electric yellow, flickered briefly but couldn't find the will to stay on.

Somewhere ahead, there was a rasping scrape of claws on stone.

The unpredictable light came on again and Emily got a look at the long, straight corridor ahead of her. The floor was carpeted with torn-up papers, trampled and filthy. About ten yards ahead, shadowed openings along the right- and left-hand walls suggested additional halls opening off in either direction.

The light went out and the scratching noise sounded again, closer. Emily stretched out her right hand, pulling her left with it, until she touched the wall. She hurried forward, letting her fingers brush against

165

stone until she felt empty space, then ducked around the corner. Then it was a struggle between speed and quiet as she moved blindly down the new hallway. She could run three or four times faster than any normal human and her reflexes were equally quicker, but one thing she couldn't do was see in the dark, so she kept her hand on the wall, hoping it would warn her of any twists and turns as they arrived.

A crashing roar shook the tunnel and as if in sympathy, the lights flickered on. Back down the hall where she'd first turned was a hunched silhouette. It had the proportions of the antlered monsters she'd fought before, with a long-snouted head atop a humanoid body, but it was larger, much larger, probably ten feet or more if it stood up straight.

In the sudden yellow glow she could see another turn-off to her left and she leaped for it, hoping she'd moved fast enough to avoid the creature's notice. She sprinted down the new hall, kicking rotting book-pages into a flurry as she went, making for a T-junction at the far end maybe fifty yards away. The lights went out again just as a second roar sounded from the way she'd been heading, as loud as the first and somehow even more vicious.

Emily skidded to a stop in the darkness, straining her aching ears for sounds of the creature's approach. She heard them, behind her, back the way she'd come from. Then the scuffling scraping sounded again down the hall where the second roar had happened. Whipping her head back and forth in panic, Emily understood: there were two of them.

A vague image like a blurry snapshot flashed in Emily's mind. There was something about the wall behind her, something she'd seen on its face before the light had gone out—that was it, the plaster had peeled away to reveal broken bricks and flaking mortar, and through the gaps, the gray shadow of an empty space.

There was no time for quiet now as she slapped her hands onto the wall and began searching for the crumbling spot she'd seen. She found it quickly enough, feeling holes where she could stick a probing finger through to the open air beyond.

"Good enough," she muttered and began to push. Bricks gave way at her touch. Their ancient mortar turned to dust and suddenly a whole section of wall fell away to clatter to the floor of whatever space waited behind them. Soon there was a space big enough for Emily to wriggle through.

She landed on her shoulders on a cold stone floor and twisted upright. Now being quiet mattered—replacing the bricks she'd pushed through was a strange game of grabbing them swiftly then putting them back gingerly, one by one, as she prayed her shackles wouldn't clank. The wall was halfway rebuilt when she heard the scraping of claws on stone start down the hallway beyond, then a matching sound coming from the other direction. Zero's monsters, whatever they were, were closing on her position. She redoubled her efforts, trying to replace bricks even more quickly without making a sound. The last brick clacked against its mates as she felt for the hole it needed to fill, then slotted in with a whisper of stone.

Emily was rigid, her hands still raised, her breath held, listening. The sounds of movement drew closer to her position, paused… then passed on, shuffling off down the way she'd originally come. A minute passed. Emily let herself breathe out.

As she did, the lights came on.

It was a glow from nowhere, with no obvious source, the same sickly yellow as elsewhere in the tunnel complex. She was in a narrow hallway, barely five feet wide and terminating in a dead end maybe forty yards away. Here the walls were whitewashed brick and the remnants of the old royal family hadn't been torn out or burned away by Zero's soldiers— Emily blinked in wonder at painted murals that ran the length of the hall on both sides. Their colors were still bright, red and green and blue, with whorls of gold that glittered as though the paint had been made with flecks of the precious metal. Among the vivid curves of landscapes and white lines of cities, human figures ran, danced, fought, and conversed.

Drawn in despite herself, Emily moved along the hall, running her fingers over the mural. It seemed to show the story of a family, generations of parents and children who grew old and gave way to their descendants,

167

who aged and died in their turn, from one end of the corridor to the other. Emily paused at a coronation scene, a young man on a throne being crowned by his mother. She was looking at a history of the royal line that had reigned before Adam came and tore everything down.

Intrigued, she followed the life of the young High King. He had a daughter, who grew up into a beautiful princess—at least her painted version was beautiful—and married a man with a crown of his own who seemed to have come from far away. The story now followed the young couple, who returned to the man's distant homeland and had a child of their own, a girl. The man's face was shown contorted with rage and he held a sword in his raised hand as his wife and their daughter cowered before his anger.

Halfway down the hall the scene shifted again. The woman now knelt before a fierce-eyed bird with a small hooked beak and slender, wicked talons, raising her daughter to it like an offering. Her face was stained with tiny paint tears. The artist's intent came through clearly across the gulf of a hundred years: she would never see her child again. Beyond that last image, there was only blank plaster, where any future stories would have been told if Adam hadn't come.

Recognition hit Emily like a war hammer to the chest, leaving her just as staggered. She'd already guessed she was looking at the story of Princess Anne, whom Viktor had told her was married off in an alliance by the last High King whom Adam dethroned. The bit with the bird had been a mystery until a flash of memory triggered by the clean plaster wall sent her back a few months to Elizabeth's neat white sitting room in the Castle Forlorn, where she'd said—how had she phrased it...? *The King of Birds carried me across the ocean on the trade winds and set me down on the sand.*

She was looking at the lineage of Elizabeth Pendragon, queen-in-exile of Albion and, apparently, of Cantelon as well. Princess Anne, the marriage of alliance to a man from far away—she must have been Elizabeth's mother, and the foreign king her father, Arthur XXIX. Faced with the fury of King Arthur at the birth of a girl, Anne had given her child up to the King of Birds, whoever that was, who had delivered her to safety in the Castle Forlorn, and there she had stayed until Michael Fletcher's near-death at the hands of the dragon had forced her to leave her room at last.

Did Elizabeth know who her mother really was? Who *she* really was? Emily guessed not—nothing in Elizabeth's behavior had suggested that Arcadia had any special meaning to her aside from the loss of her powers to Valeria Tall and Gray and the prophecy the witch had given them. But King Zero did, Emily thought. No wonder he was so threatened by Elizabeth, so obsessed with her. He'd even said something about it: "I imagine she feels entitled to the Albian throne, as well."

As well as the throne of Cantelon.

Emily forced herself to take a few slow, deep breaths to calm her racing heart. When she'd walked through the door into these tunnels, her only goal had been to survive. Now she had to do more than that: she had to get this revelation to her friends.

The far end of the hallway exploded in a shower of bricks. A filth-crusted skull head thrust its way through the gap, brick dust swirling around its ragged nasal cavity in breath-like puffs. It wasn't a stag's head like the other monsters; it looked more like a wolf skull, but gigantic, with jagged fangs of black crystal and smooth bone where there should have been eye sockets.

It pointed its snout toward Emily and pushed its way through the collapsing wall into the tunnel. Its gray-furred body was man-shaped, but it moved on all fours, splaying its fingers almost gingerly each time it set down a hand on the cold stone of the floor. Behind it, from the shadows of the hall beyond, an identical second creature poked its skeletal face through the broken opening and sniffed. This one placed its hands on either side of the gap and climbed through carefully, like a human would, though it was forced to hunch almost as low as its fellow by the ceiling against which its furred, muscular shoulders scraped.

There was only one way to go; hoping she could move faster than the things chasing her, Emily broke instantly into a sprint, her manacles rattling, her feet slapping on the stone. The nearer monster roared and both came after her, scraping plaster from the walls that were barely wider than their bodies. The lights went out, but Emily plunged on, heedless of the darkness. The things had no eyes, which meant they didn't need to see her to find her. To slow down would mean death in their taloned hands.

The lights came back on. Only a few yards ahead was another brick wall of the same make as the one she'd pushed through. There was no guessing what was beyond it; as it rushed toward her, Emily considered the possibility that she might be about to stun herself on solid subterranean stone, but there was also the chance that this end of the hall was like the other and someone had blocked off an entrance here.

That was her desperate hope as she hurled herself at the wall, tucking her head and twisting her body to connect with her shoulder.

She crashed through the brick and fell to the ground in another black hallway. The echo of her landing and the feel of the air suggested this was a larger, main corridor. Her hands scraped painfully on stone as she shoved herself to her feet. She ran.

The monsters smashed through the remnants of the wall she'd busted, one after the other. Silhouetted against the faint light of the mural hall, they paused briefly to sniff the air where brick dust swirled like yellow ghosts, then set out after her. Out of the cramped side corridor, they ran like a cross between men and gorillas, sometimes upright with outstretched hands and sometimes loping on all fours with their fingers brushing the floor.

The light came back in time for Emily to see that the hall ended in a T-junction not far ahead. She chose at random and hared to the left. The wolf-headed creatures were picking up speed. They hit the junction not long after; the leader followed her while the other split off and turned right. Emily cursed. There had to be a loop coming up that would allow that one to cut her off if she wasn't careful, but there was no guessing how or where.

A side hall opened on her left and Emily took the corner at speed. She was thoroughly lost now, running at random, and was just considering finding somewhere to make a stand when she realized she'd just passed the original hidden wall she'd broken through. Of course—she'd made three lefts since breaking out of the mural hall, forming a neat little rectangle. That gave her some sense of space and if she could just remember how to get back to the door, she might be able to get it open, or at least put it at her back when she fought the monsters.

A roar sounded from somewhere ahead of her and the lights flickered threateningly. Emily shook her head—something was off. One monster was still dogging her heels, tearing through the halls at full speed and showing no sign of falling behind. The other had gone in the other direction; it could cut her off from the side, maybe, but it shouldn't be in front. Which meant—a third?

"You've got to be kidding me," Emily gasped between ragged breaths. Her top speed was superhuman, but it wore her out like any sprinter. Dredging her memory for the turns she'd tried to memorize on her way in, she took another corner, nearly bouncing off the far wall as she skidded around in a sprint. There was a roar behind her—another ahead, maybe off to the left from a corridor that she immediately discarded as an escape option—a third from a shadowed opening on her right, and a moment after she passed it, one of the creatures burst from it and rejoined the chase.

They were herding her, taking choice away from her, forcing her to move how they wanted. And they were closing in.

The metal door came into view, but Emily knew it was a hollow victory. She was boxed in, with two monsters just behind and a third that would be coming toward her out of the darkness at any moment. It was time to stop running. She skidded to a halt by the door and for a moment she let herself feel the full weight of her desperate frustration as she put her palms on the cold steel that stood between her and safety.

The monsters came into view all at once, one from ahead and two from behind. As they approached, their nostrils making puffs in the dust-hazed dungeon air, they slowed down. With her back flat against the door, the pair of creatures was on her left and the solo third was on her right. The closer of the pair barked, a lupine sound that was also a command, and the slowly advancing lone monster yelped a response.

They were smarter than she'd given them credit for. They'd worked together perfectly, cutting off her avenues of escape one by one until they had her neatly flanked. If their size was anything to go by, any one of them would be a desperate fight for her, but they'd still worked as a pack rather than taking the chance of wasting their greatest advantage.

Emily, meanwhile, was about to die alone.

The monsters closed on her, reached her, loomed over her. The leader reached out with its clawed man-hand and grabbed her around the throat, lifting her from the floor as though she weighed nothing at all. Then she thought panic had cracked her mind, because on her right, the creature just over its pack-mate's shoulder wavered and disappeared. The third monster stood just to her left, its skull-head cocked in blind regard of her, and then it, too, faded away into nothing, leaving a swirl of dust where it had been.

There was only one left, but it seemed suddenly much larger as it roared in her face, its stinking breath crashing over her. It *was* larger, Emily realized. Had it somehow absorbed its companions? Or had they never been there at all…?

The lights went out and the monster began to squeeze.

It was incredible how strong it was. Beneath her shackled hands, its tendons were like corded steel, totally immune to her desperate clawing as she tried to break the grip that was now making her see stars burst in the darkness as she suffocated.

Something scraped behind her, then clanked. The sound was warped like a half-melted record playing on a turntable, slowing and speeding up and dropping in pitch at random. The conscious part of Emily knew that her brain was struggling to process what she was hearing and the rest of her couldn't find the strength to care. It was just too hard. So much easier to just fall asleep…

The wall fell away from her and light burst all around. The wall? No— the door, the door at her back had swung open, and somebody was pushing past her to face off with the huge wolf-headed beast that was choking the life from her. The new arrival wobbled and wavered uncertainly as though she was watching him in a fish tank, but when he raised a small, white idol and began to speak, she knew him instantly: Marlow Bright, magician of Earth.

CHAPTER 15

Marlow's spells were like prayers, Emily thought blearily. As the real world turned black all around her, memories of Harkness filled the empty space, of a little clique of Arcane students who claimed that their powers were the gift of various major and minor gods. Marlow was one of those, Emily thought, as the sound of his voice became inexplicably clearer and more pure, cutting through the buzzing that crashed like a wave over her mind. He was a holy man, working the miracle of resurrection in the name of his god Mithras as she fell into a lightless, airless abyss.

The wolf-headed monster let go and Emily fell to the stone floor. Her body reflexively tried to gulp in a double lungful of air, but succeeded only in a racking cough that spasmed up and down her body. Somebody dropped to their knees by her, put warm, dry hands on her neck, pressing more forcefully than she thought was really necessary.

Her vision was clearing and in one corner of her view there was a pair of clawed feet receding into the darkness of a stone hallway. The creature moved in a slow shuffle very different from the four-limbed lope with which it had chased her through the shadows. It turned a corner and was gone.

"Emily, can you hear me?" The voice was gentle and as warm as the touch.

"Mike..." Another spasm of coughing ran up and down Emily's body, doubling her over until it worked itself out. She swallowed and a stinging burn ran down her throat. "Michael."

"I'm here." Michael put his hand on hers. "You're going to be okay, but we need to get moving. Can you stand up?"

She stood shakily, her knees threatening to give out the whole way up, but Michael bore her weight until she had her feet under her and a steadying hand on the wall. The magician gave her a wary smile and she smiled back. The fog was clearing with every joyful breath. Next to Michael, Marlow stood with his arms crossed and his mouth set in a thin line, and behind him, peering out from around the door jamb, was Mere.

"You saved me," Emily said.

"Marlow saved you," said Michael. He looked at the Albian magician with open appreciation on his face. "What was that spell?"

Marlow opened his mouth then shut it again and shook his head.

The bottom dropped out of Emily's stomach. "What's wrong?"

Marlow turned his back on them and waved a hand in a *come on* motion.

"Marlow?" Michael said.

"I don't think he can talk," said Mere. She raised a hand in greeting. "Hello, Emily."

"He can't talk?" Emily repeated.

"Marlow, is that true?" asked Michael.

In answer, Marlow spun around, his face contorted in an unreadable expression. He opened his mouth, wide open, and tilted his head back. It took a moment for Emily to realize what he was showing them.

His tongue was gone.

#

Mere led them past the remnants of the old royal archives, retracing the route that King Zero had taken to bring her to his creations' hunting grounds. She moved confidently and Emily wondered just how much time the girl had spent exploring down here while she was supposed to be at school. Eventually they joined up with a larger trunk tunnel where a

175

few lab techs stood chatting or wheeled metal carts to and fro. Emily had pulled her sweatshirt off, tearing the sleeves to get it free from her shackles, and now carried it wrapped over the manacles in a position that she hoped made her look like any old person who'd just gotten too hot while wandering around underground, rather than someone who'd just escaped from a dungeon. The technicians ignored them.

Eventually Emily found that she was able to talk without feeling like she was swallowing needles. It still hurt and her voice was wheezy, but she had too much to say to wait any longer. She decided to start with questions.

"Mere?" she rasped.

"Yeah?" the girl said without looking back.

"What do you know about the old royal line?"

Michael gave Emily a curious look but stayed quiet.

"Not much." Mere glanced over her shoulder. "You get people like Viktor who think everything was way better back then, but everybody seems happy now, so I dunno."

"People seem happy?" Emily asked, surprised.

"Everybody is always smiling," Mere said and suddenly Emily realized just how young this girl was. She'd been Mere's age not too long ago, yet she'd probably done as much growing up in the last few months as she had in her first thirteen years. The smiles she'd seen on the faces of the adults in Beverlay, their chipper voices, were as obviously hollow as a suit of armor without a wearer. Mere couldn't see that—and why should she? She'd grown up under the reign of King Zero and Queen Adae. This was normal to her.

They came up a long, sloping tunnel into the crystalline glow of Beverlay, what Emily had come to think of as "aboveground" despite it being deep in the roots of the mountain of Olympia. A long line of adults passed them, going down into the earth to work, their eyes locked straight ahead and their faces carefully neutral as they shuffled by the strangers who walked one way while everyone else was walking the other.

They emerged into the plaza where Mere's rowhouse stood and the girl set off at a run, then remembered her guests and spun back around to wave goodbye.

"Hey!" Emily shouted. Mere cocked her head as Emily jogged over to her. She put a hand on the girl's shoulder, the chain between her manacles slumping into a new curve, and stared into her upturned face. "Thanks for everything. You have no idea how much you helped me."

"No problem." Mere shrugged, but the corners of her lips were turned up. "Be seeing you."

"See you," said Emily as Mere turned and ran to her door.

"She saved your life, you know," said Michael, watching the girl go. "She came and found us, told us you'd been taken prisoner. That kid really knows her way around the tunnels."

"The tunnels!" Emily blinked. "Michael, Marlow, I have something I need to tell you."

"You there! Visitors!"

Emily turned to see a pair of armed and armored guards approaching them across the plaza, with Eneph the lizard majordomo between them.

"What is it?" Michael asked, but Emily patted the air near her hip in what she hoped was a subduing motion.

"What seems to be the problem, officers?" Emily said, putting on her best smile.

"We're not officers," said one guard and the other gave him a disappointed look.

"King Zero sent us to find you," the second guard said. Emily's right hand immediately went for a weapon in her belt, making her chain clank as it reached full extension, and of course there was nothing there for her to grab. The guard glanced at her curiously, then continued. "He'd like you to be at dinner tonight. He said to say please."

"Oh," said Emily, blinking.

"We'd love to," Michael put in quickly.

Emily came to dinner with her wrists still in shackles and if King Zero was surprised to see her as he entered the great hall, he didn't show it. He and Queen Adae entered together and took their accustomed places on their thrones at the head of the table, which was empty except for Emily, Michael, and Marlow. Zero set his three-horned helmet on the floor.

"A toast," he said, standing. "The queen."

Adae, whose eyes had been fixed firmly on the table before her, glanced up at her husband.

"The queen," echoed Emily and Michael, and Marlow also raised his glass to drink. Instantly King Zero fixed him with a glare.

"Mr. Bright," he said, "do you not toast my wife?"

Fear widened Marlow's eyes and he took a breath.

"Marlow isn't feeling well," Emily said.

"Have you lost your voice?" Zero asked, watching Marlow with narrowed eyes. "That is a tragedy for a spellcaster."

In response, Marlow opened his mouth, his eyes locked on the king's. Zero peered between the Arcane's teeth and a barely suppressed smile crinkled his pale face.

"I see." The king leaned back. "I must say, I've never had such an odd assortment of guests to table. A woman in chains. A man whose tongue seems to have gone missing overnight. One might almost think the three of you have been up to no good." He looked over at Adae, his armor creaking. "What do you make of this, my queen?"

"I'm sure I don't know," the queen whispered, her eyes lowered.

"Well." King Zero took a sip from his goblet. "At least the food will be good."

The end of dinner was almost as much a relief as escaping from Zero's monster. Eneph showed them back to their guest chambers—he was more concerned with them sneaking off than getting lost, Emily thought—removed Emily's shackles, then slunk away with a bow. As soon as he was gone, Emily turned to her friends.

"I have to tell you something," she spat out, desperate to share the news and terrified of being interrupted again. Then she remembered that there was an even more pressing issue. "Wait—where is Elizabeth?"

Michael shook his head, his shoulders bobbing in a tiny shrug. "I haven't seen her all day."

"She was gone when I woke up," Emily said. "Shit. Okay, well, listen. I saw something down in the tunnels. I think—no, I *know*—that Elizabeth's mother was Princess Anne of Cantelon."

Marlow's eyebrows went up and Michael's brow furrowed.

"She never knew her mom," the American magician said. "But her name was Anne of Avon. I always assumed she was Albian."

"I wish I could show you this mural," Emily said. "It was like the whole story of the old royal line. Princess Anne was married off to this king from far away—I think that was Elizabeth's dad—and then the king killed her—well, I think so—but she gave her daughter to this giant bird, and—"

"The King of Birds," Michael breathed.

"Exactly," said Emily.

"Shit."

"*Exactly.*"

Michael took a long, slow breath. "Elizabeth has no idea. But this makes her the rightful queen of Cantelon as well as Albion. That's... that's a lot of kingdoms."

Emily jumped as someone tapped her on the shoulder, but it was just Marlow. He was holding up a scrap of paper with a word scrawled across it: *prophecy.*

"Prophecy?" Emily blinked. "The prophecy? What about it?"

Michael's eyes focused on nothing as he began to murmur, repeating the words of the prophecy under his breath.

"*And the queen returns home,*" he said.

"You think...?" Emily stared at him.

"It makes sense, doesn't it?" Michael said. "No man's armor—that's King Zero. Adam's daughter fleeing her throne, that part is obvious. Even

179

the crown of iron turning to gold, that could refer to a change of royal power as well."

"Kind of redundant, then, isn't it?" Emily said.

Michael shrugged. "Hey, I didn't write it. Look, we all need some rest. Today has been… something."

"What about Elizabeth?" Emily said. "I think King Zero knows she has a claim to his throne. She might be in serious trouble."

"She's okay," said Michael. "Trust me."

"How do you know?" Emily asked and Michael smiled. He stuck a hand into his pocket and pulled out a crumpled white flower. It unfolded a little as it lay in his palm. It was a rose.

"See?" Michael closed his hand around the flower. "She's okay."

"I'm still worried," Emily said. "Without her powers…"

"She's a lot more than just a few magic spells," Michael said. "For a girl who grew up with books for friends, Lizzie's tougher than you'd think. Trust me, she'll turn up, and when she does, we can start clearing up this whole mess."

#

Emily collapsed onto her bed, eager to let sleep take her and uncertain that it would. She closed her eyes, expecting to relive her day in the tunnels, maybe with the dragon of Finalhaven taking the place of the wolf-headed monster. Instead, she fell asleep instantly.

The room was black when she woke to a footfall on the plush carpet. A hazy dream-image of Jack Twelve-Fingers stroking her cheek lingered in the darkness.

"Elizabeth?" There was no response. Emily lay still and unbreathing, listening, but the sound didn't return. "Hello?"

She sat up, or tried to, but was instantly back down on the bed with something around her throat. It was slick, like fabric, and it was choking her. All the traumatic memories of her near-death experience that hadn't bothered her before got their chance now and the thought flashed insanely through her head that maybe the thing from the tunnels had come back to finish the job.

Then she realized how stupid that was.

Her leg lashed out and she was rewarded with a pained grunt as her shin connected with something soft. The tension around her neck slackened a hair and she shoved her fingers into the space that opened up. It was a tie, or a sash, or a belt, or something like that. She expected the fabric to tear away, but instead she only shredded a top layer that revealed a flat matrix of metal wire underneath. Lines of steel bit into her fingers as her assailant retightened the garrotte. She could breathe, though, and that was enough.

Emily slipped one of her hands free from the choking line, shearing skin from her fingers, and began to search in the blackness for her opponent's face. She found an ear and pulled it sharply forward as she brought her own head up. There was a sudden pain and a satisfying crack as her enemy's nose shattered on her forehead. The tension around her neck released instantly as her attacker fell away, cursing. The voice was male— and familiar.

Emily felt around beside her bed until she touched the knob of crystal that controlled the lights. The room lit up from all around revealing Grant Lopez, ambassador plenipotentiary of the Gifted Nation of Deseret, kneeling on her bedspread with both hands holding the bloody wreck of his face.

"You broke my nose," he wheezed through noisy breaths.

"You tried to kill me, you unbelievable asshole." Emily slid out of bed and dropped into an aggressive stance. "Did Zero send you?"

To her surprise, Lopez didn't cower or beg. Instead he hopped off her bed, flicked the blood from his hands, and squared up with her, hands raised in a boxer's pose.

"Does it matter?" he said. He came for her, much faster than she would have guessed from his portly build. His left hand flickered out in a testing strike that she slapped away, but instead of following up with a right like she'd expected, Lopez kicked her in the stomach with enough power to send her staggering back into the wall.

"You're a Combat," Emily gasped.

"Starling class of eighty-nine," said Lopez.

"Is that where you learned to strangle girls in bed?" Emily threw a left of her own, which Lopez easily sidestepped, and for a few seconds the space between them was a blur of punches, blocks, and counterpunches as they made a circle in the limited floor space of the guest room. Then one of Emily's jabs slipped through Lopez's defense and caught him on the ear, forcing him to backpedal as his flow was broken.

"Did Wasteland tell you to kill me?" Emily asked. "Is this about Jack? He's never going back."

Lopez shook his head, a pitying look on his face. "Good God, you kids think everything's about your little personal problems, don't you?" He tried a warning kick at Emily's head as she closed in; she slapped his polished wingtip shoe away easily but had to back off a step. "Do you know what 'plenipotentiary' means?"

"What?" Emily snorted. "No. Who cares?"

"It means the Baron trusts me"—another kick, which Emily let pass half an inch from her nose—"to do whatever"—a juke to her left, followed by a quick striking combo that consumed Emily's focus as the fighters began to circle again—"I want!" Lopez lunged, apparently going for an arm lock, and Emily tried to keep back, but her legs hit the edge of her bed and she sat down suddenly. Lopez wasn't surprised at all; instead he shifted his balance as Emily flailed to regain hers, and delivered a kick that slammed into her head like a hammer ringing a bell.

She fell back onto the bed, head spinning, and then Lopez was on top of her, lashing at her with both fists. It was all she could do to keep her guard up to absorb the blows with her hands instead of her face.

"This is so much bigger than you, girlie," Lopez said through gritted teeth as he battered away Emily's defenses. "The line of Adam has been cooped up in this little pocket dimension for too long. Zero's aiming for a comeback and whoever's on his good side is going to benefit big time."

182

His left fist slid between her raised hands and landed solidly on the bone above her eye, blurring her vision.

She didn't even see the next blow coming; stars sparked in the dim room and everything went watery.

"So I figured," Lopez grunted, "why wait to be asked? First you, then your little queen. Should make King Zero pretty happy." He was mirrored and revolving like the tumbling shapes of a kaleidoscope, but every one of those images raised its right fist for a triumphant final blow.

"Get off her!"

Lopez looked up in surprise and Emily tried to follow his gaze, but all she could see was a blinding arc of lightning that crackled and spat as it made a line from the doorway to her attacker's raised fist. Emily shut her eyes, though the white line was burned into her vision; then she felt Lopez fall heavily across her. The tang of burned meat filled her nose. Gasping in revulsion, Emily bucked and shoved the corpse off her. It landed on the floor with a soft thump. Emily stood shakily, rubbing her eyes, her heart slamming in her chest in certainty that she had another fight waiting for her.

A warm hand touched her face.

She opened her eyes to see Elizabeth looking up at her, her pale face a mask of worry in the dim crystal glow of the bedroom.

"Are you all right?" asked the queen.

"I think so," Emily said. "Did you…?"

"No," said Elizabeth. She stepped aside and Emily saw Michael slumped against the door jamb, panting and cradling his remaining hand against his chest.

"Michael!" Emily gasped. "Your hand!"

"Ruined," Michael whispered. He was right: the fingers were as black and smoking as Lopez's body and angry red burn lines ran down his cracking palm, past his wrist, and nearly to his elbow. The young magician looked at Emily and to her amazement, he smiled. "But you're alive."

"I'm so sorry," Emily said, painfully aware of how inadequate the words were. "Thank you."

"Adae was worried something like this might happen," Elizabeth said. "You should thank the queen for warning us."

"The queen!" Emily gasped, memories rushing back. "Elizabeth, there's something I need to tell you."

"It can wait," Elizabeth said. "Queen Adae wishes to speak with us. Immediately."

CHAPTER 16

They followed Elizabeth in silent midnight confusion as she led them confidently through the labyrinthine halls to see the queen. Michael walked with the remnants of his hand tucked into his armpit. Marlow, who'd slept through the whole fight and had to be roused from bed, stumbled in a tousled, half-asleep daze. Emily just watched Elizabeth, equal parts eager and anxious to spill what she'd learned earlier down below the city.

Emily's right eye was swelling where Lopez had tagged it a couple times before his sudden immolation. All things considered, though, she'd gotten off much easier than the others. Michael was crippled; Elizabeth was powerless; Marlow didn't act too bothered about going half-blind, but then again he was incapable of complaining, and Emily wouldn't have given up her depth perception for almost anything. Even the vague blurriness of her own minor wound was a constant frustration.

Queen Adae lived in a modest suite not far from the throne room at the heart of the palace. Elizabeth let them into a small sitting room that reminded Emily of Elizabeth's own front room in the Castle Forlorn. It was much darker, much heavier, with glowing crystals an inadequate stand-in for natural light, but there were shelves of books and seating for all four visitors in the form of low couches of a greenish leather. Emily knew without having to ask that the queen lived here alone; there wasn't so much as a hint of King Zero's brutality.

Elizabeth sat on a couch and Emily sat next to her. Now that she had her chance to tell Elizabeth the truth, she found herself suddenly unable to do it. It felt like a loss of innocence, like she'd be opening the doors to a gray and complicated real world for a girl who'd lived in only two little rooms her whole life. Revealing Elizabeth's heritage would put her immediately and irrevocably into conflict with King Zero, Queen Adae, maybe the entire kingdom of Cantelon. It would start a fight that wouldn't end until one of the two queens was dead. Elizabeth had to know—of course she did—but Emily didn't want to be the one to tell her.

So she kept her mouth shut.

They waited in pained silence for only a few minutes until a tall wooden door between two shelves opened to reveal Adae, alone. It occurred to Emily that they hadn't seen any guards, retainers, or even so much as a scullery maid on their late-night walk. It was hard not to feel that fate was dangling a second shot at killing the evil queen in front of her nose. Instead, she stood politely with her friends and watched as Elizabeth moved to Adae and took her hands in a comforting gesture.

Immediately Emily felt anger welling up in her stomach, rising up her throat. Adae had clearly tricked Elizabeth into friendship, made her feel at home in the palace, commiserated over whatever problems only two magical queens could understand. It was all part of whatever sick game Adae and Zero were playing, Emily knew, and that realization gave her the strength to speak.

"Elizabeth, you should step back," Emily said. "She's not safe."

"Not safe?" Queen Adae peered at her curiously.

"Seriously, Lizzie, get away." Emily stepped forward. "There's a lot you don't know."

"Please, tell us," Adae said.

Emily put her hands on Elizabeth's shoulders. She was nearly a head taller than the Albian queen and she glared at Adae over Elizabeth's head.

"Where should I start?" Emily said. "See these bruises? How about my neck? I nearly died twice today. First it was your monsters and then it was your friend Grant Lopez. Oh, and before that I was locked up for a while by your lovely husband. There's something really rotten going on in Cantelon."

"I know," said Queen Adae.

"No shit you know," Emily sneered. "You and Zero are making those monsters and sending them to Earth. Do you have any idea how many people you've hurt?"

"Yes," said Adae, her eyes lowered. A momentary doubt got in the way of Emily's righteous fury like a stone on a train track, but it was knocked aside just as quickly.

"Have you told Elizabeth that the monsters are yours?"

"Yes."

"Have you told her *why*?"

"No." Queen Adae pulled her hands from Elizabeth's and stepped away. Emily promptly put herself between the two women, making sure she looked as tall as possible as she confronted the queen. There was nothing left but to say it.

"We know that Elizabeth is the rightful queen of Cantelon."

"I'm what?"

Emily glanced back to see Elizabeth looking as shocked as she'd ever seen her, her mouth half-open, her pale face gleaming in the murk of Adae's chambers. In fact, it was the first time Emily could remember seeing the young queen show any feeling so openly; she so often seemed to exist in her own mystical headspace that normal human emotion was alien on her features.

"I'm sorry you had to find out like this," Emily said. "But it's true. I saw proof. Your mother was Princess Anne, the daughter of the High King that Adam killed. You're the last of the old royal line."

"It is true," Adae breathed.

"Ha!" Emily turned on Adae. "You admit it! It's no coincidence that the first monsters appeared near Barley Bright after Elizabeth and Michael showed up. You sent those things to kill Elizabeth. Zero said so when I was in your dungeon." She was really going now, with a furious full head of steam, and all her half guesses and assumptions tumbled out of her mouth as quickly as they fell into place. "You probably had no idea Elizabeth was even alive, did you? Nobody did, just rumors. Until we fought the dragon at the Castle Forlorn and Elizabeth had to bust out of her apartment. No hiding it then. So you started throwing monsters through the Veil."

"Why, though?" Michael said. He'd come up beside them while Emily was ranting, his hands still tucked into his armpits, glancing nervously between the three women. "Lizzie had no idea. We never even would have come here originally if not for the monsters you sent through. You could have just carried on forever with us none the wiser."

"The ambassador spilled the beans on that one," Emily said. "King Zero is planning a comeback, he said. They want territory on Earth." She shook her head. "Wow, you must have been so excited when your target showed up on your doorstep, helpless and hurt. You couldn't have planned it better if you tried."

"I did plan it," Adae said. Her voice was soft, with none of the malice Emily expected from a villain's confession. "From a certain point."

"When?" Emily crossed her arms.

"You should sit," Adae said.

"I don't think so," Emily replied.

Adae waved her hand and an irresistible force pressed on Emily's chest like a stone, pushing her backwards and shoving her down beside Marlow on a hard leather couch.

"You should sit," the queen repeated.

Elizabeth put her hand on Michael's shoulder and together they sat on a second couch across from Emily. Adae stood alone between them, her hand still raised. She took a long breath in through her mouth and blew it out of her nose, then lowered her hand.

"It started with the witch," Adae said. She made a small motion with her fingers and her form shimmered and blurred and resolved again into the tan skin and long black-and-white hair of Valeria Tall and Gray.

"You," Emily breathed.

188

"Me," Adae agreed in the witch's voice. "I took Elizabeth's powers. I made a prophecy for her."

"To trick us into coming here," Emily said. "You lied. You made us think we could... oh, God."

"No," said Adae. "It was not a trick, not a lie." She blurred again and resolved into a too-skinny boy with ash-pale skin and oversized gray clothes. Then the face of the boy who'd led them through Olympia faded back into Adae's normal queenly countenance. "It was a call. I wish to leave this place and go home. To Earth."

"Earth isn't your home," Emily said.

"I am of the line of Adam," Adae replied. "We do not belong here. We should not rule Arcadia."

"You—" Emily blinked. "You want to quit being queen?"

Adae nodded. "If I abdicate, if I renounce the throne and return to Earth, the Curse of Adam will be broken. My powers will be lost and Elizabeth's will return." She smiled. "At which point she may make the boys whole."

"Bullshit." Emily stood up and Adae didn't force her back down. "You really expect us to buy that you stole Elizabeth's powers so we'd come here and help you? Why on earth would you put together some crazy scheme to get us here? You're the queen, for God's sake! If you wanted our help, you could have just asked!"

Something flared momentarily in Adae's eyes. "The queen of Cantelon does not—" She took a sudden, sharp breath in through her nose and her face untwisted. When she continued, her voice was back under control. "The queen of Cantelon does not ask for help."

It wasn't enough for Emily. Her fury was stirring again, uncoiling, demanding to be heard. She looked at her friends with her hands spread. "You guys aren't buying this, right? It's obviously some weird plan to get us to bring her to Earth. I almost died twice, just today—they tossed me in a hole with monsters, for God's sake!"

"Was Adae there for any of that?" asked Elizabeth softly.

"No, but—" Emily shook her head in frustration. "You can't seriously think Adae doesn't know what her husband is up to. The monsters, the dungeons, the Paramount they've chained up and hacked to pieces."

"They have Astraeos?" Elizabeth turned her white face up to Emily.

"Ask your friend here," Emily said.

Elizabeth looked at Adae and Emily looked, too, and she had to admit that if Adae were faking her surprise she was doing a good job of it. The queen's mouth was open, one shaking hand raised as though to cover it, and there were tears starting in the corners of her eyes.

"I had no idea," she whispered.

"Bull," Emily insisted, but she wasn't so sure now.

"Please," Adae said. "Listen. I'm lost in this palace. You have seen how the halls twist and split and turn back on themselves. You could wander forever and never find your way out... My life here is a hundred times more tangled. King Zero makes secrets and to protect his secrets he makes lies. I make lies to protect myself in turn. He has no knowledge of why you came here, how I brought you here, and I have no knowledge of his schemes."

"But why wouldn't you just ask for help?" Emily whispered.

"But I did," said Adae. Tears made tracks down her cheeks and her hands shook as she spoke. "I didn't threaten you or hurt you. I gave you a reason to come. I made a prophecy so you would know to take me from my throne. I offered a reward for your aid. When you were unsure where to walk I flooded the river to turn your path and helped you find my bears to guide you. Why won't you just do what I want?"

"And if we take you back to Earth, everything will be fixed?" Emily's hands were by her sides and her shoulders slumped. It was as though the entire world had been flipped upside down and she'd just found her footing in the new gravity—Adae's mad story made perfect sense once you saw even a sliver of what the queen's life must be like. Whoever Adam had been, his great-granddaughter was someone else entirely. Whatever cruel upbringing had shaped the line of Adam into a series of autocrats had had the opposite effect on its youngest member. Emily's heart hurt for her.

"Yes," said Adae, startling Emily. "The curse will be undone if I abandon the throne."

"Okay!" Emily clapped her hands, making Adae jump. "I love a quick fix. Let's do it. You lead the way out of Cantelon and we can take it from there. You're going to love Marlow's farm."

"Wait," said Elizabeth.

"What?" Emily said. "No disrespect, but I thought you'd be happy I'm not trying to kill her anymore."

"We can't just leave," Elizabeth said. "My people need me."

Emily blinked. "*Your* people?"

"If I'm the rightful queen of Arcadia, they're my people as much as any Albian," said Elizabeth. "All of them—the humans, the bears, the Paramounts. If we run now, King Zero will know we've learned his plans. He'll know Queen Adae has betrayed him."

"And he'll take it out on the people under him," Michael said. "I knew a hundred people just like him growing up. If we leave now, we're putting the whole population of Arcadia in danger."

"Shit," said Emily.

"I won't leave my people under Zero's boot," said Elizabeth.

"But you're powerless," Emily said. "Marlow and Michael are in bad shape. I hear what you're saying, but..."

"We fight now or not at all," Elizabeth insisted.

"Well, my dear, you're about to get your chance."

Emily spun on her heel to see King Zero standing framed in the open door to the hallway. The king was in full armor, helmet on his head, and he carried as a shield the slab of stone his men had cut from Astraeos. As he stepped forward, his boots heavy on the carpeted floor, Emily saw that he wasn't alone.

Half a dozen knights followed him, but they didn't wear the beetle-helmed armor of Cantelon. They dressed in shiny steel and carried long, gleaming swords. Over their plate mail they wore tabards emblazoned with the dragon of Albion.

The Albian knights spread out to surround Emily and her friends and as they did, they revealed a final shock. De Soto Rigmaiden, member in good standing of the Sabre & Torch Society, stood with his knife at the throat of Aminah Mirza, whose eyes were wide and panicked.

Rigmaiden caught Emily's eye and winked.

"Surprise."

CHAPTER 17

"Rigmaiden, what the hell are you doing?" Emily's head felt empty. There was a thin line of red where the Free Stater's knife pressed against Aminah's throat and green bruises stood out on her wrists, hints of the resistance that had been crushed out of her.

"Marlow!" Aminah cried, her voice raspy. The Albian magician stood sharply, causing the knights arrayed behind King Zero to take a collective step forward. Marlow's face was horrible, pale in openmouthed shock and deeply lined and aged by misery at his inability to even speak a comforting word to his friend. His sunken eyes showed his pain and somehow Emily suspected that Aminah understood.

"Shut up," said Rigmaiden, yanking on Aminah's arm which he had pinned behind her back. She winced but said nothing. "Emily, change of plans. We're working with Arthur and his boys now. Come on over."

"That's insane," Emily said. "King Zero is the one sending those monsters to Albion. Help me take him out and... and you can have all the credit with the S&T."

Rigmaiden snorted. "Nice try. But I don't work for the S&T."

"You don't..." Emily's eyes narrowed. "Sabine Free State? Is this about your stupid war with the Grand Kingdom?"

Rigmaiden nodded. "Plan was to get Miss Pendragon on our side by supporting her claim to the throne. But these Albian boys convinced me otherwise."

"You sold us out."

"Politics." Rigmaiden shrugged. "Your queen is dead in the water."

King Zero slammed his shield on the ground. "Enough of Earth! Knights, seize the pretender."

"Wait!" Emily said. Sir Arthur and his knights hesitated. "Arthur, listen to me. Once Zero gets rid of Elizabeth, you're next. He's not just gonna sit here in Cantelon. He's coming for Earth. He's coming for Albion."

Sir Arthur raised a gauntleted hand and his men stopped moving, instead glancing at one another in uncertainty. The knight flipped open the faceplate of his ballistic helmet, revealing his green eyes, fine-boned features, long nose, and a shock of blonde hair plastered to his forehead by sweat. To Emily's surprise, his wide mouth curved up in a smile.

"You think we don't know?" Arthur shook his head. "This is an alliance of convenience, Miss Sledge. It's all been worked out. The pretender Elizabeth Pendragon is a common enemy and we're all too happy to take her off King Zero's hands. If I can kill you into the bargain, well." He slammed his faceplate shut. "That's a nice bonus."

"Take her!" screamed Zero, and the Albian knights charged.

There were six of them and they fanned out to surround Emily and her friends as they moved into the sitting room. Emily gestured for Elizabeth, Michael, and Marlow to get behind her; she backed them all toward the far wall as they huddled together. Queen Adae stayed apart, letting them move away from her as though she were no part of their group.

One of the Albians—Sir Rowan, Emily thought—lunged for her, longsword leading. Rather than dodge or block, Emily stepped into the attack and grabbed the knight by his wrist. With a vicious yank she pulled him off-balance; his leading foot met hers and he crashed to his knees. Emily spun on her heel and kicked the sword from his hand; it slid across the carpet and stopped at Michael's feet.

Sir Arthur came for her as Sir Rowan struggled to his feet. Emily put him back down with a heel to his helmet then spun to meet Arthur, reaching out an open hand to Michael as she turned. Arthur charged her with his sword raised and as he brought it down in a two-handed chop she caught the flash of steel in her peripheral vision. Her grip closed around the blade of Sir Rowan's sword, thrown by Michael, and she swung it up to sloppily deflect Arthur's blow as stinging lines of red appeared on her fingers.

Sir Arthur took a step back, refusing to overbalance despite the surprise of her parry and giving Emily a moment to get a proper grip on the sword. They came together a half-second later, steel clashing on steel as Arthur turned Emily's lunge and swung his free fist at her head. She twisted out of the way and bull-rushed the knight who, while taller, wasn't much heavier than she was. Arthur staggered backwards but kept his footing and Emily pressed the attack, bringing her sword up for a quick stab at the exposed joint at the knight's hip. His own blade flashed down to slide hers away; he was a hell of a swordsman, much faster than she remembered.

Sir Rowan had regained his feet and retreated behind his companions. Now two other knights were closing on her, trying to box her in. A wide, arcing slash of her sword reminded them to keep their distance. They stood like that for a frozen moment, the three knights like trainers trying to break a wild animal, knowing they can overpower it together but each afraid to make the first move.

"Out of my way!" King Zero bulled through the ring of knights. He had a long-handled sort of war hammer in his right hand, with a long spike sticking from the back of the hammerhead, and his left bore the huge stone shield made from Astraeos's armor. It was six inches thick, as wide as he was and almost as tall; just lifting the thing would have been a challenge even for Emily.

She knew her sword would be no good against that massive shield, but she attacked anyway. She feinted left, hoping to draw out the king's hammer or at least get him to move his shield, but he didn't take the bait. She didn't even try a swing at him, instead bouncing back to square off with him again.

Behind her, the knights had taken advantage of the distraction to surround Elizabeth and the boys. Adae still stood apart, apparently unnoticed by the Albians in their focus on their own royalty. Emily's moment to assess the situation had passed, though, as King Zero rushed forward, his shield raised. The massive thing had to be slowing him down, as did his stone armor, but to move like that under all that weight suggested an absolutely colossal strength. Emily did *not* want to get hit by that war hammer.

Instead, she sidestepped, blessing her superior speed as the king turned to chase her. She took a few more steps back, letting him follow closely but staying just out of reach of the hammer, until she felt her back collide with one of Queen Adae's bookshelves. She bent her knees and grabbed a breath.

King Zero swung his hammer; it blurred as it cut through the air toward her. Emily leaped straight up and the hammer clipped her foot with a crack before crashing into the bookshelf. Emily's ankle bent painfully as she landed on the shaft of the hammer, but she kept her balance. Zero looked up, his eyes wide under his horned helmet. Emily twisted and grabbed a shelf, knocking books aside with her sword as she fixed her grip, then threw herself backwards.

The bookshelf came away from the wall as she arced over the king, bringing the furniture with her. Books cascaded down over Zero, bouncing off his raised shield. A thick leather-bound tome impaled on one of the horns of his helmet, then he disappeared as the shelf itself crashed over him.

The wind was knocked from Emily's lungs as she hit the carpet on her back. She'd lost her sword somewhere in the fall and she spasmed in shock as a shape loomed over her, but it resolved into Queen Adae, reaching out a helping hand. Emily grabbed it and pulled herself to her feet. The Albian knights had turned in surprise at the sound of toppling furniture; the ex-squire Daniel had flipped his faceplate open and wore a look of openmouthed shock. But they still had her friend surrounded.

"Let's go," said Adae, tugging at Emily's arm. "Let's go!"

"Go?" Emily blinked. Beneath the fallen bookshelf, King Zero stirred.

"To Earth!" Adae's eyes were frantic, her voice barely under control. "Take me to Earth. We can come back for your friends once I'm safe."

"Hell no," Emily said. "You heard Lizzie: we fight together or not at all." She turned to face the panicked queen head on. "Listen to me. You took her power, so use it."

"Use it?" Adae blinked. The bookshelf rose, spilling books as Zero pushed it up and off him.

"*Do something!*" Emily shouted. Adae jumped in surprise, but the panic cleared from her eyes. She put both her hands up, palms out, murmured a few hasty words in a breathless voice, then clapped.

The sound was like a gunshot in the little sitting room. Emily's ears rang, but under the whine she recognized silence. The room was still.

"What did you do?" she gasped.

"Come on!" Adae was already running for the door; she paused only to beckon with a desperate hand. Emily glanced over her shoulder and realized that the queen was gesturing to her friends, who were picking their way carefully between the raised swords of the Albian knights, who stood completely motionless like a set of matching statues.

Under the bookshelf, King Zero crouched half-hunched, caught in the act of lifting the shelf off himself with his back. The single remaining book slid from its place and clattered on top of the pile of its mates. He, too, was frozen.

Emily didn't need to see any more. She followed her friends from the room at a sprint.

Their feet hammered on stone as they ran through the halls of the palace. Emily had quickly overtaken Adae, who was gasping for breath and shiny with sweat. Emily grabbed her arm and slung it over her own shoulder to support the queen as they ran, but she soon realized that Adae was more than just winded.

"You've never cast a spell like that, have you?" she asked as they cut around a corner into a parallel hall one layer deeper into the circular labyrinth of the palace.

"So much power," gasped Adae.

"She needs it back," Emily said.

"I… I can't…" Adae's eyes unfocused and rather than finish her sentence, she fainted in Emily's arms.

"She's out!" Emily shouted as she heaved the queen's body over her shoulders in a fireman's carry.

"Her spell will break," Michael called from the back of the group, where he was helping Elizabeth keep up.

"We can't stay here." Emily slowed her pace to let the others catch up. "Once Zero starts moving there'll be guards everywhere. We need to get out of Cantelon. I'm sorry, Lizzie."

Elizabeth shook her head. "Don't be sorry. Just promise me we'll return."

Emily nodded. "As soon as we can. Okay. Lizzie, you know the way out. Michael, you're with her. Set the pace and *keep moving*. Marlow's in the middle. Adae and I are rear guard."

"Can you fight like that?" Michael's brow was furrowed.

"Don't worry," Emily said, "I can just throw her at them." Then, "I'm kidding!" a second later, after a look at her friends' faces. "Come on, move it!"

Elizabeth led them through the twisting halls of the palace and out onto the streets of Beverlay. They sprinted past a pair of stunned guards, who seemed to have a momentary internal debate that ended with the decision that they'd been told to keep trouble out, not in. The long, straight avenues of the city took them through residential plazas and between rowhouses of stone and crystal as they fled for the edge of town.

Soon they reached the long, long ramp that spiraled up the wall of the crater in which the city lay. They pounded up it, but the Arcanes quickly tired, and Emily found herself at the head of the group once again despite her burden. Halfway up the ramp, Michael fell to his knees, gasping and heaving as though about to puke.

"Come on, Michael!" Emily shouted. "I know it hurts, just—"

"Look!" Elizabeth pointed down the ramp, which curved down to the ground maybe a quarter mile below them. At its foot, King Zero and the half dozen Albians were just beginning their ascent, followed by Rigmaiden, who was shoving a stumbling Aminah before him. A mob of armored guards trailed maybe fifty yards behind them, struggling to keep up.

"Shit," Emily said. "Time to go."

She pulled Michael to his feet and with a tight grip on his arm, began to run again.

By the time they reached the cavern below the Counselor's throne room in Barbary Cross, King Zero and the knights were barely a hundred yards behind them. Emily led the way into the long, echoing cave, Adae still across her shoulders and the three Arcanes stumbling after her.

Across the cavern Hyperion's stone boots, each the size of a car, stood in the ruddy gloom. As far as Emily could tell the Paramount hadn't moved since making a staircase of its body to let them down into Cantelon. With any luck it'd let them back up again.

Emily reached Hyperion's left foot and heaved herself up it, laid Adae gently on top, then reached down to pull Elizabeth up. Michael came after her, then Marlow, who glanced over his shoulder at the approaching Albians as Emily lifted him. She knew what he was thinking, but Aminah was invisible in the shadows.

The foot moved.

Adae screamed as she jerked awake. Why the motion of the foot would stir her after all the running and climbing she'd slept through, Emily couldn't guess, but the queen of Cantelon sat bolt upright and almost toppled off Hyperion's boot before Emily grabbed her arm.

"Who dares?" rumbled a voice like a rockslide from high above their heads.

"I am Elizabeth Pendragon, queen of Albion and Cantelon," said Elizabeth, her face raised. "Your friend."

Emily spared a look back at the cavern and saw their pursuers halfway across and closing fast.

"Pendragon queen," said Hyperion. "Did you find my brother?"

"We did," said Elizabeth. "He is a prisoner of King Zero in Beverlay. We were unable to help him. I am sorry."

"I will go to Beverlay," boomed Hyperion. King Zero had nearly reached them. The Albian knights fanned out behind him, making to surround the Paramount's foot and trap their quarry on it.

"No need, monster!" roared Zero, skidding to a stop just below Emily. He clashed his war hammer against the huge shield made of Hyperion's brother. "I am King Zero of Cantelon and you will make me a fine suit of armor!"

"Hyperion, we need to escape," Emily called, hoping the colossus could hear her over the sounds of armor clanking and weapons being drawn. It didn't respond.

"Hyperion, please help us," said Elizabeth and there was a sound like a hundred millstones grinding as the Paramount kneeled. It lowered a hand and as soon as it came within reach, Emily jumped aboard and began pulling her friends after her.

"Someday you have to tell me how you get him to listen," she said as she hauled Elizabeth up next to her.

"I start by listening," said the queen. Emily reached down for Marlow's hand as an arrow spanged off the Paramount's stone palm barely a foot from her. The Cantelon soldiers had caught up and their sergeant was shouting them into some sort of order as they strung bows and pulled full quivers from their backs. The next arrow to come would be one of twenty.

Hyperion's hand began to rise, lifting the huddled companions with it. The soldiers released a flight of arrows that soared past or broke on the back of the great stone hand as the Albian knights started scaling the Paramount's leg. By the time Emily leaped down into the Counselor's throne room they'd reached its hips; the colossus was clearly focused on helping Elizabeth escape rather than fighting off her pursuers.

Queen Adae jumped into Emily's waiting arms and Michael and Elizabeth followed together, with Marlow coming last as usual. Unburdened of its human cargo, Hyperion turned its attention to King Zero and the knights, filling the air with dust as it slapped at the climbing Albians with a sound like buildings collapsing. Peering over the lip of the pit that connected the throne room and the cavern below, Emily watched with glee as the knights fell away, but her satisfaction quickly turned sour when half the squad of Cantelon soldiers sent arrows at her while a dozen ran forward with ladders and grappling hooks on long ropes.

Emily ducked back to let the arrows pass. Up and down the rim of the pit the hooks appeared, thunking into the stone floor, and then the tops of ladders rose up from the shadowed depths. Emily kicked one of the ladders over as she bolted back to her friends, who had taken cover behind the broken throne of the Counselor.

"We gotta go!" she shouted.

"Hyperion—" Michael began.

"If anyone can handle them, it's him," Emily said. "There's way too many for me. Come on."

She shoved the others ahead of her, herding them out of the throne room like wayward children as the first knights came over the edge of the pit. Hyperion's eyes flared like torches in the gloom and searing beams of blue-white light blazed from them, shearing a Cantelon soldier in half as he came up a ladder.

They spilled into the waiting room of the Counselor's temple and from there out onto the small plaza that fronted it. The long central avenue of Barbary Cross sloped down and away from them, a straight shot to the exit from the city onto the gray side of Olympia. They had days of travel ahead of them if they meant to reach Earth, but there was nothing to do but start.

They'd just crossed the plaza when the temple behind them exploded in a whirlwind of dust and shards of stone. From the wreckage rose Hyperion, its arms outstretched with a soldier in each fist, which it smashed together and let drop. At its full height it was taller than the buildings of the city. The Paramount roared and its voice shook the ground.

"Holy..." Emily breathed.

Six knights in dust-grayed plate armor charged from the collapsing temple, led by King Zero with his war hammer held high. They skidded to a halt in the plaza and turned back to face their giant foe, forming up into a neat line with the king at the center and a few steps in front.

Hyperion loomed above them, raised a man-sized fist, and brought it down to crush the king. He should have moved—could have dodged as the fist came down, Emily had seen how fast he could move—but instead he raised his shield and put it between him and Hyperion.

The blow landed like a bomb going off. The shockwave rippled through the street like water and hid King Zero in a great gout of dust. The remains of the Counselor's temple were tossed in the air to resettle into a new shambles. All around the plaza windows burst, raining glittering glass over the knights. A tall rowhouse slouched, then gave up, collapsing down on itself until it was half its original height.

The dust settled, revealing King Zero unmoved.

He stepped back, letting Hyperion's fist slump to the ground. The Paramount was stunned, or at least it wasn't moving. From the wreckage of the temple about half the squad of Cantelon soldiers emerged with dogged determination and sent a flight of arrows at Hyperion. Rather than glancing off, they stuck quivering in its stone hide.

Sir Arthur began shouting orders and three of his knights split off to handle Emily and her charges as Arthur and his other two men warily approached the Paramount. Shaking off her own shock, Emily waved for her friends to start running again. Michael staggered to his feet, pulling Elizabeth up in the crook of his elbow; Marlow and Adae leaned on each other uncertainly.

"Come on, move it!" Emily said.

"We can't keep running." Michael shook his head. His face was gray with dust. "My legs are like jelly. Adae is barely conscious."

"Can she—now would be a great time for a spell," Emily tried, but Michael just stared at her. A glance showed the knights closing in, their swords at the ready. "Okay, I'll hold them off. Just move. Please."

"Emily—" Elizabeth began, but she was cut off by a gravelly roar that echoed through the city. Hyperion had come back to life.

Sir Arthur hung from the Paramount's arm by one hand, his sword dangling from the other. The colossus kicked one of the other knights away as another flight of arrows pricked its back. King Zero darted forward to strike Hyperion's leg with his hammer, sending a shower of blue sparks flying, then dodged back before the Paramount could retaliate.

Hyperion shook its arm and Arthur fell free. One of his knights— Daniel, Emily guessed—bolted forward to try to catch him and they crashed to the ground together in a tangle of steel. The colossus raised a foot to stomp both men at once. Seeing their captain in danger, the three Albians dispatched to deal with Emily sprinted to his side. Not for the first time, Emily felt a pang of sadness that she'd continually found herself at odds with the Albian knighthood. Fearless and loyal, they would have made good friends if they weren't always trying to kill her.

Hyperion brought its foot down just as the knights pulled Sir Arthur free. He was thrashing as they dragged him away and Emily suddenly saw why: Daniel was still in danger. The squire-turned-knight looked up as the huge stone boot came down and at the last second he grabbed his sword from the cobbles beside him and jabbed it straight up.

Daniel disappeared under Hyperion's foot. The Paramount roared, a different sound this time—pain? Then, slowly, the colossus fell backwards. Daniel's sword glinted from the sole of its foot; it seemed to hang in the air forever, suspended mid-collapse, until inevitably it hit the ground with a thunder that rattled Emily's numb ears.

King Zero was the first to react, darting across the plaza to where the Paramount's head lay amid shattered paving stones. He let his shield go, took up a two-handed grip on his war hammer, and brought its spiked head down like a woodcutter. The spike pierced Hyperion's left eye, which shattered with a burst of crackling blue light that surrounded the king in a momentary nimbus, flared, and then died. Zero roared in triumph, wrenched his hammer free, and brought it down again into the Paramount's other eye.

Hyperion was still.

King Zero turned and stalked across the square, dragging his hammer across the cobbles. He was headed for Emily and while Sir Arthur was occupied with what remained of Daniel, the other four knights were in motion again, flanking the king as he approached.

"Now, Emily," said Zero. "You and I—"

Hyperion's left arm lashed out and its hand grabbed the king, enclosing him in a stony grip.

"Flee," Hyperion said, its blind eyes locked with Emily's.

"Let me go!" Zero roared, but the Paramount was dead, its hand frozen around the king.

"Time to go," Emily said as the Albian knights paused, uncertain. She turned to her friends, shoving them into motion. "Time to go!"

"Running away?" Zero called. "Really? Aren't you forgetting someone?"

From behind the mob of Cantelon soldiers, De Soto Rigmaiden appeared. He'd tied Aminah's hands behind her back and stuck a gag in her mouth. King Zero began to laugh and he took his time enjoying himself while Emily stared in horror at her captive friend.

"Twenty-four hours!" Zero shouted as Emily began to run. "Twenty-four hours to surrender, or I'll cut the girl's throat!"

Chapter 18

The crumbling gray buildings of Barbary Cross blurred together as Emily hustled her group down the central avenue. The rusted gate out of the city was in sight and a vague plan was forming in Emily's head involving the Paramount named Crius who slept there. So she didn't see the hooded figure who stepped into the street until she'd almost bowled him over.

"Emily Sledge," the man said, gesturing to a narrow alley that cut between two tall townhouses. "This way."

"Uh, no thanks," Emily said. She moved to go around but was blocked.

"Please, come," the hooded figure said. "All of you."

Emily glanced back at her friends. Elizabeth nodded, Michael shrugged, and Marlow just stared. Past them there was no sign of immediate pursuit by the Albians or King Zero and his men.

"Fine," she said. "But make it quick."

The priest, or so she thought of him, led them into the alley. It was choked with rubble and filth and ended at a cracked stone wall where another person huddled beneath a matching hooded cloak, this one a light gray instead of the deep black of the first. As she approached, the disheveled figure looked up and a faint cloud of dust rose from his head then settled over his shoulders. The cloak itself was black, Emily realized, but this priest was covered head to foot in a layer of heavy gray dust.

"What do you want?" Emily asked, crossing her arms. In response the gray priest, his invisible gaze still set on Emily, opened his cloak. At first,

Emily thought he was carrying a baby or a curled-up child, as grayed by dust as the priest himself. Then she realized she was looking at the top half of a humanoid figure. Its face was smooth, its body neuter, and it ended at the waist as though it had been neatly severed by a guillotine. It was the Counselor.

"You have brought destruction to Barbary Cross," the Counselor said, its voice neutral, the red light in its chest pulsing in time with its words. It was hard to be sure, but Emily thought the light was fainter than the last time she'd seen it.

"I—I'm sorry," Emily stammered. "We didn't mean to."

"We are all that remain of the priesthood," said the black-robed man who'd brought them down the alley. "We rescued the Counselor from the wreckage of your fight with Hyperion... or we tried to. It is dying."

"I'm sorry," Emily said. "I really am. We never wanted a fight, but we had no choice. King Zero attacked us when we tried to help Adae get out."

The Counselor's heart light fluttered. "The queen of Cantelon is here?"

Emily glanced at Elizabeth and Adae behind her, sweat-sheened and feverish. "Yeah."

"The line of Adam walks the streets of Barbary Cross." There was almost a hint of sadness in the Counselor's voice. "I have failed."

"It's not too late," Emily said. "Listen to me. We can drive out Zero and the knights, we just need a little help. Hyperion is... they killed him. But the other Paramounts can stop him, I know they can. You can control them, right? Turn them on and point them in the right direction and I'll do the rest."

The Counselor's smooth face turned away, as though it were staring off into infinity. "I cannot do that."

"What?" Emily blinked. "Why the hell not?"

"I have shut them down," the Counselor said. "Permanently. The Paramounts will never fight again."

"Why would you do that?" Emily shook her head in disbelief. "After a hundred years growing moss, now is when we actually need them!"

"I will tell you," said the Counselor. "If you will listen." The featureless head faced her again. "After the people of Olympia created the Paramounts, they argued over how best to use them. Should they attack Adam and his army? Should they hide behind the walls of the city with the Paramounts to protect them? They could not decide.

"So they beseeched their artificers for an answer and those makers created me." The Counselor's heart light flared brightly for a moment. "The people of Olympia ceded all authority to me. I was given absolute power over Barbary Cross, its people, and its defenses, with my sole charge to keep it safe from outsiders.

"When Adam attacked, he could not best the Paramounts, and in time he gave up. But Adam was not the only threat that waited in the outside world. Any visitor might be a danger to my people. Under my direction, the Paramounts drove them all away. In time, they stopped coming all together and Olympia knew peace. I was pleased to watch the Paramounts sleep, to watch the moss and brush grow upon them."

"So, what—you don't want to wake them up, is that it?" Emily crossed her arms. "Because let me tell you—"

"That is not it," the Counselor said. "When Hyperion fought King Zero, my temple crumbled. Worse, many other buildings fell and were lost. The act of resistance itself brought destruction. Our defenses do as much damage as our enemies."

"You can't be serious," Emily said.

"Waking the others—Crius, Cronos, Coeos—would mean the end of Olympia."

"Olympia is screwed anyway if we don't do something," Emily insisted. "King Zero is gonna conquer all of Arcadia and then he's coming for Earth. You can't just sit by and let him do it!"

"We will not fight," the Counselor said. "We will let King Zero pass through Olympia safely."

"I can't believe you won't help us." Emily's voice was a whisper.

"We are helping you already," the Counselor said.

"What?" Emily snorted. "How?"

"We are letting you pass through Olympia safely."

"Fine." Emily turned her back on the Counselor and its ragged priests. "We're done here. Come on."

She stomped off down the alley, cursing the waste of time that had been her conversation with the Counselor. Behind her, Elizabeth, Michael, Marlow, and Adae said their goodbyes and got ready to start running again.

As promised, Crius did nothing to stop them as they passed through the gate of Barbary Cross. A new stillness had settled over the Paramount and a pair of gray birds twittered from atop its head. There was no sign of King Zero or the Albians as they descended the slopes of Olympia. Cronos, who still sat with its hand raised at the boulder-ridden foot of the mountain, was as motionless as its sibling.

The eternal green of Arborea was a welcome sight as Emily and her friends struck out across the meadow. For a while it was enough just to leave the gray and black lands behind them, to feel the warmth of the sun as it crossed the wide blue sky. But as Emily realized that Zero had given up the chase, her mind began to insist that she reckon with exactly why.

She called a halt in the shadow of the last of Olympia's boulders. Elizabeth and Michael immediately sat and leaned against the rock; Marlow watched Emily with his arms crossed as Adae peered around in fascination.

"We need a plan," Emily said. "Adae, I assume Zero's not just bluffing about killing Aminah?"

"What?" said the queen, blinking. "No. No, he's serious. You can't rule by fear if you don't follow through."

Emily nodded. "Thought so. Okay, if I were him, I would post up in the deepest hole in Beverlay and let my enemies come to me. Is there any way to get Aminah back without straight up walking into Zero's trap?"

The pained silence that followed was all the answer Emily needed.

"Fine," she said. "We're heading back to Cantelon."

"What is *that*?" gasped Adae. Emily looked in alarm to see the queen pointing to a short, spindly tree covered in spidery yellow blooms.

"Witch hazel," Elizabeth said and Marlow nodded. "Blooming out of season."

"Witch hazel, of course!" Adae clapped with childlike glee as she ran to the tree. "I remember you!"

"Remember…?" Emily said.

"I planted this tree," Adae said, "years ago when I was little. Before I became queen. My mother, Queen Nothing, loved to take me walking. We'd be gone from Beverlay for weeks at a time, exploring Arcadia. Learning the land, she called it. The king was always angry when we returned— gone too long, he'd say—but it was worth it."

"How long has it been?" Emily asked.

"Years," Adae said. "Years. I knew from the moment King Adama introduced me to Zero that he wouldn't like me going out walking. And I had all the work of being queen to keep me busy."

"I don't know how many trees you planted," Emily said, "but a lot of them seem to have survived. There are weird plants all over Arborea."

"Zero was so handsome when I met him," Adae continued, as though Emily hadn't spoken. "All I'd known was that he was a powerful warlord who served my father. I was so pleased when I saw him. I knew he would be cruel, all King Adama's warlords were, but it was a good match, or so father said. My mother wept and wept, but when the time came, she dried her eyes."

"That's awful," Emily said.

"It is?"

"Uh, guys?" Michael said. "We've got company."

Company took the form of some two dozen bears, fully armed and armored with bucket helms and spears. They quickly encircled the humans with their weapons lowered, making a ring of glittering steel, a view Emily had gotten all too used to during her time in Arcadia.

She sighed. "Now what?"

"We find." There was a ripple of motion among the animals and a great black-furred bear pushed his way between his inferiors into the center of the circle. He towered above Emily; the black-and-white plume bobbing atop his helmet blocked out the sun. It was Skaros, she realized, the warband leader who'd captured them originally. "You run, but we find. Always find."

"Oh," Emily said. She'd nearly forgotten about their escape from the bears' castle. "Right. Well, look, we kind of have a lot going on right now. Can we get back to you in a couple days?"

"No," rumbled Skaros. "You come now."

"Do something," Adae said, grabbing Emily's arm in a tight-fingered grip. Emily was about to shush her when she realized who she was talking to.

"Wait!" Emily straightened up and looked Skaros in the eye, or at least tried to. "You're not in charge here."

"Are not?" Skaros's eyes narrowed.

"Nope." Emily stepped aside, letting the bear get a better look at Adae. "This is Queen Adae, great-granddaughter of Adam and your queen." Adae raised her chin and peered up at the armored bear. In return, Skaros squinted down at her, his head cocked.

"Is not," he said finally. "You come now."

"What?" Emily said. "Yes, she is. Tell him, Adae."

"I am your queen," Adae said.

"No," said Skaros. "Adam was of the divine. Was of power, magic. A clan leader and war maker. You are... not."

"Rude," said Emily, but the bear ignored her.

"How dare you," Adae said. "I am your queen!"

"Where are soldiers?" Skaros asked. "Servants? Where is king? Is not here." He shrugged, his shoulders rippling like a hill in an earthquake. "So. Not queen. Do not say again. Now come."

"Emily—" Michael started, but Adae's voice drowned him out.

"You dare question me, Queen Adae of Cantelon, daughter of King Adama, of the line of Adam?" She wasn't exactly shouting, but she was certainly projecting. It was actually pretty impressive, Emily thought.

"Prove," said Skaros.

"Very well," said Adae. Her voice had dropped in volume but not in intensity. "I will prove my lineage to you. Watch and be ashamed."

Adae spread her hands, palms up, as though standing in a summer rain. But instead of falling from the sky, it came up from the ground: just sparks at first, like embers floating off a campfire, then lines of light that burst one by one from the ground around the queen, stabbing up into the sky like spears of every color.

Adae's feet left the ground; she rose slowly as the stabbing lights bent into curves that arced around her to make interlocking circles, spinning around her on a dozen offset axes so they continually intersected and broke apart again, until their blurring paths formed a translucent globe around the queen that was every color at once and then simply white.

The bears stared in gape-mouthed awe at the hovering orb of light; then it flared and some shielded their eyes while others fell back, turning their heads, or dropped to the ground and buried their faces in the grass. Soon only Skaros was able to watch the blazing globe. Its light caught the subtle hues in his black fur, making him shimmer like the dark crystal of Cantelon with a thousand colors that had been invisible until now. His face was a mask of wonder, his eyes wide and clear.

With a jolt, Emily realized that she was squeezing Marlow's hand, but the magician didn't seem to have noticed. Beside them, Elizabeth had her arms around Michael, enfolding him protectively as they watched the arcane spectacle.

The sphere of light disappeared and Adae fell. Emily darted forward; the queen landed in her arms in a graceless flop. She was unconscious again, her face shining with sweat and her skin a bit greenish, but breathing evenly. Emily laid her gently on the grass, then turned her face up to see Skaros staring down at them with a frown creasing his long face.

"A pretty trick," he rumbled.

"A trick?" Emily stood, brushing grass from her pants. "Seriously?"

"Many and many are the magicians who come," Skaros said. "Light and lightning are their tools."

"You felt it, though," Emily said. Something had changed about the bear, though she couldn't put her finger on it. His eyes seemed brighter. "I know you did."

"Many magicians," Skaros repeated. "None are of Adam."

Adam—the name bounced off something in Emily's mind, a realization that had waited patiently since Adae had cast her first spell in her sitting room. Her breath caught as she realized what exactly the queen had been trying to prove.

"The Curse of Adam," Emily said. "Anybody who uses a spell has to pay for it, unless they're descended from Adam, right?"

"Is so," Skaros agreed, his eyes narrowed. "And?"

"And—well, look at her!" Emily gestured to the woman who lay unconscious at her feet. "Okay, she keeps knocking herself out, I'll give you that. But that spell was... I don't even know how powerful. Look at her. Did she pay for it?"

Skaros's black-lipped frown deepened and he bent over to peer at Adae. Emily watched his eyes rove over her form, checking her limbs, her hands and feet, her face. Finally he nudged the body with his huge foot. The queen rolled onto her side, muttered something, and began to snore.

"Unhurt," Skaros said.

"Exactly!" Emily pointed at him. "Admit it—only the line of Adam could get away with a spell like that."

Silently, Skaros knelt. On his knees he was about Emily's height and for a moment their eyes locked, then he turned his gaze to the sleeping woman below him. He took off his plumed helmet and set it on the grass at his side, then reached out for Adae. Emily's heart skipped a beat, but before she could react she understood, and she let Skaros lift the queen's body.

The great bear cradled Adae in his arms, hugging her to his chest like a father with a baby. She sighed and nuzzled into his fur. Watching him,

212

Emily realized what had changed about Skaros. He seemed somehow more human, either more intelligent or just more empathetic. A memory of Aidos, the bears' storyteller, floated up—hadn't he said something about Adam making them more human? The phrase he'd used sounded in Emily's thoughts in Aidos's rich voice: *a piece of the divine.*

"Why is she here?" Skaros asked, his voice a low purr like an idling engine.

"We had to run away," Emily breathed. "From Cantelon, from King Zero. He wants to conquer everything, all of Arcadia and then Earth."

"What is Earth?" the bear said.

"Oh, uh, never mind. The point is, we had to run from him."

Skaros cocked his head, looking like a confused dog. "Why? He is the king."

Emily sighed. "Okay, think of it this way. He wants to conquer everything. Where's he gonna start? Right here in Arborea. He and his soldiers and his weird monsters are going to come here and take everything. Your spears, your armor, your castles, everything."

"He is the king." Skaros cocked his head the other way. "The chosen of the line of Adam. Our spears are his. Our armor is his. Our castles are his. We welcome him."

Emily looked at her friends helplessly. Marlow shook his head slowly, his eyebrows raised, and Elizabeth just stared at the bear dwarfing the woman in his arms. Emily caught Michael's eye and his brow furrowed sympathetically, then he stepped forward to stand beside her as he addressed Skaros.

"He hurt her," he said. Skaros looked up, his dark eyes round. "That's why we had to run away. King Zero hurts Adae. Every day. Not with his hands, but with his words, do you understand?"

"Hurts with words?" the bear said.

"Yes," said Michael. "He won't let her be free, so she had to run away."

"But she is of the line of Adam."

"He doesn't care," Emily said, willing the bear to comprehend. "He... puts her in a cage with his words."

Skaros stood. Adae slid off his chest and slumped into his arms, so that he held her parallel to the ground, her loose black hair falling in waves to the ground, the hem of her dress stirring in the faint breath of the breeze.

The other warrior bears picked themselves up, got to their feet, and crowded around their captain. They peered around his back, over his shoulders, into his arms, all trying to get a glimpse of their queen. Skaros roared and Emily thought of Hyperion. Then they all roared, together, their voices making an earth-quaking chorus of animal rage.

Adae snorted and her head jerked up. "Where are we?" she gasped, looking around with a wide-eyed stare.

"Arborea," Emily said quickly. "It's okay, you're safe."

"No," said Adae. She twisted out of Skaros's arms and dropped to the grass. "My husband will come for me. Why aren't we in the castle?"

"We just ran away—"

"The bears' castle!" Adae snapped. She looked up at Skaros. "Take me there now. Today has been exhausting. We'll rest for the night and in the morning we'll begin our journey to Earth."

"Absolutely not!" Emily said.

Adae frowned. "I beg your pardon?"

"I said no," Emily said. "We're not going to Earth."

"Emily," Adae said slowly, "would you prefer to go alone or with an entire army of bears to protect you?"

"I'd *prefer* to go after we rescue my friend," Emily said between gritted teeth. "You heard Zero. We have less than a day before he kills Aminah. There's nowhere near enough time to get home first."

"You're suggesting we assault Cantelon like this?" She pointed at Michael, Marlow, and Elizabeth in turn. "No hands, no tongue, no powers. Bring me to Earth. Adam's Curse will break, Elizabeth's powers will return, and I shall remain there while you launch your rescue mission."

"There won't *be* a rescue mission if Aminah dies." Michael had let his arms fall to his sides and his scorched hand was opening and closing again and again. Marlow stepped up next to his friend, his chin high, his face tight.

"I'm in charge here, Emily said so." Adae's hands were clenched into fists and she looked about ready to stamp her foot. "I say we're going to Earth."

"Adae, listen—" Emily tried.

"I'm feeling threatened," the queen said. "Skaros, please help me."

The bear, who had been watching the exchange with curious eyes, nodded and grabbed a spear from one of his warriors. He leveled it at Emily and the other bears followed suit. They surrounded Queen Adae like a bristling hedge, its many steel thorns pointed at the other humans.

"Adae, please," Emily tried again. "I don't blame you for wanting to get out of here. I want to run, too. I want to go get help. I want to go home. But I can't. My friend has a sword hanging over her head and she's waiting for us to save her."

"I don't trust you," Adae said, her eyes flickering over all of them but landing on Elizabeth. "You're up to something. I'm offering you your power back and you don't want it. Skaros, take them."

The bear gestured to his warriors and half a dozen of them stepped forward. One grabbed Elizabeth, hoisting her over its shoulder in a mock fireman's carry before she could object. Two more put heavy paws on Marlow's and Michael's shoulders; one Arcane did nothing to resist and the other, with his ruined arms, simply couldn't.

Three bears pressed their spear tips into Emily's chest.

"Adae, look at me." Emily put her hands up, palms out, in what she hoped was a nonthreatening gesture. "We just want to get our friend back, that's all."

"But *why?*"

"Because—listen to me!" She pointed at Adae and immediately two dozen spears pointed back at her. She ignored them. "We could have just left you in Cantelon after you fainted the first time. Remember? But we didn't. As a matter of fact, I had to literally *carry you* out of the palace, through the entire city, up that stupid ramp, and through a bunch of tunnels, with your husband and those Albian assholes chasing us the whole way. I could have just left you there—actually, I'm starting to wish I had!"

Adae had gone quiet and her eyes were wide, but Emily wasn't done yet.

"Look, is it easier to go it alone? Hell yeah it is. It's exhausting having to worry about other people. But what's the point of fighting if you're just doing it for yourself? Because it's exciting? Because it feels good to win? Because it makes that little voice in your head shut up for a while?

"That's not enough. If you have power over other people, if you're stronger, or smarter, or you just happened to be put in charge through no fault of anybody's—you have to use that power to lift them up, not put them down.

"Adae, you impress the hell out of me. You figured out you don't have to be like your ancestors and that's amazing. But it takes work. If you're gonna give up your throne, that means giving up getting your way all the time. I'm telling you this as your friend: I need you to decide if it's worth it and I need you to decide now, because with or without you, when this conversation is over, I'm going to rescue Aminah."

CHAPTER 19

Queen Adae stood speechless behind her bristling ring of warriors, her brow furrowed and her mouth slightly open. The bears whose spear tips pricked Emily's chest stared stonily ahead. Skaros shifted his grip on his own weapon, aiming it directly at Emily's heart, leveling it so the flat arrow-shaped blade would slip neatly between her ribs on the first strike.

"I have never in my life been spoken to this way," said Adae. "I am queen in Cantelon. No one denies me."

"First time for everything," Emily said, her face still flushed, her mood apocalyptic.

"You deny me, yet you claim to love me," Adae continued, her voice thoughtful. "It is a paradox."

"It's not," Emily said. A wave of nauseous panic crashed in her stomach; Adae was clearly intelligent, had all the power of her own lineage and Elizabeth's, and she was even older than Michael and Marlow, yet she could be as moody as a toddler. "Real friendship doesn't mean always saying yes, it means being honest."

"You honestly think I am wrong?"

"Yeah."

"Hm." Adae reached out her hand and put it on Skaros's arm. The bear glanced back at her, spent a moment taking in her face, then lowered his spear. His warriors followed suit. The queen's eyes met Emily's and she smiled. "First time for everything."

Emily let out the breath she'd been holding and felt her shoulders sag. "So you won't stop us?"

"I still think it would be better to get where you're going with an army of bears around you," Adae said. "But I suppose a platoon will have to do."

"You mean—"

"Skaros, I would like you and your warriors to help us throw down King Zero." The queen and her bear looked at each other, Adae craning her neck to peer up as Skaros pressed his chin nearly to his chest to see the woman far below. "Will you do this for me?"

"You are of Adam," Skaros said. "We will kill and die for you."

"I hope that won't be necessary," Elizabeth said, stepping forward to take Adae's hands, queen to queen. "Thank you, Adae. We are in your debt."

"So what's the plan?" asked Michael. "We should be able to get back in through Barbary Cross."

Emily shook her head. "They'll be expecting us. Adae, there must be other ways in."

"There are many, but King Zero knows them, too." Adae frowned. "He will have guards watching every entrance, except..."

"Except what?" Emily asked.

"The Gates of the Sky."

"Well *that* sounds fun." Emily sighed. "Okay, let's hear it."

#

Eight hours later, Emily found herself wishing for about the hundredth time that they'd just made a frontal assault on the tunnels of Cantelon.

At least that would have killed us quickly.

The climb up the side of Olympia hadn't been so bad, at first. The mountain was huge, its rise gradual, and there were plenty of jagged rocks to clamber over or hold onto when the slope grew too steep to simply hike up. But the higher they got, the sharper the angle of the mountain grew, forcing them first to scramble on all fours and finally to sidle along narrow ledges looking for spots to pull themselves up a few painful feet to rest, gasping for breath, before starting the process all over again to find the next way up.

And it was cold, colder than the deep underground gloom of Cantelon, even colder than the foul-weathered nights she'd spent in Maine that summer. The ever-present haze of Olympia hid the sun and the thin air did nothing to carry the summer warmth of Arborea. As she watched her friends sweating and shivering simultaneously, Emily worried that they'd end up dead of exposure before King Zero and his men could ever find them.

Only one thing lightened her mood, though it weighed her down physically: a huge spear, a bear spear, strapped across her back. Skaros and his warriors had been well equipped on their hunt for the runaway humans and under Adae's orders they were happy to share their surplus weapons. Marlow and Michael carried swords that had passed for daggers to the bears and Elizabeth had a thin-bladed knife that Skaros used to fillet game.

Emily would have been happier in armor, but there was no quick way to make the huge breastplates and bucket helms of the bears fit a person, even if she could bear their weight. Even more, she found herself wishing for a hammer. It had always been her weapon of choice, from the time she'd won her first tournament at Harkness, with a weight and heft that were comforting in the do-or-die situations she seemed to have a knack for winding up in.

Still, she had a spear, a good one, and as she pushed Marlow up into a little divot gouged in the cliffside above her head, she saw a sweet sight against the persistent gray of the mountain and sky: an iron gate, painted bright blue, wide enough for a truck to drive through and twice as tall.

"The Gates of the Sky," Adae said, pointing.

"Why would you make that?" Michael asked, panting.

"I haven't been here since my coronation," Adae said. "*Open the gates as wide as the sky, and let the king and queen come by,* that's what Adam said, so he had them built. They're only used for coronations."

"Okay," Michael said, hitching his foot up onto a protruding rock at hip-height. With a grunt, he shoved himself up into a standing position and grabbed the hand Marlow offered him from above. "But *how?*"

"Everyone gathers at the base of the mountain," Adae said, "all the people, the animals, everybody. Then the new king or queen comes out through the gates to greet them and prove their lineage."

"Prove their—" Emily began.

"Like this." Adae shoved off from the face of the mountain and fell into the open air.

"Adae!" A memory of her fight with the wyverns of Deseret flashed through Emily's mind as she flung out a hand to try and catch the queen, but it was too late.

Adae was flying.

She laughed as she rose the last few yards to the gate. Her hair had come loose from its ties and it whipped around her head in lashing black waves as the high winds caught it. She looked as though she were standing still, balanced on one foot, but she floated easily. The gate swung open on silent hinges as she approached, revealing a dark tunnel into the mountain. Adae alighted gently on the floor of the tunnel, then turned to regard the rest of the group still struggling up the slope.

"Come along!" she called. "It's warmer up here!"

"Maybe you should have just killed her," Michael grunted.

It *was* warmer in the tunnel, though that may have just been Emily's body burning with the exertion of hauling three full-grown adults the last ten yards up the mountainside, then climbing back down to shove two dozen armored bears along as they scrabbled and clawed their own way up. Or maybe, she admitted, it was the glow of satisfaction at a job well done. They'd all made it through the Gates of the Sky and Adae had been right: the dusty tunnel that spiraled down into the heart of the mountain was unguarded and looked as though nobody had been there since the last coronation.

Emily led the way, pushing aside crystalline cobwebs that crackled and splintered into glittering lines as they floated to the floor. The tunnel made a neat corkscrew that took them down the height they'd so painfully climbed in a fraction of the time, then continued down into the roots of the earth.

An hour's walk brought them to a tall archway that opened onto the same shelf from which Emily and her friends had first seen Beverlay; the entrance they'd used that time lay somewhere miles away, across the sparkling lights of the city in its underground valley. It seemed dark, though; last time they'd seen it, Beverlay was lit up like any aboveground metropolis, but now its pinprick lights were few, with wide swathes of black between them.

It took another half hour to reach the top of the nearest ramp to lead to the floor of the canyon and by the time she'd herded the magicians and the bears down it, Emily was growing anxious that they'd miss King Zero's deadline simply by their inability to get anywhere faster than an exhausted shuffle.

"The guards must all be watching the entrances," Emily said to Adae as they led the way toward the city side by side. The stone basin where the city sat was as deserted as the high rim and the ramp, and there were no signs of movement from the streets and buildings ahead.

"My thought precisely," Adae said. "Might I ask where you trained? You have the mind of a soldier, though not the bearing."

"Harkness Academy." Emily smiled. "Old Montrose's ears are burning right now."

"Harkness," Adae repeated. "That is on Earth?"

"Yeah, New Hampshire."

"I would like to visit New Hampshire," Adae said.

"I'll take you myself, if we—when this is over." Emily held up a hand. "Now shush. Please. Your majesty."

They entered the outskirts of the city, walking slowly between the first low buildings. As far as Emily could tell, they were the only things moving in Beverlay, until somewhere above her head a window shut with the click of a lock, sharp in the silence of the street.

"They're hiding," she said.

"They know a battle is coming," Adae agreed.

The humans and the bears headed for the palace in the center of the city, following empty streets and passing through empty squares. As they drew closer, the buildings began to look familiar to Emily, and as they emerged from a narrow side street she realized they'd entered the plaza where Mere's house stood.

"Wait," she said and Adae raised a hand, causing all the bears to come to a stumbling, crashing halt. As if on cue, the door of Mere's rowhouse opened and the girl came running out to throw her arms around Emily in a flying hug.

"You're back!"

"I'm back," Emily agreed.

"Mere, come back here!" The girl's mother stood in the doorway, face pinched with worry, her hand slightly raised as though unwilling to commit to a full wave. Her father, still wearing the drab gray of a technician in Zero's underground laboratory, said something inaudible to his wife and stepped out into the plaza.

"You need to come back inside," he said as he approached. He put his hands on Mere's shoulders; they were splotchy with faint purple stains and lined with small scars. He had a long face, with deep lines and deeper eyes. "And you all need to move on."

"What's going on?" Emily asked.

Mere's father glanced up and down the deserted square. His eyes flickered up to the window of a facing rowhouse, where a brown curtain fell back into place. When he spoke, his voice was hushed. "King Zero is up to something. He sent his soldiers through last night, clearing the city and getting everyone inside. They're all either in the palace or watching the entrances. The work down below has been ended as well…"

"The work?" Emily repeated.

"Emily!" That was Michael, pointing with a rigid finger to the empty space above their heads where a flight of arrows reached the top of their long arc and began their descent, aimed exactly where Emily was standing.

There was no time to move, so she shoved Mere to the ground and pushed her father away, then yanked the long spear from her back. Twirling it over and around her wrist in a simple spin, she made a blurring shield that scattered the arrows as they came clattering in. A few badly aimed ones stuck into the ground on either side of her and Mere, but a glance showed her that the girl's father had reached the safety of his doorway.

Up the long avenue that ran toward the palace, De Soto Rigmaiden stood at the head of a phalanx of Albian knights. The old Free Stater was dressed the way he'd always been, in dirty jeans and a torn serape, but instead of the battered wooden shield he'd borne in Albion he carried a new one of rune-carved gray steel that matched those the knights wore. Behind them, about a dozen of King Zero's soldiers were nocking new arrows. Aminah was nowhere to be seen.

Emily hustled Mere toward her house as a sergeant gave a cry and the thrum of bows heralded the next attack. Rigmaiden and the knights charged as the arrows soared over their heads. Mere ducked through her door. Emily bounced back into the center of the square, putting herself between her opponents and the magicians at her back. Michael urged Marlow and Elizabeth toward the narrow street they'd come from as Adae stood watching. The bears boiled forward around her, setting their own spears and adjusting their helmets as they prepared to meet the charge.

Another few spins of her spear drove the incoming arrows in all directions. The charge would reach her before the Cantelon soldiers, moving at human speed, could send another flight her way. With any luck they would realize they were out of the fight and stay far back.

The speed of the bears' counter-charge ruffled Emily's hair as they passed her. A moment later they met the knights and the neat lines on both sides collapsed into a roiling, slashing melee. The bears fell instantly into a savagery that made Emily glad she'd never gone to war against them as she watched the clash unfold.

Bear spears were quickly discarded as they shattered against Albian shields and the animals reverted to their slashing claws. Sir Arthur caught a paw on the edge of his shield, pushed it wide, then cut the tips from three spears with a single slash of his sword. The bear whose blow he'd just deflected flung itself bodily at him, but he set his feet and shoved back as the huge creature bore down on his shield.

Arthur disappeared from Emily's view as another bear crowded in on him. Then a sword exploded from that animal's back and another of Arthur's knights bulled his way past the ravaged creature as he tore his weapon free from its side. A third knight, carrying a bear spear instead of his sword, met up with his comrade and together they formed a miniature shield wall as they began laying into the bears' flank.

Emily hefted her spear, thinking she could catch the knights unawares, when a thought flashed through her mind: where had Rigmaiden gone? He'd been at the front of the charge, but must have skittered off somewhere before the lines collided. Spinning around to look for him, Emily found Adae instead, her hands working a complex spell, her face locked in concentration.

The queen shouted a final word, flinging her arms above her head, fingers spread. A blazing dart of flame shot from each finger and streaked toward the fray, leaving trails of orange light in Emily's vision. The missiles weaved around the bears as though they were target-locked, ducking and spinning as they homed in on the Albian knights. At the last moment, the knight carrying the spear noticed what was coming for him and shouted a warning.

Too slow, Emily thought with satisfaction, but then something unexpected happened. The knight had raised his shield in what looked like a desperate bid for protection, but it was low, too low—until the magic dart angled sharply down and dove for the shield rather than its bearer. A moment later it connected in a splash of magical pyrotechnics and when

Emily lowered the arm that had shielded her eyes from the burst, both the knight and his shield were unharmed.

"What just happened?" Emily said. Blooming color and light within the melee showed the spots where each knight's shield caught one or two of the arcane blasts. The Albians fought on, unfazed, even rejuvenated by their show of invincibility as they redoubled their assault on the bears and began to drive the animals back into the plaza and toward Emily and Adae.

"Those shields," Adae gasped. She was wilting like a flower, sweat dripping from the end of her nose, though to her credit she was conscious and still standing. "What are they made from?"

"Astraeos," Emily said in a flash of insight. The shields she'd thought were gray steel were actually stone. "The Paramount your husband captured. Zero has a shield like that."

"The Paramounts were made to resist Adam's magic," Adae said. "They must—" She cut her own thought short with a shriek. Emily spun around to see Rigmaiden at the mouth of the side street where Elizabeth and the boys had fled, his back to them, raising his machete as he stalked after the magicians.

"Adae—"

"Go!" said the queen. "I'll help the bears."

Emily ran. Michael and Marlow stood between Rigmaiden and Elizabeth with their swords raised; Michael's hand was shaking, making his blade waver. Rigmaiden had paused with his weapon up; he said something Emily couldn't hear and Michael shook his head in response.

She threw her spear.

It hummed as it flew, perfectly aimed right between Rigmaiden's shoulder blades. A moment before it struck, Marlow's eyes widened in surprise. Rigmaiden spun instantly, moving so fast that his arm was a blur as he slapped the spear from the air with his stone shield. It spun away to the side and skittered off across the pavement.

"You," he said.

"She's just a girl!" Emily called, moving warily toward Rigmaiden. "Sabine isn't worth it."

"And the S&T is?" The Free Stater spat on the ground. "No land, no loyalty, no honor."

"That doesn't give you the right—"

"The right?" Rigmaiden snorted and hefted his machete. "I do what it takes to defend my people, no more, no less."

"By killing a girl?"

"Looks like two girls." The old fighter gave his weapon an experimental swing as he advanced on Emily. "Unless you got something up your sleeve."

"Actually," said Emily as the sword that Michael had just thrown arced over Rigmaiden's head, "I do."

She caught the sword as Rigmaiden charged. Her blade came up as his came down and they clashed with a shriek of steel. Sneering, Rigmaiden shoved her with his shield, sending her stumbling as their lock broke, but she kept her feet and bounced back for a quick lunge of her own. The Free Stater turned it with his machete but couldn't manage a riposte.

The next few seconds saw a flurry of sparking metal as their blades met again and again. Despite his age and sloppy appearance, Rigmaiden had excellent technique and his attacks came from all sides, darting over and around the rim of the shield that he kept perfectly placed over his core. His advantage was just too great, Emily realized, as another of her counterstrikes bounced off gray stone.

She went on the attack, forcing Rigmaiden to keep his shield up as her blade came at him from every angle. She had no expectation of getting through his impeccable defense; she just needed to distract him as she slowly turned under the guise of shifting her footing and he turned with her. Soon she had her back to the spot where her spear lay on the pavement maybe ten yards away.

Rigmaiden's next attack was a sudden lunge, giving her just the opening she needed to break free as she skipped backwards out of range. The skip turned into a flat-out sprint, exposing her back for a single precarious moment before she reached the spear. Dropping her sword, she grabbed the spear as she spun, and as she came back up the tip of her weapon thunked an inch into Rigmaiden's shield, only a few feet away.

Emily wrenched her spear free and backstepped, putting space between her and her foe. Peering at her over the lip of his shield, Rigmaiden frowned. The tactical math had changed; he had the defense, but she had the reach, and for now, a little breathing room.

A roar across the plaza caught both fighters' attention. The great bear Skaros toppled backwards, blood spraying from a gash across his face as his split helmet flew from his head. Sir Arthur, his armor red and dripping, leaped onto the bear's stomach and plunged his longsword through his neck, then tore it free in a lash of gore. His men raised a ragged cheer as Skaros's warriors fell back, terrified by the death of their leader.

"Pathetic!" Arthur shouted, swinging his sword in a looping arc that encompassed all the bear warriors accusingly. From somewhere on the other side of the fight, a half dozen blazing magic darts appeared, then exploded in harmless fireworks on Arthur's rune-carved shield. The knight snorted, then leaped from Skaros's belly and raised his sword and the killing began again.

Sir Rowan emerged from the bloody melee, trotting over with his visor raised and a dripping sword at his side. Eyeing Emily and Rigmaiden's standoff, he raised his sword and called out, "Need an assist, Sabine?"

"No," Rigmaiden growled, his eyes still locked on Emily's.

Rowan blinked. "You're quite certain? She's fierce."

"Thanks," Emily said, watching the knight for any sudden movements from the corner of her eye.

"I'm sure," Rigmaiden said.

"Have it your way," said Sir Rowan with a shrug. He hefted his shield and turned back to the fray. "But make it quick."

The knight twirled his sword as he jogged toward the fight, where the bears had rallied and were tearing into the Albians with renewed savagery. He paused a moment to assess the scene, then, with the superhuman movements of a well-trained Combat Gifted, jogged three steps, leaped ten feet in the air, and raised his arm for a blow that would shear an unaware bear's head from its neck.

Emily's spear burst through the knight's back and out his chest, spraying blood over the startled bear, who was hit by Sir Rowan's tumbling body and fell backwards into the fray under the weight of the knight's armor and shield.

"Fierce," said Emily, and then Rigmaiden was on her. His shield, swung horizontally, clipped the side of her head, stunning her as his machete darted in low and caught her in the back of the leg. Emily gasped with pain as her Achilles tendon parted. She dropped to one knee then toppled over onto her butt.

Rigmaiden lashed out with his machete and Emily thought her life was over, but then there was a teeth-rattling clang as the Free Stater deflected another flying sword that had come within inches of his head. Emily dared a glance over her shoulder to see Marlow standing sheepish and empty-handed. Still, it was the distraction she needed to climb to her feet and run.

It was more of a high-speed hobble, she admitted as Rigmaiden started after her, but she was able to keep just ahead of the older fighter as she crossed the plaza with no destination in mind. It was enough to keep Rigmaiden away from Elizabeth. Maybe he would take long enough killing Emily that the queen could escape.

Her gaze fell on the crystal bench where she'd once sat with Mere, still skewed a bit off true from when she'd lifted it and set it back down. She jumped for it, but her cut heel betrayed her and instead of clearing the bench she crashed into it with her shins and tumbled over the top to land chest-first on the pavement beyond.

Rigmaiden appeared around the side of the bench just as Emily righted herself. She scrambled backwards as fast as she could, but the Free Stater was faster and he brought his machete down in an overhand chop aimed at her head. Emily grabbed a foot of the bench and yanked, dragging it into the path of the machete as she fell back away from it. The corner of the bench clipped Rigmaiden's arm and he cursed as the weapon sliced through empty air an inch from Emily's ear.

His next attack was better aimed. The tip of the machete dove for Emily's heart and all she could do was try to grab the old fighter's arm. Her fingers locked around his wrist as the blade bit into her chest just below her collarbone. Pain blossomed in a burning flower. Emily tried to ignore it as she pulled Rigmaiden down with a sharp yank. He stumbled and crashed into her and they hit the ground in a heap.

With a gasp of surprise, Emily realized the machete was still protruding from her chest, standing straight out like a soldier at attention. In the back of her mind, the dry voice of Professor Montrose giving a combat anatomy lecture suggested that perhaps the weapon had lodged in a rib. Shoving Rigmaiden away from her even as he tried to stand on his own, Emily wrapped her fingers around the handle of the machete, clenched her teeth, and pulled.

It came free with a lash of pain, a pulse of blood, and an unexpected *crack*. Emily's vision blurred and refocused as she held the weapon out, warding Rigmaiden away, but he acted faster than she expected as he aimed a swift kick at her wrist. His toe connected and her arm went instantly numb from elbow to fingertips. The machete dropped from her limp hand and Rigmaiden snatched it from the air.

Emily dropped back and away to avoid the slash that came next and her head bounced off the pavement. She tried to scramble out of range but her shoulder collided with something hard. A desperate hand waved behind her met a crystal pole—one of the lampposts she'd noticed in her early explorations of the city.

"Any last words?" Rigmaiden asked, raising the machete.

"Oh, that's a perfect setup," Emily panted.

"What?" Rigmaiden's lip curled in a sneer.

"It's hammer time."

Emily's hand closed around the lamppost and she yanked with muscle-ripping strength as she exploded upward in a sit-up that became a sloppy haymaker as the glowing pole tore free of the pavement, taking a chunk of stone with it, and crashed into the side of the surprised Free Stater's head, sending him toppling over the back of the bench and sliding to the stone ground beyond.

She stood, using the lamppost as a crutch, and her slashed heel nearly gave out under her. On the other side of the bench, Rigmaiden lay sprawled on the pavement, eyes closed, rolling his head slowly from side to side. A little blood leaked from his nose and he coughed. His machete lay near his hand, so Emily stepped around the bench and kicked it away.

"Where's Aminah?"

"Zero has her," Rigmaiden muttered, showing broken teeth.

"*Where?*" Emily let the jagged stone head of her makeshift hammer drop next to Rigmaiden's head, just inside his peripheral vision.

"Don't know." Rigmaiden coughed again, spattering blood on his serape. He tried to push himself up into a sitting position but his eyes went hazy and he slumped back to the pavement. "He likes her. Said he might start his own royal line."

"Gross." Emily turned away, then paused. "Lie on your side or you'll choke to death."

Across the square a huge mound of bodies lay where the knights and bears had clashed, a mix of fur and steel all sprayed with blood and deathly still. At some point during Emily's duel with Rigmaiden the fight had ended, apparently in total annihilation for both sides.

One of the bears moved, arching its back as though trying to rise. A candle flame of hope lit in Emily's chest, then was snuffed as quickly as she saw that the bear was dead and the motion was from a knight shoving his way out and up from under the massive furred corpse.

His helmet was missing, his fair hair plastered to his skull with a pinkish mix of sweat and blood. His sword was gone; his shield was gone. The tabard he'd worn showing the dragon rampant of Albion was missing, revealing battered, claw-marked armor stained with a gruesome rainbow whose spectrum ran from brown to red.

"Arthur," Emily said.

"Emily." Sir Arthur staggered down the pile of bodies, slipped halfway down and slid the rest of the way to the pavement. He swiped at his hair with a gauntleted hand—the other glove was missing—but failed to push it from his eyes.

"You did this," the knight said, his voice pinched and slurring. His long nose was askew and turning purple. "You killed them all. Rhys and Rowan, Connor and Oliver."

"The bears—"

"You killed all my friends!" Arthur shouted. He paced toward her on unsteady feet. "Daniel was just a kid."

"I didn't!" The accusation felt like an iron band around her chest, crushing her, denying her air.

Sir Arthur raised a shaking hand, extended a single pointing finger that pierced her heart like an arrow. "You killed Max!"

Emily fell to her knees, tears cutting through the sweat and grime on her face. The righteous fury in her belly had burned out, leaving only an empty space, and she was falling into it, into herself, collapsing like a black hole. In the darkness there was motion, the face of the dragon swimming up from the darkness. Its mouth was open; the jaws that had bitten the Marcher Lord in half and crushed Sir Maximilian were coming for her.

"No, she didn't," someone said and reality crashed over Emily like a bucket of ice water. The blood-washed plaza in the great cavern of Beverlay, lit by softly glowing crystal and silent in the aftermath of battle—*that* was real. Michael Fletcher standing with a gentle hand on her shoulder was real. Not the dragon. *Not* the dragon.

"She saved us," Elizabeth said. "All of us that she could. She would have saved Sir Maximilian if it were possible."

"She killed him," Arthur said, his voice like a child calling from another room.

"The dragon killed him," Elizabeth said. "Go home, Arthur."

And to Emily's astonishment, he did. The knight gave her one last lingering look and then he turned and walked away, disappearing into the mazy streets of Beverlay with empty hands, naked in his armor.

"Are you okay?" Michael asked, helping Emily to her feet.

"I think so," Emily said. "My heel is—is fine. My chest… You?"

"Fine." Michael smiled and patted Marlow on the back as the Albian magician joined them. "Where's Adae?"

"Here," said the queen of Cantelon. She lay slumped against the pile of bodies that was all that was left of her loyal platoon of bears and the men they'd fought. Her face was greenish-pale under its usual umber and her eyes were bleary and red.

Emily crossed the plaza and reached out a hand to help Adae to her feet. "Can you walk?"

"I think so." Adae wiped blood from her eyes. "I think so."

Emily let her eyes rove over the dead heap until they settled on what she needed. Wading in among the bodies, she picked up a long bear spear and one of the knights' stone shields, its runic carvings chipped and battered but still legible.

"In that case," she said, "let's go save Aminah."

CHAPTER 20

Nobody stopped them on their way to the throne room. Nobody dared. The soldiers of Cantelon scattered at their approach, unwilling to get caught in a clash between gods. The guards at the front gate of the palace stared straight ahead as they passed through. The front hall was as empty as the streets of Beverlay and as silent, except for the click of their feet on the white parquet floor.

They passed through the wide double door at the end of the hall and entered the throne room. The bright glow that had previously bathed the chamber was gone, leaving it in sloping, pooling shadow. Emily and Adae led the way as the group approached King Zero on his throne of iron and crystal, walking between the high columns of gray Olympian stone.

Aminah sat on Queen Adae's throne. There were no guards, no obvious threat, not even a shackle on her ankle to show her status as prisoner, but it was obvious all the same. Her face was defeated, her square jaw clenched as though she were biting back all the dangerous things she wanted to say. She wore a dress that had likely been Adae's, black with gold stitching, and a necklace of dangling crystals. There was a green-and-purple bruise on her right arm.

King Zero was dressed in armor like nothing Emily had seen before. It was massive, covering his entire body with foot-thick, shield-sized slabs of stone that Emily recognized as the skin of the Paramount Astraeos. They overlapped at every joint and jutted up in a semicircle around his exposed head and they scraped and grated on each other as the king stood and extended his hand in a gesture of welcome.

"I've been waiting," he said. His three-horned helmet sat at his feet and a huge flat-tipped sword leaned against one arm of his throne.

"Let her go," Michael said.

"Let her go?" Zero snorted a laugh. "Aminah is no prisoner. She's to be my queen. She has no reason to leave." He turned to the Albian woman who sat stony-faced at his side. "Isn't that right?"

"Why would I leave?" Aminah said. Her voice was thick and dull and she stared straight ahead.

"What did you do to her?" Emily asked, but Zero just gave a half-smile that made shadowy creases in his pale face.

"There are two people in this room with a claim to that throne," said Adae, stepping forward. "And you are neither of them. Zero, it is my intent to abdicate the throne, and without me at your side, you have no right to call yourself king. I am giving you this chance to step down and relinquish your false claim. Otherwise, I"—she glanced over her shoulder—"*we* will remove you."

Zero gestured to Elizabeth with a massive gauntlet. "You think this girl has a better claim than I do? There are higher laws than the right of birth. Adam seized this throne by blood and magic. It hasn't belonged to the old line for a hundred years."

"Then you will lose the throne by blood and magic," Elizabeth said.

Zero spread his arms, rage distorting his face. Emily darted forward to put herself in front of the king, her shield raised and the butt of her spear planted on the floor to absorb the shock of his likely charge. Zero snapped his fingers and his helmet and sword leaped up and flew to him as though pulled by magnets; the weapon settled in his left hand as he snatched the helmet with his right and slammed it down over his head.

He moved slowly, coming down the steps of the throne dais like a glacier swallowing the earth. When he reached the last step, he pointed his sword at Elizabeth, the threat obvious. The helmeted head turned to

Emily, the king's cold eyes and thin-lipped frown visible behind the vee-shaped opening of his mask.

Zero was in no hurry and let Emily come limping out to meet him at the foot of the dais. She caught the first overhand swing of his sword on the lip of her new shield, crossing it over her body to meet the left-handed attack; the blade bit an inch into the stone but came free instantly, testament to its razor edge. Her counterattack, stabbing out with her spear at an awkward angle, clicked off Zero's armor without even making a mark.

The sword came in again in a straight stab, an attack meant for a light, sharp-pointed blade but far more terrifying with the full weight of the king and his huge weapon behind it. Emily ducked behind her shield in a half-crouch and caught the thrust square in its center with a sound like the first thundercrack in an empty sky. The sheer force of the blow drove her back a few steps and made her teeth rattle.

"You have no right to bear that shield!" the king roared. He whipped his sword around and brought it down again and Emily knocked it away with the shield, knowing her spear would shatter if asked to catch that massive blade. Zero's sword went wide, cleaving the air at Emily's side, but she'd overbalanced and stumbled to her right as momentum carried her that way.

Zero's free hand shot out and his stone gauntlet closed around Emily's neck.

He lifted, raising her until she hung by her neck two feet off the floor, struggling and kicking. She refused to let go of her spear and shield, the only defenses she had, but she could feel her hands weakening as her body burned through its little store of oxygen. Black night edged into her vision.

A rushing mass of crystal and iron crashed into the king's back, making him stagger. He dropped Emily, who hit the ground in a gasping heap and rolled to the side as Zero toppled under the weight of Queen Adae's throne. Crystal exploded into flying shards as the king and the chair hit the ground together.

Up the dais steps, Aminah stood panting with her hands on her knees.

235

Zero stood, brushing bits of rainbow and black from his armor, and turned to look at the Albian woman who now stood with her square jaw set and defiance burning in her eyes under a spilling curtain of sheer black hair. Emily staggered to her feet, letting air rush into her burning chest as she resettled her grip on her weapon.

But Zero wasn't interested in her. He stomped up the steps toward Aminah, raising his sword. She paled but didn't flinch.

"Hey!" Emily yelled.

Zero ignored her. He towered over Aminah as though she were a child.

"I could have loved you," he said and brought the sword down.

Jagged spikes of stone erupted from the dais between Zero and Aminah, spraying chips and raising a cloud of dust, knocking the king's blade away. Aminah fell to her knees and disappeared as the stalagmites rose up all around her. They reached up, up, and bent inwards as though reaching out to touch each other. Soon Aminah was completely hidden inside a rough dome of rock.

"*Who?!*" Zero roared, spinning to confront his attackers. Emily followed the king's furious gaze as it landed on Marlow, who stood a few yards back with his little white icon of Mithras raised high over his head in one hand and the other stretched out toward Aminah. He was smiling.

The Albian magician held that pose for a breath, then another, and then Emily realized he wasn't moving. His body was rigid. It was hard to tell in the shadows of the throne room, but his skin looked ashy, even gray. Zero saw it too and he began to laugh.

"The Curse of Adam holds true," he said. "Even Mithras cannot protect you."

"Then I will do what the cursed cannot," said Adae, stepping forward. As she spoke she wove complex shapes in the air with her fingers and where they passed they left faint rainbows behind. The rainbows made a shape like a Celtic knot, twining and looping until the whole work was the size of Emily's shield and still growing. Adae's face was tight with exertion, sweat gleaming on her brow, her shoulders rigid and quivering even as she kept her arms flowing.

The queen shouted and the glowing shape rushed forward, growing even bigger as it did. It flew at Zero, threatening to engulf him like a net thrown by a gladiator. To Emily's surprise, the king did nothing to avoid or even deflect the spell. Instead he stood still and let the magic settle over him, folding over and around him like a blanket.

Adae's shoulders slumped. She fell to her knees.

The rainbow weave that covered Zero began to fade, its colors blending into the gray of the king's armor, the lines of magic sinking into the stone as though it were water. Emily checked her grip on her spear, readying herself to meet any new attack, though she was unsure how to stop Zero before he could reach Adae.

Under his helmet, the king smiled. "I built this armor for you, Adae," he said. The queen looked up from the floor. "I always said you gave me strength, my queen. Do you like it?"

"The Paramount," Adae murmured, her back rising and falling with ragged breaths. "You stole its skin."

"Yes," Zero agreed. "Astraeos, I believe its name was. Quite a thing. They were built to defend against Adam originally, but I always suspected they would work just as well against his children."

"Then you planned…" Adae shook her head, unable to finish.

"To destroy you?" Zero snorted. "Yes, of course. You were too willful to share my throne with forever. But it's so much more than that, don't you see? *You give me strength.*" He laughed. "Quite literally, now. Adam was never able to defeat the Paramounts because they drew power from his magic. My armor does much the same. The more you fight back, the stronger I get, do you see?"

The last remnants of Adae's spell faded into nothing, leaving no indication that she'd done anything at all except for her own slumped, spent form kneeling on the cold floor of the throne room. Her head drooped.

Zero came down the dais steps to stand before Adae. The queen barely seemed to register his approach. She was conscious, Emily realized, but she'd spent all her power on her last spell as surely as when she'd passed out during their escape.

237

Emily tensed, preparing for a charge, when a knife came spinning past her shoulder in an awkward overhand throw. Zero didn't even spare it a glance, just let it bounce off his armor and clatter to the floor. Emily glanced back to see Elizabeth, wide-eyed, with her arm still outstretched from her failed attack.

"Don't worry, Albion," he said. His eyes were locked on Adae. "You're next."

Zero reached down with a huge stone gauntlet and grabbed the queen of Cantelon. He heaved her into the air and for a moment Emily thought he was going to choke the queen as he'd done to her, but then she realized he had caught her by the collar and was simply dangling her before his face. Adae's eyes fluttered, open but heavy-lidded and bleary. A thin smile bloomed on the king's face.

Zero's stone armor rasped as he brought Adae's face close to his. He peered at her, his sharp, cold eyes boring into her smeared and wandering ones. Then he slammed his sword into the ground with a short, sharp motion that caught even Emily off-guard. It stuck there, quivering, as he used his free hand to remove his helmet.

"One last kiss," he said.

Adae's head lolled backwards, rolling so that she faced over her own right shoulder, looking back at Emily and the others. Her mouth fell open and her lips were moving. The barest whisper escaped from between them.

"Help me."

Emily threw her spear, aiming for Zero's white face, which hovered just beyond Adae's shoulder. The weapon sliced the air. Zero's eyes slid from Adae's face to the incoming missile. He turned, just a fraction of a degree, a motion that suggested more disappointment than anger. The spear crashed into one of the protrusions of stone that jutted up around the king's neck. Rainbow light crackled out from the armor, making a sudden web around the spear, which flashed once with white fire then crumbled into ash that fell at the king's feet.

238

Horrified, Emily staggered back. She was weaponless, hopeless in the face of Zero's power. A few steps brought her stumbling into Elizabeth, who, rather than move with her, stood her ground and put a steadying hand on Emily's shoulder.

"Can you get me to my knife?" the queen asked.

"Yeah, but—"

Elizabeth held up a hand. "Just keep me safe."

"But against that armor…" Emily shook her head.

"Lizzie," said Michael. He stood at her shoulder, flexing his cracked right hand, worry creasing his face. "Please. Let me go. I'm taller, I'm stronger—"

"I'm the queen," Elizabeth said. "My love, my sweet love. You have carried me since the day I gave up my magic. It's past time I learned to carry myself." She laid a pale, slender hand on Michael's cheek. "Adae will need your help. Look after her."

"But the curse—"

"I know you will do what you feel is right." Elizabeth smiled and popped up on tiptoes to kiss Michael's lips. The young magician smiled, too, despite himself.

Elizabeth turned to Emily. "Shall we?"

Emily hefted her shield and together they charged. King Zero looked away from Adae as they approached, then tossed the queen to the side and set himself to meet the attack. Adae hit the floor, slid a few feet, and lay still; from the corner of her eye, Emily saw Michael moving slowly in that direction.

Emily hit Zero shield-first.

Elizabeth slipped to the side and out of Emily's sight as the fighters collided in a shower of rainbow sparks and stone dust. There was no time to think; Zero's gauntleted fists came down at her like a meteor shower. It was all she could do to keep her shield between her and the king's hammer-blows. Each strike drove her back but she pressed forward relentlessly, her lips frozen in a snarl and her eyes blind to everything but her enemy's movements.

Multicolored energy crackled as Zero hit her shield like a jackhammer. His face was a mask of fury and now and then a moment would slip by when the king could have gotten around Emily's flagging defenses if he'd only moved his focus off her battered shield, but he almost seemed to be fighting it instead of the girl behind it.

The great slab of stone was growing heavier. Emily shook it off as a sign of her waning stamina—her arms were shaking with each numbing blow from the king—but something was scratching at the back of her mind. An arc of red-green lightning crawled up her arm, making the hairs stand on end, and Emily realized what she was feeling.

The shield is stealing his energy.

It made sense, as much as magic ever made sense. Zero's armor had absorbed Adae's magic, but Emily's shield was made to do the same. With each blow they traded power back and forth, but as the king was overflowing, Emily took more than she gave back as his fists hammered her. Soon they would be equal and then it was anyone's game.

The king's left came in a little high. Emily ducked out of the way and exploded upwards, straightening to her full height, her slashed heel screaming in protest. She caught Zero's extended arm on her shoulder with a sharp crack, pushing inside his guard, and flipped the shield up so she could ram it toward him edge-on.

He twisted at the last second, trying to deflect the blow that was aimed straight at his heart, but he couldn't dodge it. The rim of the shield crashed into the king's side. Rainbows burst like fireworks; chips of stone sprayed in all directions, blinding Emily. The shock drove up her arms, shot through her hurt shoulder like a flaming lance, set her chest searing. She fell away, driven as much by the force of the impact as by her own loss of balance.

The floor came up to meet her and her head bounced off stone, doubling the room for a nauseating moment until she could blink the swimming shapes away. She sat up. King Zero stood, apparently unmoved in the cloud of dust, streamers of energy playing over his stone plates. But as

240

the haze cleared, Emily saw a line of white in the gray: a crack in the king's armor.

Elizabeth appeared, knife in hand. Emily's head buzzed with pain, but a thought broke through the noise: the queen of Albion had found what she was looking for. Elizabeth didn't hesitate as she slipped her narrow blade into the gash in Zero's side. The king's mouth gaped as she dug in, her teeth showing in a vicious grin, pressing her attack as ruby blood spilled in lush pulses over her hand.

Zero fell to his knees and Elizabeth went down with him like a terrier with a rat in its grip. He toppled over, the weight of his armor dragging him down, and crashed to the floor on his back. Elizabeth fell too so that she lay on his chest, her eyes locked on his, the handle of the knife still in her hand. The king opened his mouth, but no sound emerged. A last feeble spit of blood came from his side.

Elizabeth I Pendragon, queen of Albion and Cantelon, stood. King Zero did not.

CHAPTER 21

There was silence in the throne room, aside from the faint tinkle of settling dust. Then, from within the jagged hemisphere of stone on the dais, came an anxious voice.

"Uh… hello?"

Emily and Elizabeth shared a look.

"Aminah!" Emily limped up the steps. "It's okay, it's over! Just hang on." She paced around Marlow's protective dome, looking for any way in. There were gaps between the stalagmites, some of them wide enough to slip a hand or even an arm through, but none big enough for a person to squeeze in or out.

Emily sighed. It seemed a fighter's job was never done. She cracked her knuckles, rolled her neck, and got to work. Fifteen minutes later she was reaching a battered hand through a ragged hole in the rock to help Aminah step out. The Albian woman smiled her thanks, but her brown eyes could barely stay on Emily's face as they roved the room looking for Marlow. Her gaze found the gray, frozen shape of the man, his hand still raised, the smile still on his face. Aminah raised her own hand in a little wave. Marlow didn't move.

The moment of realization was as plain as day on her expressive face: her smile inverted; her eyebrows fell; her eyes widened. Her lifted hand drooped and fell to her side.

"Marlow?"

Nobody spoke as Aminah moved slowly down the dais steps and crossed the floor, passing King Zero's crumpled body without a glance, to stand before the statue that had been Marlow Bright. She raised her hand and placed it on Marlow's stone cheek. A tear glittered in the shadow at the corner of her eye; she blinked and it disappeared.

"What happened?" she said, rounding on Elizabeth.

"The Curse of Adam," Elizabeth said. "No one not of the line of Adam may cast a spell here without paying a price."

"Did he know?"

Elizabeth lowered her head. "He knew."

"Fine," Aminah said. "Fine." She sniffed and wiped her nose with the sleeve of her sweater, then turned away.

"Michael, your hand!" That was Adae, sitting up shakily where Zero had thrown her during the fight. Michael knelt by her side, watching her carefully, and for a moment Emily couldn't see what had upset the queen. Then Michael shifted, revealing the empty fabric of his sleeves dangling over his knees. His right hand was gone—no, not just the hand, the entire forearm up to his elbow, just the same as when he'd healed Emily after her fight with the bears.

"It's all right," Michael said, but Adae was weeping openly, her head in her hands.

"I'm so sorry," she said between racking sobs. "For everything Adam did. For everything my father did, and Zero. This horrible bloodline..." She looked up, her face half-hidden by her hands and streaked with tears. "You should have let me die, Michael."

Michael stood, straightening his legs with a grunt. He looked down at Adae with a puckish half-smile on his face. "Come on, it's okay. Can you stand up? I'd give you a hand, but..." He shrugged.

Adae blinked up at him, her eyes wide with disbelief at his kindness, and then she began to laugh. She was still sobbing, but they were no longer tears of sorrow and self-pity. Watching the queen, Emily found herself wondering just how often in her life anyone had ever done something for Adae without expecting anything in return, had smiled at her without any secret motive behind the facade of friendship. It was hard to imagine a young Adae laughing with friends her age, or playing with the father who would go on to marry her to a brutal warlord.

Adae stood, her eyes far away. "When I abdicate the throne, the Curse will break and my prophecy will be fulfilled. Maybe Elizabeth can help once her power returns. Get me to Earth. Now." She smiled and her eyes met Emily's. "Please."

#

The wagon bumped along a long gravel road, pulled by a team of pink crystal lizards and flanked by two columns of beetle-helmeted Cantelon soldiers. They'd left Beverlay via a wide stone gate near the foot of Olympia, passing by a one-armed Paramount that stood straight and tall with birds building nests on its shoulders and the cross guard of its sword. Adae had watched it go past in silent wonder.

The wagon's exterior, of simple wood panels painted gray and unadorned by any royal insignia, had been chosen to avoid attention, though Emily secretly thought that Adae's insistence on bringing an honor guard with them sort of mooted that plan entirely. Still, it beat rolling around in one of the queen's opulent carriages and for all the drabness of its outside, the inside of the wagon was as plush as any luxury car.

Elizabeth and Michael sat cuddling on a cushioned bench, watching through a narrow window as the great peak of Olympia receded against the blue sky. Emily shared a second bench with Adae, who was full of questions about Earth. Only Aminah opted for discomfort; she sat on the wooden floor at the feet of the petrified Marlow, who had been lifted and set carefully into a corner of the wagon by a team of straining guardsmen.

"You think the bears will leave us alone?" Emily asked for the third or fourth time. She was tired of fighting, for now at least; whatever desperation had urged her into danger again and again seemed to have burned itself out for the time being. She was content to sit, and talk, and close her eyes and doze off to the sounds of birds and insects that wafted in through the windows on Arborea's warm breezes.

"They respect strength," Adae said. "They always have."

"Will they accept me as queen?" Elizabeth said. Michael snorted sleepily and nuzzled his head deeper into the crook of Elizabeth's arm; she stroked his hair idly.

"I'm not sure," Adae said. "They still think Adam will come back for them some day. It's heartbreaking."

"Is it?" said Aminah from the floor.

They rode in silence for a while. Eventually Michael woke up, looked around sheepishly, then stood and stretched before settling back in at Elizabeth's side. He caught Emily's eye and gave her a smile.

"Bet you're gonna have fun trying to fit this all in your report to the Sabre & Torch."

"Actually, I've been thinking about that," Emily said. "With everything that happened with Rigmaiden, there'll probably be an investigation. Statements, testimony, questioning... he said, she said, who hit who with what light fixtures. You know."

"Sounds awful," Michael agreed. Rigmaiden had been gone when they came back through Beverlay, only his battered John Deere hat left behind beneath the bench in the plaza where he and Emily fought.

"So I was thinking," Emily went on, "what if I didn't go back?"

"Seriously?" Michael raised an eyebrow. "You wanted to join the S&T so bad you gave up a nice life with Jack on Finalhaven. Now you're getting chased off by paperwork?"

"I wasn't..." Emily scrunched up her face, searching for the right words. "I didn't know what I wanted, back then." *Back then*—only a few months ago, although they'd been very long, dangerous months. "Or I knew what I wanted, but not what I needed. I always thought I wanted to go solo, but now I'm not so sure. You know?"

"I know." Michael smiled. "So what are you gonna do instead?"

"Well..." Emily glanced at Elizabeth, who was watching her with steady eyes. "I was thinking maybe I could stay here." Elizabeth's gaze didn't waver. Emily cleared her throat. "Help get you set up as queen. The soldiers have a lot to learn, no offense, Adae. Plus we don't know how many of Zero's monsters are still lurking under the city. And I mean, somebody has to knock some sense into those bears, right?"

"Emily Sledge," Elizabeth said, "how would you like to be a knight?"

#

Elizabeth's white hand matched the marble column she stood caressing thoughtfully. Its ornate top had long since broken off and toppled to the ground, there to be attractively half-hidden by a spurt of long grass and wildflowers. A matching pillar stood about three feet away; half of a carved arch still extended from its crown, reaching toward its headless mate in eternal frustration. The pair sat alone on the top of a gently rounded hill that stood high above its fellows, giving the impression of a doorway leading into the open blue sky.

Emily stood at Elizabeth's right hand, glancing down the long slope of the hill with a hand shielding her eyes. Her previous complacency had worn off somewhat and she found herself not entirely willing to believe that the land that had been the scene of so much drama and violence would let them leave without a final assault. The soldiers from Cantelon who stood in a ring around Adae and the five from Earth should have soothed her fear, but her mind was still hung up on thinking of the warriors with their antlered helmets and flat swords as enemies. It would take time to get away from that.

A handful of sweating soldiers set Marlow's frozen form in front of the columns. Adae, who had absolutely refused to let Emily help, thanked them with a smile and dismissed them.

"That's all, then," said the Queen of Cantelon. "I'm ready."

"I'll go first," Emily said. She took a deep breath and stepped between the columns. She'd thought she was prepared for it, but the wrenching feeling of passing through the portal still caught her off guard; as the world twisted and untwisted around her, she imagined for a dizzy moment that she knew exactly what a wrung dishcloth must feel like.

The sitting room at Barley Bright unfolded around her as she stumbled to keep her balance. It was a wreck, even worse than she'd left it after the first fight with Sir Arthur and his knights. Both the leather armchair and the couch were toppled onto their backs, the rug was bunched up in the center of the floor, and Marlow's Roman carving had fallen from the mantle and cracked in half. The windows were all shattered and broken glass glittered beneath them in the slanting sun of a fresh country morning.

"What?" Aminah said at Emily's shoulder. "I fought back."

"I can see." Emily laughed. "Not bad against seven Gifted fighters."

"Thanks, I—oh, Lord!" A terrible retching sound cut Aminah off and Emily peered past her in alarm to see Adae doubled over and puking onto the floor. The queen's face was greenish and sheened with sweat and her long black hair tumbled in waves around her face as she fell to her knees.

Aminah followed her promptly to the floor, grabbing a bunch of Adae's hair with one hand and pulling it away from the growing puddle of sick. The queen retched a few more times, producing something purple with flecks of gold, then swallowed a huge gulp of air and belched noisily.

"Feel better?" Aminah asked.

"Maybe," said Adae.

"Right then." Aminah snorted. "Come on, on our feet. Let's get you some proper clothes." She stood with Adae hanging shakily from her arm and together they stepped carefully around the splinters of a busted chair and headed for the door to the kitchen.

"Where shall we put this, ma'am?"

Two soldiers flanked the petrified Marlow; one was leaned over with his hands on his knees, breathing deeply but carefully, while the other, to his credit, only looked a little ill. Elizabeth, apparently entirely unbothered by their trip out of the painting, took in the wrecked sitting room with one hand on her chin. Eventually she pointed.

"The couch, I think. Thank you."

With Emily's assistance they got Marlow settled on the couch in an approximation of comfort, his frozen smile and raised holy symbol pointing roughly at the ceiling. Emily thought for a moment that she ought to put a blanket over him, then decided that of all the magician's problems, being cold probably wasn't one.

The sound of running water rose from the kitchen and over it, Aminah saying, "You've a lot to learn about life on Earth!" accompanied by a laugh from Adae. Turning away from Marlow, Emily caught a soldier's boots disappearing into the painting over the mantle. Then he was gone, leaving her alone with Michael and Elizabeth.

"How do you feel?" Michael glanced at Emily, but the question was clearly meant for Elizabeth.

"The Curse of Adam is broken," Elizabeth said. "You must have felt it when Adae passed through."

"I did." Michael shook his head. "But that's not what I asked."

The young queen took a long breath in through her nose and stretched her arms out in front of her. She rolled her hands through a few gentle circles, as though warming up her wrists, then forced her fingers into a series of awkward arcane positions.

Nothing happened.

"Your powers," Michael said.

"Nothing," Elizabeth agreed. Emily felt the bottom falling out from her stomach, but instead of the matching despair she expected to see on Elizabeth's face, there was a faraway look of concentration. The queen's lips moved in a whisper and then she repeated herself at volume as her eyes met Michael's.

"*And the queen returns home,*" she said.

"The prophecy?" Emily asked.

Michael nodded. "Prophecies are powerful magic, but they're tricky. They never mean quite what you think, or maybe they do, but they mean something else as well. Once a true prophecy is spoken, it's binding. So when Adae said *the queen returns home*, she was probably thinking of getting to Earth, but that might not be all."

Emily blinked. "What else?"

"*The crown of iron turns to gold*," Elizabeth said. "Michael, my heart, there's nothing I want more than to rebuild your hands for you. Even Marlow is within the realm of saving, if Mithras will give him back. But it seems that first, there is the small matter of my coronation."

A clatter of glass made Emily jump and she spun in alarm as adrenaline flooded her veins. But there was no enemy. A fox—*the* fox, Emily realized, the one Marlow had talked with in the forest—stood silhouetted against the morning sun in a broken window. Its tail stuck straight up and it eyed the humans warily, ears back. Then its black-eyed gaze fell on Marlow and it yipped as it leaped from the windowsill and dashed across the floor to hop up onto the couch. It licked Marlow's stone face once, sniffed at his ear, then curled into a ball on his chest and promptly fell asleep.

#

The moss under her feet was springy and cool, the perfect balm against the summer warmth that slanted in green beams through the emerald foliage above their heads. Emily took a long, slow breath, feeling the clean air of Arborea tingle in her nose. It was a world worth saving, she thought.

Michael wore an expression much like how Emily imagined her face looked at that moment. His face was raised, his unbound dreds hanging to his shoulders, his eyes closed and a smile curving his lips. In a plain white T-shirt, his missing arms were painfully obvious, just smooth stumps above the joint of the elbow. Not for the first time, Emily wondered how strong Michael must be, to be able to find joy despite the sacrifices he'd made. What had he been through, before, that had been even worse than this?

Elizabeth led the way through a familiar stand of slender birches, their trunks white and peeling. The three friends emerged blinking into full sunlight not long after, a few hundred yards from a glittering river. They'd come through in the same spot as the first time, when Emily and Elizabeth fled from the Albian knights. She hadn't had the time then to really appreciate the beauty of Arborea, with its rolling hills and picturesque white ruins. The air was clearer here, the colors brighter, everything a little sharper.

They set out along the foot of the hills and crossed the river at the ford Marlow had found. Emily accompanied Michael across, making sure he didn't have trouble with his balance, and he thanked her on the other side despite not needing her help.

Not far from the riverbank stood a shrub that even Emily immediately recognized as witch hazel, but there was something different about this one. The flowers she'd come to expect, yellow-legged spiderlike things, had all fallen from its branches and lay in bright piles on the grass. Something new was growing on the bush, little half-open buds like cups made of tight green stalks, each with a starburst of color within.

"Zinnias," Elizabeth said, brushing her fingers over one. She smiled. "A summer bloom."

They were at least a few miles from the hill where they'd passed through to Earth, where Adae had ordered her soldiers to await their return. The distance went by quickly, in companionable silence, but Emily found concerns about her impending knighthood rolling uncomfortably in her thoughts. She couldn't quite find the words to express them, so instead she asked a question.

"Do you guys ever miss the Castle Forlorn?"

Michael and Elizabeth, who'd been walking a few feet ahead with the queen's arm around the magician's waist, paused and turned in such perfect sync that Emily had to smile.

"Hell no," Michael said.

"Every day," Elizabeth said at the same time.

"You weren't trapped there as long as I was," Michael told Emily. "I loved the castle at first—the old stones, the sandbar, the food. But it was like a prison by the end."

"Yeah," Emily said. "But do you miss the people, ever?"

Michael raised an eyebrow. "Do you?"

Emily felt a flush creeping up her neck and into her cheeks, but she mentally ordered it to retreat.

These are my friends, she reminded herself firmly.

"I miss Jack," she said and Michael's face crinkled in a smile. "But it's not just that. I know it was awful on Finalhaven, but it was... simple? Right? I mean, Alder was insane and Liu was kind of a hardass but there's something to be said for not being in charge."

"Getting cold feet, Sir Emily?" Michael laughed. "They're not coronating *you*, you know that, right?"

They'd come in sight of the wagon, surrounded by soldiers waiting faithfully, if lazily, under the warm sun. They'd spread across the hillside, helmets in the grass at their sides or by their feet, and a few had even removed the bigger pieces of their armor. Outside their strange, insectoid ceramic casings, the men of Cantelon looked remarkably small and human as they talked, laughed, and shared food.

"That reminds me," Emily said. "Michael, are you gonna be—I mean—"

"King Michael the First?" He smiled. "It has a ring to it, doesn't it? But no. I'll be Michael, Prince Consort."

"Not bad for a boy from Detroit."

"Not bad at all." Michael stretched, looking up at the sky. "Except for all the planning. A coronation and a wedding in one year... whoof."

"Emily," Elizabeth said suddenly. "You're not ready to settle down."

"I'm not?" Emily blinked at the sharp change in topic.

"Of course not." Elizabeth's gaze was steady. "You'll be knighted, of course, as soon as I am queen. And I'd like to make you captain of my household guard, which will grant you a position on my inner council. But the title will be nominal at first. You'll be back on Earth while Michael and I get the kingdom in order."

"Earth? Why? What do you mean?" Emily, floundering, was reminded strangely of her job interviews the day before Harkness graduation.

"I have work for you," Elizabeth said. "A job for my sworn captain." Her eyes were steely, her mouth set in a firm line. "After I'm coronated in Arcadia, it will be time to see about my other crown."

#

The dust and cobwebs had been cleared from the ramp that led in a long, looping spiral from Beverlay up to the peak of Olympia and the Gates of the Sky. The people of the city lined the walls of the first dozen turns of the tunnel, waiting eagerly for their chance to see their new queen. After them, half the soldiery of Cantelon stood at sharp attention with buffed armor and polished swords and spears. Near the top, where the light of the bright sky beyond the Gates still filtered through the gloom, stood King Zero's handful of warlords, sour-faced and beady-eyed.

Emily, dressed in new armor of her own and trailing a few feet behind Elizabeth and Michael, kept one hand on the pommel of her sword in what she hoped was a casual manner. It was hard to know what to expect from the strange people of Beverlay, where the soldiers' loyalties lay, which of the warlords would submit and which might seize a convenient opportunity to declare himself king with a crown snatched from Elizabeth's dead hands.

Motion in the crowd drew her eye and her stomach lurched as a shape broke free of the line and rushed toward her—but it was Mere, her father trailing sheepishly behind, running out to hug Emily before being dragged lovingly back into place. Emily winked as she passed by.

She hadn't seen Mere until now, despite exploring Beverlay more thoroughly while Michael and Elizabeth planned the coronation. The city's wonders were much more evident without the burden of a deadly mission on her shoulders and its people had seemed to breathe easier around her. If Emily had to guess she would have pegged the mood of Elizabeth's new subjects as relief. Their manic good cheer was fading—it was somehow encouraging to see children slouching in wholesome bore-dom under the eyes of their irritated parents.

The last of the commoners disappeared around a curve as the soldiers came into view. They'd been given their final instructions by Adae before she'd left the city and seemed to be following orders to a tee. If the regime change bothered them, it didn't show on their still and somber faces.

Emily blinked in the sudden sunshine as she came around the last turn. A dozen warlords in ceremonial black armor carved in the shapes of terrible animals and monsters lined the last approach to the Gates of the Sky. Watching their expressions closely, she was reminded of Marshall Alder, who had seemed like a man born too late as his beloved Lancers put aside their dragon-slaying and became little more than a social club. These captains and generals had a similar vibe.

A warlord in a bright white cloak and crystal armor that perfectly matched his deep purple eyes stood nearest to the Gates, only a foot from the sheer drop down the face of Olympia. His age-lined face was deeply tanned, brown against his sun-bleached blonde buzzcut. He caught Emily staring at him and their eyes locked.

He winked.

Elizabeth and Michael reached the end of the ramp. The purple-armored warrior bent and picked up a flat, lacquered wooden box from the stone at his feet. He flipped the top open and drew out the circlet of black iron that Emily had last seen around Adae's head. He handed it to Elizabeth, who contemplated it for a moment then threw it out into the open air.

It spun for a moment against the blue sky, then disappeared among the gray rocks of Olympia far below. Trying to follow its arc, Emily saw instead the mass of surging color at the base of the mountain. It was impossible to make out any details, but she knew that down there were the people of Olympia and Arborea, as well as animals and whatever other mythical creatures dwelled in this strange pocket of reality.

The warlord snapped the box closed and set it back down. His gaze held Elizabeth's for a long, searching moment, until, apparently satisfied by whatever he saw in the young woman's eyes, he reached into his cloak and revealed a second circlet, this one of gleaming red-gold.

He placed it into Elizabeth's hands with much more reverence than he'd shown handling the iron crown and the queen accepted it in the same fashion. She murmured a word of thanks to the warrior, glanced at Michael with a secret smile, and placed the golden band on her head.

A breathless pause came and went as Elizabeth stood gazing out over the slopes of Olympia and the green hills of Arborea beyond. Then, as unceremoniously as if she'd been walking to the fridge for a drink, she stepped over the terminal edge of the ramp.

She dropped with heart-stopping suddenness, disappearing below the line of the cliff before Emily could even think to cry out. Elizabeth had fallen, Emily thought in wild panic, she was even now breaking into pieces on the jagged rocks a thousand feet below, and the whole thing had been a ruse or a scheme or simply a horrible, horrible mistake.

Then she saw long, bone-white hair fluttering like a flag of victory, bound only by a golden crown. She saw narrow, freckled shoulders in a white dress stitched with green, gray, and gold. She saw slender arms outstretched to catch the sun and she heard the roar of approval from the crowd far below, and she understood.

Elizabeth should have fallen. Instead, she flew.

ABOUT THE AUTHOR

Nathaniel Webb, aka Nat20, is an author, musician, and game designer. As a lead guitarist, he has toured and recorded with numerous acts including Grammy-nominated singers Beth Hart and Jana Mashonee and Colombian pop star Marre. His published writing includes the GameLit novel *Expedition: Summerlands*, various short stories and novellas, and adventures and supplements for the tabletop RPGs *Shadow of the Demon Lord* and *Godless*.

A graduate of Phillips Exeter Academy and Wesleyan University, Nathaniel lives in Portland, Maine with his wife and son under a massive pile of cats. He can be found @nat20w on Twitter and Facebook, where he mostly talks about games, writing, and obscure 80s progressive rock.

CPSIA information can be obtained
at www.ICGtesting.com
Printed in the USA
LVHW030344090421
683894LV00011B/341

9 781839 190810